WHY DOES EVERYONE STEAL MY LIGHTER?

ALSO BY MICHAEL JOHNSTON

Fight, Kid!

WHY DOES EVERYONE STEAL MY LIGHTER?

MICHAEL JOHNSTON

For anyone who has ever played in a band

Keep on dreamin' boy, 'cause when you stop dreamin'
it's time to die.

SHANNON HOON

CAST OF CHARACTERS

Zach Long: Guitar
Luke Strange: Vocals and Bass
Harry Wood: Drums
Bartholomew Louise "Bart" Zenobel: Piano
Todd Shift: Manager

1

E Street Sushi
Durham, NH
12/31/91

Capacity: 215
Tickets Sold: 215

Zach and Luke sat inside their small unheated two-bedroom apartment and worked on lyric rewrites for the fourth time that week, and if a fire had been set to the pages, they'd still be cold. Unable to rhyme anything with the word "orange" no matter how many dictionaries they stole from the library, their scratched-out spiral notebooks sat before them like the Bible written in Mandarin, the words on the pages as comprehensive as the hash smoke that fumed from the lit joint in the bottle cap that substituted as an ash tray, their young band in a similar predicament as the faint blue ink that spelled out disaster.

New Year's Eve was in three weeks: a joyous night to celebrate the coming of renewed possibilities and self-made goals, a night so powerful that it provided even the shittiest of cover bands an excuse to gather a sizable audience one night a year, and Texas Flip had nothing in the pipeline worth their time or effort.

Problem for acts like them, though—whose draw exceeded no further than the relatives and friends who had seen them seven times already—was that the crowds they brought in on a good night weren't large enough to fill the bigger clubs in town. And so instead of being proactive about it and booking their own show at a smaller venue with plenty of time to promote and draw a broader audience and make an even bigger name for themselves, they did what most lazy bands do—nothing— and hoped for the best.

Weird that a phone call would save them.

"Hello?"

"Dylan Mutters just called me!" Harry screamed.

Luke cradled the cold phone between his shoulder and ear and rubbed his even colder hands for warmth. "Cool. Who's Dylan Mutters again?"

"Seriously?" Harry asked, surprised but not surprised. "You know who Dylan is, dude. He's my buddy. That has that band. In New Hampshire . . . We've played with them, like, six times, dude."

"The Dylan Mutters Band?"

"Exactly."

"Why did he name the band after himself again?"

"Who cares, Luke. Do you have any more questions, or can I tell you why he called me?"

"Ha!"

"He asked me if we had a New Year's Eve show booked."

"What did you tell him?"

"I told him the truth—that we don't."

"Yeah . . ."

"He wants us to be the second band on a bill he is putting together."

"What did you say?"

"I said I would talk to you guys first. That's why I'm calling."

"Who is that?" Zach asked from his position on the couch, a one-foot green plastic bong gripped tight in his left hand, blue Bic lighter in his right. A trail of smoke from his last hit lingered in the cylindrical glaze and leaked from its top like a blocked chimney. Then he cleared it.

"It's Harry. Says we might have a lead for a New Year's Eve show." To Harry: "Where's it at?"

"Durham."

"North Carolina?"

"Are you a complete fucking moron? The dude goes to college in New Hampshire. Why would he book a show in North Carolina?"

Durham was four and a half hours away from Oneonta. Without snow.

When you're a young band, any show is a good show, even if it's half a workday away. That's what being in a young band is all about: playing shitty shows for shitty pay in shitty places to shitty people. It was easy to see that this gig—independent of the nine-hour total driving time they'd be dealing with— would be ten times more successful than anything Texas Flip would have booked on their own at this stage.

Zach spoke up for them all. "We don't have any other options. And we've driven farther for worse."

Harry could hear their guitarist in the background over the phone, and he liked what he heard. He was also on a pay phone. "Should I hit him back?" he asked Luke. "I know Bart's down; I'm with him right now."

Luke looked at Zach and gave a quick head nod. "Let's do it."

Dylan Mutters and his bandmates all attended the University of New Hampshire, placating the local scene of college kids with their weak variation of shwaggy, mediocre, acoustic rock and roll. They booked shows with Texas Flip in Oneonta whenever they were on tour and would help reciprocate with gigs to fill up their friends' calendar on those few excursions outside their familiar hangouts. Cool group of guys for the most part, though the crowds they drew could be somewhat polarizing: college bros in salmon-colored polo shirts and yachting shoes—guys who spent the weekend on their doctor fathers' sailboats, wearing hats with slogans like SMOOTH SEAS DON'T MAKE GOOD SAILORS, and shotgunned Coors Light at the frat house afterward; these piranhas operated in sick tandem with the mass of sorority girls who were equally as gripped with the Dylan Mutters Band.

An explanation as to *why* escaped most everyone else.

If you had asked Zach his opinion about the band's music, he would have told you they sucked ass. But Dylan could sing in key while playing an acoustic guitar, and they also had a cello player, so the arithmetic behind the Dylan Mutters Band's early "success" was rather easy to compute. And because sometimes it really *is* that easy.

"Did he say what venue it's at?" Zach asked Luke to ask Harry.

"It's at a sushi restaurant," Harry said.

Luke did a double take. "A *sushi* restaurant? In New Hampshire?"

"That's what he said."

"Fuck it," Luke held. "We've played worse."

It was true. They had.

Harry fell in line with this agreement. "Cool. I'll call Dylan back tonight. Also, ask Zach if it's chill to get the directions to the restaurant faxed over to his work."

In addition to his job as a waiter three nights a week at an Applebee's, Zach had also been working weekend shifts at Oneonta Self-Storage. The pipe dream was to save up enough money to buy a black-with-white-trim 1979 Gibson Les Paul Custom, this job's only promised reward.

Zach was playing with his dick when Dylan's fax arrived a couple of days later: a list of directions, the telephone number for the restaurant, and very specific instructions as to where to park.

"Should we call them?" Harry asked at band practice the following evening in a rehearsal room they rented by the hour. He was as unsure as the rest of them. "Maybe double-check everything?"

Shaky about the whole affair and looking for peace of mind from someone other than Dylan, Zach agreed, for there was nothing else to do. "Probably wouldn't be a bad idea. I'll call them."

His call was collect.

The phone rang seven times before a youngish-sounding girl with an accent straight from the lobster shores of Maine answered. "Ayuh—E Street Sushi, this is Sandra. How can I help ya?"

"Hey, Sandra," said Zach, a little thrown by her accent, "my name is Zach, and I play in the band Texas Flip. Our buddies in the Dylan Mutters Band"—even saying it out loud felt strange—"have a show booked at your restaurant on New Year's Eve, and we're playing it too."

Sandra didn't say anything in return. She coughed, but that was it.

"So, I, um . . . I'm just calling to confirm everything, because, well, we've actually never played in a restaurant before. How does it work exactly?"

Zach was genuine with his question.

So was Sandra.

"Ya show up, and you, uh, play."

"Thanks," he fibbed, "that about answers all the questions I had. We'll see you in a couple of weeks."

The rest of the band was busy with the intro to a song that had been eating their time for the last two hours when he entered back into their stratosphere with the hard news and a storyteller's spirit. "We're all set. Should be super easy. Harry— if you could confirm everything with Dylan regarding load-in, sound check, all that stuff; we should be good otherwise. Don't think we have to do any promotion either."

E Street Sushi, located on a street that didn't even contain the letter *E*, was a fresh-fish joint in the afternoons and evenings and transformed into an all-ages music venue every Friday and Saturday night. The stage pulled out of the wall like a giant Murphy bed, and bands had to bring their own PA system, microphones, microphone stands, and microphone cables if they, or the crowd, wanted to hear their crappy lyrics over their too-loud instruments. Tables were cleared and patrons told in a gruff manner to finish their meals or pay the six-dollar cover if they wanted to stay for the show.

"Gonna be fun," Zach said.

The rest of the band agreed.

The scenic panorama as the band (and Luke's girlfriend, Abbe) departed Oneonta for Durham belonged on a postcard that no one should have to receive from anyone ever. They left town midmorning, and the Dunkin' Donuts coffee in their hands provided more warmth than the car's heating system as the sun stretched itself awake before their eyes, naked and alone.

Arriving five hours later at the nondescript one-story brick building that might have been mistaken for a massage parlor if they hadn't known better, their hopes high and heads higher, Bart dutifully followed the faxed-over instructions that led to the designated BAND PARKING ZONE, painted behind the izakaya —a spray-painted letter *L* that now read BLAND PARKING ZONE —and parked the Chevy with an abrupt exaggeration; his socked foot more connected to the brake pedal than the tires to the wintry ground.

Everybody lit a cigarette.

Having landed at the rear of the building, Texas Flip was opposite the parallel-running, thickly treed street that belonged to the front entrance, and therefore had not seen the line of two hundred people wrapped around the side of the eatery, at 3:00 P.M. on a Tuesday, in 23-degree temperature, with high winds and a sun unseen.

But then they did, and the cold made Siberia seem reasonable.

The hippies and their hairy-arm-pitted girlfriends kicked hacky sacks and blasted *Waiting for Columbus* on a boom box like it was the middle of summer and Abbe's blond hair curtained as she searched her purse for a match to light the Capri cigarette suspended from her lips, her red nails scrabbling. "That's, like . . . a *lot* of people," she said, her attitude taller than her boyfriend. "Are they all here for you guys?"

"Nah, babe," Luke said, finding it hard to believe himself, "they're here for Dylan's band."

Dylan Mutters had sensed Texas Flip's arrival blocks away,

like a dog knowing its owner was back from vacation. From behind a dumpster meant for grease waste, where he'd been smoking weed with a one-hitter, he leaped in the air with a joyous glee, an invisible Frisbee caught between his lips. "What's up, fuckers!" he screamed loud enough for them to hear through closed windows and dark chatter. "Took you long enough!" Approaching their station wagon with a dramatic gusto, he impaled their warm bubble of trust with a spear of pesky confidence. "You guys ready to rage tonight? Shit's gonna be epic!"

The dude was like a wet sock: unbearable for any conversation longer than needed, an irritation for only being himself and nothing else. And tragically for Texas Flip, they had arrived early for once.

"Yeah, man," Zach said, "we're stoked too. Do we load in thr—"

"We got my band," Dylan interrupted, "you guys, and the openers, Funky Hunky! I'd be super pumped if I was in the audience tonight. To see my band *and* Texas Flip on the same bill?! Crazy, bro!"

"Yeah," Zach said. "*Crazy* . . . So that door ov—"

"Cool if Funky Hunky uses your drum kit?"

Dylan's question, a bee sting to the cochlea, shocked Zach's brain like a finger does in damp electrics. For a moment he felt suspended in air, until he collapsed and cracked like an egg. He had to shake his head to make sure it was still there and what Dylan Mutters had just asked him was, in fact, correct. One of the biggest mortal sins in live music: never, under any circumstances ever, is it all right for a last-minute request, by any band on a bill, to use another band's drum kit. Ever. Simple courtesy, weeks of advanced warning—if there was enough time beforehand to book the show, print flyers, and promote it for a month, then there was enough time for the drummer to ask if they could use another band's drum kit.

And even then, don't do it.

Dylan's breath smelled worse than hot garbage on a hotter day, and Zach inched away as far as he could without looking obvious and wished he had a toothbrush to give. "You gotta ask Harry," he said, not happy with the last-minute request, but also not the one to be bothered by it. "I also thought Farhead was ope—"

"Nah," Dylan interrupted again, "they canceled last minute. But Funky Hunky is awesome. Motown/funk kinda thing. Good buddies of ours. They're gonna be epic, bro!"

Zach promised himself that if Dylan said the word "epic" one more time, he would kick him in the shin hard enough to break the bone. If the bone didn't break, it would break on his second kick. Calling to Harry over his shoulder, he asked, "My brother! Cool if the openers use your drum kit tonight?"

"Yeah, whatever," Harry replied immediately, more irritated by the rug for his drum kit and its ability to get stuck on any surface it touched rather than the safety of the actual kit itself. "One thing, though. Can you tell their drummer to go easy on my gear? I just bought a new kit. Don't want it getting messed up."

Shocked was Zach.

"Without a doubt!" Dylan promised.

"And if he can use his own breakables too."

"A hundred percent," Dylan agreed. "Their drummer is the coolest dude I've ever met. And I'll take personal responsibility for all your gear."

"Sooooo, are all of those people here for you?" Abbe asked Dylan, the lit Capri separating her top and bottom lip, her voice as if cigarettes could talk.

Dylan's attention gripped by the presence of a female, he looked Abbe up and down, oblivious that Luke was standing right next to her with his hand in the ass pocket of her jeans. "Ha-ha, yeah," he said, "they seem to follow us wherever we go. A bunch of weirdos, if you ask me. But who gives a shit if they keep buying my shirts, right?!" He allowed Abbe time to laugh before he asked, "What size are you anyways?"

"Back off," Luke said. "She's with me."

"Whoa!" Dylan announced, taken by surprise at this reaction, and retreated from Texas Flip's lead singer with his hands up in the air as a form of capitulation—"All good, man! All *good* . . ."—and patiently stepped backward toward the restaurant, soft as silk. His approaching disappearance feet away, he looked over his shoulder for a piece of equipment he could maybe help carry in before not caring anymore. "I'll, um . . . I'll see you dudes later," he said, opening the door to the building slowly. His eyes locked on Luke until his escape into the building was successful. "And thanks again for letting us use your kit, Larry!"

Desirous of peace in New Hampshire, Zach restarted the process of unloading their gear from the station wagon before Luke unloaded on Dylan's face. "I hate that guy," Texas Flip's singer squealed with an unnatural rile.

Zach handed him his bass case and pedal board.

"You didn't have to be such an asshole," Abbe said. "He seemed nice . . . Kinda cute too."

Zach gave her a small gray backpack that held Luke's cables in hopes of shutting her up.

It didn't.

So then he handed her Luke's tripod boom microphone stand, Gallien-Krueger 800RB 300/100W bi-amp bass amp head, and Harry's cymbal bag.

Then she did.

"Is that the door we bring our shit in through?" Luke asked, pointing at the doorway that said LOAD-IN ENTRANCE but might as well have said DOOR YOU BRING YOUR SHIT IN THROUGH.

"We're going to be all good tonight, right, dude?" Zach asked.

Luke's eyes shot shuriken toward Abbe. In his mind, they slit her throat. "We're all good."

Biceps tired from carrying his Marshall JCM900 100W hi-gain dual reverb head only ten yards from the Chevy to the load-in entrance, Zach put the vulnerable tube amp down on the wet asphalt in front of the heavy door and stretched his mangled back, ready for another smoke, a dump, or both simultaneously. With his hand in his pocket and an ache in his shoulder, the manner in which he reacted to the load-in door opening fast—its sharp, rusted edge colliding with the master volume knob of the amplifier, rattling the reverb tank and hardware with a frightening ring, and tearing a penny-sized chunk out of its black Tolex, thus dropping its resale value immediately in half—was not as reactive as it might have been otherwise. Unfortunate, really. A woman who looked like a more beaten-down Liza Minnelli spoke loudly from the doorway.

"Hello, gentlemen. Load your geeyuh in heeyah and put it ovuh in dat far cawhnuh. Make it quick, right?"

"Are you Wendy?" Zach asked, taken aback by the woman who most likely had broken his most valuable possession.

Her hair spoke more volumes than there were of *National Geographic*. "Who de hell else would I be?" she responded. "Anymawh quesshuns or what? No? Great. Yuh with me?"

Zach gave Bart a weary look. "Yeah," he said. "We're with you."

"Good. Also, do not make eye contact wit' any of de people who are still eatin'. Doawhs aren't until eight thirty, so dey still got some mawh time tuh waste my time. Yuh got me so fahr? And fifteen percent off sushi fawh all de band members —right?"

"Um, okay," Zach stuttered, afraid of her like he would be

of a mama grizzly bear with three cubs in Yellowstone. "We were told doors were at seven thirty and the show would start at nine."

"We were also told it would be fifty percent off sushi for band members," Luke piped in.

"Well, yuh were told wrong."

"Sounds great," Zach answered agreeably. "Thanks again for everything."

"Yeah, whatevuh," Wendy said, and closed the load-in door, which could only be opened from the inside.

"Seems like a nice lady," Harry said. "I'll go through the front and open it back up."

The load-in zone/emergency exit of E Street Sushi, when open, led directly into the dining area—not the kitchen or a hallway, but straight into the restaurant itself. And that, in turn, made ignoring the patrons munching away on their B-grade sushi ten feet away from where bands loaded their gear in through an impossibility. The Dylan Mutters Band's equipment already set up onstage fully mic'd and tuned, Texas Flip was then told by the sound guy, Curt, that their gear would need to be front lined and that the first two bands would be given only ten-minute line checks while Dylan's band would be afforded a forty-five-minute sound check complete with lights and videographer. This would also occur when the changeover in clientele was to take place. Families and friends, having enjoyed a nice evening out and paying their bills so they could turn themselves in before the long night to follow, would be forced to make their exit as college students drunk off Bud Light tall cans and high off glue passed them by in the opposite direction; frightened parents shielding their children's eyes from the losers they would become when they themselves attended a state university.

～

Out in the back parking lot, Zach spread out on the rear bench seat inside the station wagon reading a beat-up copy of *Zen and the Art of Motorcycle Maintenance* by the light of a streetlamp. The engine was running and the heat blasted what little it could extend, and he felt confident in his decision to not remain indoors and undergo more irreversible damage to his hearing via another band's sound check.

The clock on the dashboard was off by eleven minutes, but the dreadful moment he'd been pushing off like a teeth cleaning had finally come: Zach needed to show his face for the opening band. Rubbing the bags from under his eyes away and over his shoulder, he bit at a hangnail on his playing hand's index finger, laced up his shoes, scratched his nuts then his ass, and prepared himself for another big night in a small city. It had begun to snow while he was reading and was now coming down at a steady clip, and the moon glowed like it wanted to go to sleep itself. The shallow footprints he left behind filled back up quicker than new ones could form, as he slogged through the rear parking lot around to the front entrance, presenting the stamp on his right hand to the military-grade bouncer checking ID and taking money. He moved through the condensed crowd, well over whatever the legal capacity for the restaurant was, and cozied up at the bar next to Harry, arriving right in time for the show to start and to catch the sole bartender for a beer.

Before he could take a sip and crack a joke to Harry about Dylan's breath, the house lights turned down, the PA turned up, and Funky Hunky's lead singer turned on, grabbing his floral-draped microphone with the vigor of a younger David Lee Roth. Standing erect with his legs in a V, he screamed, "What's up, Durham!" into the audibly clipping mic. "Who's ready to get this fucking party started!"

On this cue, the band busted into a cover of "Jump," by Van Halen.

Their guitarist, who was also playing the keyboard, started the song in the wrong key and looked like an even uglier version of the guitar player from Mötley Crüe. Also sharing the tiny stage with him was a bass player doing his best Michael Anthony tribute—Jack Daniel's bottle on top of his amp, red overalls, and hair that could trap bees—but it was their drummer, all six-five of him, who soon stole the show from no one.

And he was also beating the shit out of Harry's drums.

"What's he doing to my kit?!" Texas Flip's drummer yelled over an out-of-tune C-major chord.

His sole drink ticket spent, Zach flagged down the bartender, smacked three dollars down on the bar, and asked for another Hamm's.

"We're out," the conspicuously young girl behind the bar hollered over the frantic sounds coming from the stage. "All I have left is Olympia."

A crappy beer more respected than the crappy city where it was made, Zach accepted, took a large swig, and cursed his luck.

Funky Hunky started their second song, "Panama."

Zach winced.

"It'll be cool," he assured Harry. "I don't think Dylan would have booked a bunch of assholes to play with us!" He had to scream his point over the music and hope he wasn't too loud to be heard by others. What ended up louder, though, was their drummer blasting his kick pedal clean through Harry's bass drumhead.

"Are you kidding me?!"

Harry's face looked as if the kick pedal had hit him in the dick instead. He shoved through the crowd with force, reaching the front of the audience and planting himself smack dab in view of Funky Hunky's drummer, who, dismissing Harry as no one, continued to bash away at not-his-drums with an increased intensity. *"Panama! Pana-mah-ah-ah-ah-ah-ah!"*

screeched from the PA system, flat and full of a repellant passion, and Zach's shouts to Harry over the band not less than five feet from them became lost in the miasma of this audible turd sandwich that most people considered entertainment.

"Dude, just wait till their set is over, and then talk to him!" The music grew louder and drowned out both their sensibilities with a banal swell of kitsch. "You know how hard I worked to buy that kit?!" Harry yelled into Zach's left ear, its canal a battering ram for his pent-up retribution. "Nah, man, I told Dylan to tell this idiot specifically not to screw up my shit. Now I'm pissed!"

They stood through an original song, two more Van Halen covers, and a finale of "Smells Like Teen Spirit" that no one had asked for (or particularly wanted to hear) before the suffering was finally over. No one in the audience clued in to the inevitable confrontation that had been frothing over for the last twenty minutes, Harry was up on the stage before the last notes of the set could ring out, beelining it to their drummer seated behind his abused kit, who was now rather aware that Harry, a brick wall of outrage, was ready to smash in his face. He raised his left arm in defense for a blow to come at any moment. It was hard for Zach to hear what was being said—Harry looked to be seconds from sending a right cross of irreversible damage to the other drummer's skull, but for some reason held back from the full-frontal assault at the absolute last second; his fist clenched, but his arm slacked in a bent form of embarrassing submission. Following a couple transfers of defensive discourse, it then appeared as though Funky Hunky's drummer had begun to also let his guard down too, the situation maybe simmering itself out, a kettle taken off the electric stovetop. This appeared all well and good, until the guilty party stood up from his drum throne like Bill Walton at a concert and, with no warning and no form, open-hand slapped Harry straight in his precious ear. Shocked but not ruffled, Texas

Flip's drummer took the blow like a backyard wrestling champ and, cool as a cucumber, punched the other drummer square on the nose; the force sent the goon tumbling back into the wall, taking down Harry's rack tom, DW snare drum, and Zildjian eighteen-inch K crash cymbal into a heap on the stage with him.

The room had emptied—that fifteen-minute break when bands changed gear and cigarettes were chain-smoked outside —and left scarcely a witness to this act of violence other than Zach and the rest of the dudes in Funky Hunky, fraught with indecision, bullfighters without a bull. They stood open-mouthed and as useless as a DVD rewinder as their bandmate lay on the floor like a burrito smothered in his own broken arrogance. But they were brothers in arms, holding a three-to-one advantage and at least one instrument, so they, naturally, aimed their anger at Harry. They swarmed in defense of their fallen comrade, assaulting the vulnerable combatant limb by limb under the cause of sodality and alcohol; mercilessly beating the crap out of an outnumbered Harry with fists, kicks, and sticky cheap shots. Zach, with the best of intentions and a closed fist, then ran up onto the stage to provide the neutral force this Royal Rumble needed to be a fair decision.

He had reacted in enough time to possibly stop the brawl, or at least pause it and save the rest of the night's show from being ruined. But within a flash, he was blinded.

The world no longer turning, darkness consumed him like a heavy wool blanket. Unsure whether to scream or cry, the burning on his skin disabled him from attempting either. The feeling of a thousand bees stung his face all at once and his ability to breathe became diminished, the dry chemicals on his tongue placing his taste buds into a deep freeze. He tried with all his might to straighten his attention and assess what was happening, but the pain on his skin was too persistent, the covering on his eyes too thick, the smell too foul, and so he was prevented from logical reason and submitted himself to this mysterious trauma of incapacitation. Vision stolen in the interim, he was able to gauge by the decrease of verbal volume in the room that the altercation of drummers had perhaps begun to dwindle down to a deadlock, and so he wiped away a cakey substance from off his eyelids with his forearm to get a better view of a fuzzy situation. He blinked—looking left, then right, his sight functional—and refocused on a scene of five dudes and all their equipment covered in what looked to be twenty pounds of sheeny off-white pterodactyl ejaculate.

"Holy shit!" David Lee Roth Jr. yelled. "That bitch is *crazy*! She's gonna spray us again!"

At the side of the stage, standing with a fire extinguisher in her hands pointed directly at Zach, was the female bartender. "I'll shoot the next asshole that moves a muscle!"

It was at this moment that Dylan, who had been outside during the whole debacle, walked back inside, unsure if there had been a fire or a bukkake filming. He screamed at Zach for no reason other than he was closest and had the fire extinguisher pointed at him. "Bro, what the hell?! You guys are supposed to start in ten minutes! Why is everything covered in foam?"

"It's not foam," Harry said, wiping his face for the eleventh time. "It's fire retardant. And we're covered in it because *this* band's drummer, broke *my* brand-new kick drum."

"Fuck you, man," Funky Hunky's drummer roared back, rubbing a glob of retardant from his eyes and flicking it to the stage like a load of dinosaur cum. "You said I could use your kit! And why the hell did that chick spray us with a fire extinguisher?!"

Everyone's attention turned to the bartender, who was still pointing the extinguisher's nozzle at Zach for no reason other than he was closest. "I'm sorry!" she said through a visible shakiness. "I freaked out, and I didn't know what else to do. It looked like you guys were going to kill each other, and I didn't have a gun so I thought this would work."

"A *gun*?!" Harry exclaimed. "What were you gonna do with a gun?!"

"I should have just listened to my dad and gotten that job at the sushi restaurant in the mall!" she wailed to herself through snot bubbles and more shaking. "I'm just not cool enough for rock music!" The nozzle's aim was off Zach and now up in the air. "I hate him!" She sprayed the fire extinguisher again, covering the ceiling above her; the rest of them covered themselves.

"What is goin' on in here?!" Wendy yelled from the entrance of the kitchen. "Everyone get out of here! *Now!*"

Startled, the lot of them were too scared to explain the situation, much less put up an argument with her, and hightailed it outside as expeditiously as possible. The scene outside was even stranger than it was inside: a parking lot filled with burnouts, drunks, stoners, and vagrants. It was also at this time that these same individuals who had paid the entrance fee were beginning to make their way back inside the restaurant for Texas Flip's set. Wendy's voice rang out loud and clear to all from the restaurant's front entrance that this would *not* be the case.

"Sawhry tuh break de news tuh everyone, but de rest of de show is canceled! Dere will be *no* refunds—so doan even tink about asking!" Her attention turned back to the guilty party, the bands: "Yuh all have ten minutes tuh pack up your shit and get out of here befawh I call de cops. And I ain't fuckin' around!"

The crowd, flabbergasted at this quick turn of events, were made to watch their holiday plans shatter like a thin sheet of ice holding up a snowman. With no direction that might lead them down a new road of redemption, their night, as they all knew it, was over.

Luke and Bart, absent during this entire fracas—doing

drugs in the bathroom presumably—were shocked at seeing this spectacle for the first time. "Why are you dudes covered in bird shit?" the singer asked.

Wading in a sea of suffocating temper, Zach squawked, "Can we just get out of here? I'll explain in the car. And find Abbe. She's driving."

To the luck of all involved, Abbe didn't drink alcohol, although she did everything else she could get her hands on (including half the college baseball team). This knowledge, etched into their ape brains with a rusty device, made everyone in the band behave like the responsible adults they were becoming, which meant they had begun drinking immediately upon their arrival at E Street Sushi. Unknowingly signing herself up to be captain of their ship through three states, in the snow, on a dark highway, in the middle of the night, on New Year's Eve, Abbe's tolerance for them would need to be much higher than their tolerance to the Four Roses whiskey they'd been sipping all night via Bart's flask.

The gear was back inside the Chevy in less than three minutes, fast as any NASCAR pit team. Zach—the staidest of the bunch and with the most capacity to navigate their route back home—joined Abbe in the front seat, more to calm his nerves than to calm hers about driving home. With the radio dialed to Dick Clark and passengers of varying toxicity levels buckled in, ready to sail far away from these rough waters and back to the safer shores of Oneonta, a slick exit would prove difficult. Hundreds of imbeciles dawdled around the parking lot and clogged up their exit lane with lumpy bodies full of grilled cheese sandwiches and slathered in patchouli oil. Texas Flip was not only stuck in place but, worse, with one another, rattling around in a cage and searching for a way out. "*Texas Flip sucks!*" and "*This is bullshit!*" could be heard from various faces in the crowd, the gathering becoming more hostile the longer their station wagon remained immobile. Before someone could throw an obsidian crystal through the windshield, Dylan emerged from within the dense pack like the Second Coming of Jesus Christ, docking himself at the front of this group and in front of Texas Flip, a blackhead of provocation no pressure could squeeze out.

"Don't worry, everyone!" he screeched into the two hands that formed a cone around his mouth. "Let's all be chill!" The herd of sheeple before him, this commonality parked in front of the idling Chevy, shifted undecidedly. He appealed to his assembly further, a performer finding his groove. "The Dylan Mutters Band will be playing an impromptu acoustic set in the parking lot instead! And it will be *EPIC!*"

"Run him over if you have to," Zach appealed to Abbe.

"Screw Texas Flip!" Dylan yelled louder. "The Dylan Mutters Band is going to bring you the hot jams! Going to be epic!" His rant over, the man of the night began to withdraw with his posse and created enough of a gap for the Caprice's front left fender to fit through by an inch.

"Drive *now!*" Zach ordered, loud and firm.

With this sharp direction, Abbe smashed her size 7 Converse on the gas pedal, the rear tires slipping with dirty words in the seven inches of snow accumulated on the ground thus far, before catching and sending the car flying into hyperspace. A sashimi knife slice through the crowd, they drove fast out of that traumatic suburban sprawl and up an on-ramp onto I-95S. The friction inside the station wagon was tense, to put it lightly. Last bits of smegma stuck in his hair like forgotten semen after a sexual act, Zach combed it out with crisp fingers and lit a smoke, his eyes closing, the fight to stay open lost. The rest of the band already on the brink of an intoxicated paralysis, their heads dipped to the left, slumber upon them sooner than expected, literally less than ten minutes of leaving, and then Abbe started in with the questions she'd been putting off since she had turned the ignition over.

"What happened in there? What's all over you guys? Did you beat up that jerk, Harry? Come on, someone answer me!"

"I was going to," Texas Flip's drummer said with parched lips, "but that bartender sprayed me before I could."

Switching lanes without looking, Abbe lit a cigarette and then put on her turn signal. "I bet you were," she said loudly over the honking, taking a supportive look at her boyfriend in the rearview mirror, unflustered from nearly killing all of them in a crash. "And you, sugar baby? You were a good boy, right? You don't like getting into scuffles anyways."

His head resting against the rear window, Luke drew genitalia in the fog created from his breath and breathed balls through his nose. "Nah, babe," he answered willingly. "I was taking a shit when it went down."

They were heading in a southwest direction, somewhere near Worcester—past the McMansions, housewives, and bars of Xanax—Bart, Harry, and Luke not having shown signs of life for half an hour. Abbe and Zach, up front, their eyes closed to slits and fighting to stay open, had cruised in silence long enough for them to hear it, and for it now to be awkward. Foraging for lame chatter like when your drink's already been paid for during a bad date, Abbe broke the stillness with a pickax of fury. "I can't believe Harry got into a fight. What was he thinking? Idiot." She turned the radio dial and the last seconds of "Hot for Teacher," faded out in the car speakers. "And that bartender . . . What a bitch!"

Zach eyed the fuel gauge with an unconcealed wariness and leaned over her non-seat-belted body to try to get a better look; wafts of smoke and pheromones pervaded from her cowl-neck sweater. "How are we on gas?" he asked.

The broken needle in perpetual fluctuation between ¼ and

¾ no matter the amount of gasoline in the tank, to accurately guess its real level was a near impossibility.

"Um," Abbe said, looking down at the dashboard with a mixture of puzzlement and curiosity, almost as if she had never once looked at a gas gauge before. "It says we're at a quarter of a tank. That's good, right?"

"We need to get gas at the next rest stop," Zach told her rather than suggested. Suggestions were useless in times like these.

"Okay," she said, and lit her fourteenth cigarette of the drive per the lipstick-covered butts in the ashtray.

A deer darted across the highway, then craned its head back at the passing car, thankful to be alive.

Zach craned his head back, wishing he were a dead deer.

She flicked her ash back into the vehicle and onto Bart's T-shirt. "I think we passed a rest stop a little while back," Abbe said. "There was a sign that said the next one was in thirty-eight miles. Or maybe eight . . . I forget."

"We did? Was I asleep?"

"I don't know."

"The next one is in thirty-eight miles?! How far back was the last rest stop?"

"I don't know. Probably twenty minutes ago. Or maybe thirty? We'll be *fiiiiiine.*"

An earlier butt fell out of the ashtray as she stubbed this newest one in. They passed a sign for a correctional facility; its warning—DO NOT PICK UP HITCHHIKERS—a harbinger for the plethora of possibilities that could occur if they ran out of gas. Zach's ass felt aflame and was on the edge of his seat searching for a station he knew to be dozens of miles away. Hand with a new cigarette out the window and the other twirling her hair, Abbe steered with her free elbow as four innocent souls hung in the balance on the off chance she sneezed. Snow drifted slowly down.

The highway held little assurance that the tires would do their job.

"Isn't there supposed to be, like, a light that tells you you're out of gas or something?"

A deep fear perfused Zach's lower intestine and entered his bloodstream. He could feel the alarm in his knees. "The gas light doesn't work . . ."

The first putter of the engine affirmed that.

Abbe freaked. "Ohhhh myyy gawwwwd! What's happening?!"

The engine sputtered once more, smoot puffing from the exhaust like a dirty whoopee cushion.

"Oh my god, are we gonna die?!"

Wrapped up in some dusty wool, a grizzled Bart emerged from his cuckoo cocoon, out of mind but in with time. Abbe's old ash fell away with his new motions. "We're about to run out of gas, aren't we?"

The question did not sit well with their driver.

"Oh my gawd! Oh my gawd! Ohhhh myyyy gawwwwwd!"

"Abbe!" Zach yelled. "Please be quiet! And, Bart, shut up! We're gonna be fine. Drive a little slower, get in the right lane, and put on the hazards."

The engine puttered hard again and then, summarily, put itself to sleep.

"Sounds like we ran out of gas."

"*Fuck you, Bart!*" Abbe and Zach screamed collectively.

Zach clicked the gear shift into neutral. "Abbe, coast onto the shoulder and park," he commanded.

"I told you we should have gotten gas!" spouted an awoken Luke.

"Shut up!" his girlfriend shrieked back at him. "You didn't say anything. You were passed out! And while we're at it, don't tell me you weren't eyeing that bartender all night!"

"Everyone *stop*!" Zach screamed. "For the love of God,

everyone please shut your goddamn mouths! Abbe, pull over right there."

"Where?"

"The *shoulder*, Abbe! Pull over onto the shoulder!"

Huddled between Harry and Bart like the middle of an ice-cream sandwich of losers, Luke added fuel to the wrong fire: "How did we run out of gas? Did you *not* look at the fuel gauge? What were you two doing up there the whole time?"

The station wagon safely parked on the shoulder, Zach undid his seat belt, stepped outside, licked the tip of his index finger, and held it in the air, gauging the temperature at well below freezing. He strained to see through the mist of windy snow and sleet for a single headlight in either direction, hyper-aware that his right big toe was already beginning to numb. Out of sequence and out of focus, images of a toeless life came ablaze before him. So did scenes from *Deliverance*.

He spoke to the crew through frantic pronunciations: "I'll wave down the next car that passes by. Maybe they can give one of us a lift to that rest stop. Bring back some gas."

It was almost midnight on New Year's Eve; a future of them stranded for a long while was completely part of their question. His big toe losing more feeling with each breath, Zach crunched it up and down in his wet Airwalk shoe, keeping the circulation of blood from ceasing its natural flow and his toe from entering a class of necrosis. The waiting game would last ten more minutes, when the eventual headlights of a Walmart delivery truck carrying baby formula and handgun ammunition turned the bend and began its descent upon their stalled position, two halos off in the distance like an oasis in the desert. The illuminations on the front of the semi stirred Zach's stomach with liberation more so than his white blood cells could. He flagged down the Teamster with a Dylan Mutters Band T-shirt he'd wiped the fire retardant off his body with, the driver honking his horn twice in acknowledgment, and moved out of the way, allowing the truck to pull over a couple of feet behind them.

"How goes it, partner?" the driver asked, his elbow sticking out of the rolled-down window. "Looks like ya done got yoself in a bit ov a pickle there."

He wore a camouflage jacket and a matching camouflage hat that had a picture of a deer in the crosshairs of a hunting rifle printed on its panel, tying it all together with an aptly fit mullet and gumline. He could have been Richard Ramirez for all Zach cared.

"Hey, man!" the young musician said eagerly. "Yes—yes, we are. Thank you so much for stopping. We ran out of gas. Is there any way you could give me a lift to a station? I think there's one a couple of miles down the road."

"Ov course!" the driver said. "'N' I have a spare gas tank back there y'all ken fill up too!"

Eyeing the car of passed-out dudes and the attractive female driver, lighting matches and staring into the flames like an infant, he asked, "Is it just ya?"

Before Zach could say yes, Abbe yelped from the Chevy. "I'll come too!"

"Nah, that's cool," Zach said to her. "You can hang here. It shouldn't take too long."

Out of the car she went.

"But I wanna come! They're all passed out, and it's probably warm as a key lime pie in the cab of that truck!"

Key lime pie, a dish usually served cold. The voice of reason inside Zach told him Abbe's involvement would undoubtedly muddle up his objective and also reminded him that he didn't really like her. Luke had been a fool to get involved with her in the first place, but to be a fan of hers wasn't Zach's job or prerogative. He was Luke's bandmate and best friend. Of course he wasn't going to like Abbe. No one likes his bandmate's girlfriend.

"She ken come," the driver said, imagining the taste of dessert fresh on his lips. "Plenty av roawum back there faw the both av y'all. Hop on in, preyytty thing! Let me just get Cleo's awful big ass up here."

Cleo, his full-grown female Rottweiler, resided in the cramped rear bucket seat and popped her weighty head out at the quick mention of her name.

"Aww!" Abbe cried out. "Puppy!!"

The trucker opened the door of the cab for Cleo, and following the directions of her owner, she jumped outside to relieve herself next to Zach's leg; this dog all too familiar with their routine on many a dark, twisted night. "Don't wawry—she already done took a shit an hour ago."

"You *really* don't have to come," Zach petitioned, praying Abbe would change her mind. "It might be a while."

"I'm coming."

They gathered their belongings from the station wagon and climbed into the back of the truck cab, which was covered in french fry grease and Cleo's fur and spermicidal lubricant, but it was the hybrid smell of Pine-Sol and salted nuts that flowed off the truck driver like feculence that made Zach gag. Abbe thumbed through an old *Playboy*. Cleo hopped back into the truck. The driver put the transmission into first gear and rolled them away from their broken-down mess with a smile.

"So how'd y'all run out ov gas on New Year's Eve?" he asked, picking his nose aggressively as if it contained raw silver and flicking a booger worth remembering onto the floor by his feet, the mucus landing on the brake pedal.

"Our fuel gauge is broken," Zach answered quickly, so as not to throw blame toward Abbe, "and it slipped our minds . . . It's been a long night." He stopped speaking there, none too keen to expound on their story any further.

"Looks like it . . . Y'all a-headin' back frawum some pawrty er something?"

Awfully quiet since their ride began, Abbe eyed the pack of Marlboro Reds sitting atop the dashboard with the focus of a hawk on a mouse covered in peanut butter and wrapped in chocolate.

"Y'all ken have one, preyytty thing," the driver said, noticing her focal point. "No need to be shy."

She accepted the cigarette like you'd accept a fifteen-dollar gift card—suspicious but comforted. "Their band was playing a show in Durham, but the drummer got in a fight with another band's drummer, and then we all got kicked out."

The driver spat out a gob of chewing tobacco from the side of his mouth and into a Gatorade bottle half full of brown liquid that was in the cupholder. He never picked up the bottle. His aim was immaculate. "Naw shit. What's the name av y'all's band?"

"Texas Flip."

"Huh?"

"I'm Abbe and this is Zach. What's your name?"

"The name is Rufus. Rufus Springsteen."

"*Springsteen?*" Zach asked. "Like Bruce Springsteen?"

"He's my third cousin."

"No way!" Abbe sprang up. "I love Bruce Springsteen!"

"Now do ya, honey?"

"Looks like that's the rest stop," Zach said, throwing them both off.

From a distance, the lit-up Sunoco sign was like a renounced haven, its $1.13/gallon sign the silver lining this night so greatly needed. Off the exit ramp with more speed than needed, the truck pulled into the station faster than the wheel bearings could handle and came to a sudden stop in front of the only out-of-service pump out of all twenty-six available pumps. Abbe exited first, followed by Cleo, and then Zach, extra gas can in hand.

"Do you have any cash?" he asked her.

"Yeah, I got eighteen bucks."

"Cool. Can I have it? I'll pay inside."

He didn't tell her that Luke would be the one who would have to pay her back.

A lit cigarette in his hand and fresh Skoal in his mouth, Rufus walked with Abbe over to a working pump, and Cleo sniffed between a bush and an empty sixty-four-ounce soda cup. The air warmed and the sky darkened. The underground storage tanks leaked in silence, the world unaware. Only a match needed. "Where y'all a-heading off ta tanite anyways?"

"We're driving back home to Oneonta," Abbe said, pointing at the green-colored handle. "I use this one, right?"

"Oneonta? Goddamn ay hate that place! Screwed some lot lizard there back in 'eighty-three; done gave me ah vishus case ov herpes. Sharlene were hur name."

"Sorry to hear that," she said, and started to pump the gas into the can.

Cleo trotted over to Rufus with a large piece of rope clenched in her mouth, probably found behind a dumpster; her yellow teeth gnawed at it savagely—teeth that could kill a lion. "Aw, does little Cleo wanta play tug-of-war with hur daddy?"

"How long have you had her for?" Abbe asked, capping off the small gasoline canister and screwing on its top. A little bit spilled out on the ground, a puddle of insignificance. Rufus ashed in it.

"Since she was a pup. And she's only bitten three folk hur whowl life too, wouldn't ya believe it!"

"Wow, only three?"

Zach returned with a Dr Pepper, a Slim Jim, and the cheapest pack of cigarettes they sold, fully prepared to get back to the station wagon before he and Abbe were murdered and their bodies ground up for Cleo to eat. They piled back into the cab, the dog riding shotgun once again, her exhalations the night's most audible noise, and the truck maneuvered onto the turnabout through crunchy gravel, the highway peaceful as the night was otherwise quiet.

Abbe nudged Zach in the leg with a puckish beam in her smile. It exuded *I gotta tell you something*. And then she did. "Hey, I gotta tell you something."

"What's up?" Zach asked, and accidentally dropped his half-eaten Slim Jim on the floor, mutt hair and crystal meth elements hugging its tubular form. He almost picked it up.

"I took some E like an hour ago." Abbe's index finger pointed to her lips. "*Wild*, right?"

"You what?" Zach asked, positive he had misheard—*had* to have misheard.

She covered her eyes with both hands. "I'm rolling my face off right now . . ."

"You took Ecstasy before you were going to drive all of us back home?!"

"Two hits . . . Is that baaaad? I took them right before Harry got us kicked out. How could I know I was going to have to drive home right then?" She looked up and then down and then up again, and her tongue never went back inside her mouth.

"What are y'all whispering about back there?" Rufus asked.

"Nothing!" Zach replied. "Thanks for everything, Rufus. Can't tell you how much we appreciate all of this."

Abbe scooted over closer, her lips touching Zach's earlobe. "I've always thought you were really sexy," she whispered, and grabbed his crotch. "Don't say anything . . . You make me so hot."

His manhood in her grasp, he was unable to move from the fear of a thousand deaths or an early orgasm, the power she held in her hand that strong. "What the hell are you doing?" Zach pleaded with his life as his cock pleaded with his brain.

"Let me just rub it."

"Get off me. You're Luke's girlfriend!"

Abbe grabbed harder and inched closer. "Luke doesn't know how to fuck me. He can't even keep it up. And Kloe told me about you." Zach's dick started to get hard with thoughts of being tied up to her sorority sister's bed and Abbe felt it too. "See? You like it," she continued in his ear, each enunciation sending more blood to his already massive erection. "Let's have some fun."

Oblivious to the sexual assault happening behind him, Rufus hummed "My Girl," by the Temptations, as Abbe started to unzip Zach's zipper one tooth at a time, the sound it made louder with each drop. His hands tried as little as possible to stop her, and before he knew it his dick was out, his precum splattered her hand, and Luke's girlfriend's mouth—wider than the Gulf of Mexico—was around it.

Cleo, sitting serenely in the front seat, turned around consequent to the audible gasp Zach gave out, tilting her head questioningly, thinking maybe he had a treat for her also. He stared back at the dog, doing his hardest to speak telepathically and relay the message of *turn back around, this isn't happening* in whatever language the dog might understand.

Their station wagon came into view before Zach came into Abbe's mouth. The truck's lights shined bright on the heap of passed-out drunks who lay together in a snake pit of alcohol and cannabis.

"Look!" he yelled. "We're here!"

Abbe lifted her head and wiped the corners of her lips. "Bummer. You were close."

"You can drop us off right there!" Zach ordered Rufus, his dick still erect and poking through his open fly.

"Sure thing, brothuurr. Give that awful old thing a fill up, ayn' you can all be on ur way."

His cock still half out of his pants, Zach departed the truck cabin before Abbe and tried to delete from memory the last fifteen minutes of his life. Their vehicle's flashers still on, its battery fighting for life, he walked with a bent torso to hide his culpability and poured the gas from the small canister into the Chevy's tank with precise aim, returning the can back to Rufus with not a drop to spare. "Thanks again for everything, man. You have no idea how much you helped us out."

"Naw problem there, brothuurr. Just make sure you remembuurr little old Rufus when y'all become big rock stars, and nahwt like that hack Bruce!" Honking his horn with his elbow, he rolled the truck out with a burst of acceleration, howling, "Keep on rockin' in the free werld!" and turned back onto the highway with not even so much as a glance over his shoulder to oncoming traffic. Upright in the front seat, Cleo gave Zach a wink in the window, shook her head, and licked a meaty paw, and the twosome continued their journey to wherever the road was taking them next. Probably a house with red doors.

At the sound of gasoline being poured, Luke had woken up, drunker than before, and had slouched out of the Chevy in the interim. With a small, compacted ball of snow in his hands, he hollered, "Took you long enough!" and launched the sphere of ice directly at an unsuspecting Zach. His aim off by measurements of feet, the ice pellet struck Zach directly on his previously erect and now flaccid dick, and his earlier pain of guilt was a new pain of exasperation. "Oh *shit!*" Luke yelped, shocked his aim was that bad.

Zach kneeled to the ground and absorbed the low blow as best he could. Impossibly.

"Lu—k . . . Why would—you doooo thhhhhat?"

"Dude, my bad . . . Totally my bad, bro! My aim. Wow."

"Let's *leave!*" Zach screamed in agony, one knee to the pavement, hand holding his stomach. "Abbe, I'm driving . . . Give me the keys." Crawling into the driver's seat wounded, but not defeated, Zach lit up a smoke, but not even the nicotine could control his heartbeat. He put the key in the ignition, heard the car's battery beep with most of its life drained, and turned it over.

Nothing happened.

He turned the key back toward him, and then once more, harder and with a jiggle of his wrist, turned over the ignition, and still, nothing happened. The wind stopped blowing and the snow stopped snowing. Zach looked in the rearview mirror and Abbe's eyes met his. Hers were the size of quarters. They held nothing.

"What *kind* of gas did you pump into the can?" he asked, wishing he didn't have to. Wishing he didn't already know the answer.

Abbe looked at Luke, who was seated next to her. And then at Harry, who was passed out. And then at Bart, who was in the front seat. She never looked at Zach.

"Diesel?"

2

The Exit Sign
Las Vegas, NV
10/25/93

Capacity: 110
Tickets Sold: 0

From behind the steering wheel, his sight blinded in part by the sun and in part by his hair, the words that flowed from Luke's mouth like warm tiramisu made him sound more useless than he already was, but not as useless as warm tiramisu.

"It's only one thirty. We've got *plenty* of time."

Luke was the worst driver from the shallow pool at their disposal, no question about it, but he was also the only person in the band free from the years-long stain of a DUI. A subpar relief pitcher at best, last in the rotation when the other players were forced to take a lawful hiatus from the road, they trusted him to perform the basic motor functions of driving a fifteen-seat Ford Club Wagon with a trailer down a mountainside at 60 mph how they did breakfast from Subway. But he was of great use when any one of them was too tired, hungover, or stoned to drive. Or when he was the least of all three.

The Arizona desert's burnt sienna was a torture caught in the front of Zach's throat. He sat a foot from Luke's right ear, thundering pleas for a life too young to be snuffed out: "Will you please slow down!"

Earwax and Pearl Jam on the radio drowned him out.

Todd leaned forward into the front of the van with a cup of gas station brew held in range of a foreseeable spill onto their only road map, crinkled and lying across the top of Zach's legs. The reflection of light off the road made squinting a necessary chore. But it didn't make being a dick an assignment as well. "Are you *sure* you didn't miss the exit?" he asked Luke, scanning outside the windshield with a hand over his eyes to block the sunshine he so loathed. He prodded further like a costive enema. "These mountains make it feel like we're going the wrong way."

One eye on the road, the other on Todd in his peripheral, Luke said, "I don't know, man, maybe? Chill . . . we'll figure it out. What's the map say?"

Snuggled tight in the turtle-shell opening between the front seats, Todd's right elbow accidentally hit the map off Zach's lap as he reversed back into the rear of the van; the chart fell into that dark abyss between the seat and the middle compartment, its fortune bound with the black void.

"I don't know," the guitarist said, annoyed beyond repair, his fingertips tickling the just-out-of-reach map's top edge. He threw blame with a venomous harpoon. "Todd just knocked it off my lap, and now it's in between the seats."

"You ain't getting that shit out," Harry teased, his face buried in a dirty pillow on the van's last bench seat, eyes as red as his hair.

Todd's impatience for Luke's patience reduced to naught. "I can't *chill* because you took the wrong highway out of Phoenix. And oh yeah, it's 105 fucking degrees outside and our A/C is broken because Harry's father's a drunk." Stirring up an already sore subject to score spiteful brownie points, this above-board reminder from Todd—that Harry's father was indeed an alcoholic—added no more solution to their problem.

"Meh," was all the response the culprit's son would wager.

The A/C in their van had been broken for more months than there were on a calendar. Everyone too cheap (and broke) to get it fixed, this source of invariable contention stemmed from yet another act of kindness not asked of someone who also couldn't afford to fix their A/C.

After a show in Harry's hometown at the Wyckoff Music Hall attended by mostly family, high school friends, and work associates, Harry Sr. (in the act of clumsy chitchat while Texas Flip loaded their gear back into their van) asked the question more quintessential to dads than the ownership of a leather braid belt: "How's the van holding up?" A man with no more in life to aim for or star to hope on, Harry Sr. glowed bright inside once again as these young'uns disclosed to him their van's cooling fan issues and its capability to eat gasoline like liquid Reese's chocolate. Somehow sober after five old-fashioneds, the sixty-three-year-old leaned on the Ford's right front fender and burped with good intentions. "Harry Jr. never told you guys about my mechanical skills? I'm a wizard with tools."

The damage he'd do would be financially irreversible.

Back in the Arizona desert, this decision came back to haunt them more than any 7-Eleven taquito ever could. "Didn't the map say to head north on I-17?" Luke asked with the persuasiveness of a liar on the witness stand, the urine in his bladder pushing against his kidneys in sore persistence.

Todd made sure to stagger in circuit breaker halts between every fourth or so word to emphasize the irritation they all felt. And to also prevent himself from choking out Luke. "Maps don't talk . . . they just show you . . . the best route . . . to get from point A . . . to point B . . . If we had taken US-93N. . . like the map showed . . . if that's what had happened . . . and not what is currently happening . . . then yes . . . you'd be correct . . . But by the looks of it . . . we're nowhere near . . . where we're supposed to be."

Zach tried harder to dig the map out in between rests of breath, his heartbeat in rhythm with Todd's dialogue. After minutes of steady defeat, he at last grabbed hold of the destroyed booklet, now folded in half, and carved the air with it like a paper ax, slicing their doubt in half and thus delivering the evidence that this situation would now be under control.

"Is that the map?" Luke asked, desperate to get Todd off his dick.

Zach unfolded the sticky papers like a newly found fossil, the chart opening right back to its previous diagram of the most destitute landmass our great land has to offer. He caught sight of a mile marker and was able to map out their current course with an uncut fingernail and protractor precision. The dead coyote on the side of the highway, its carcass savaged by blow flies, summed up their prognosis without error. "Shit," he said. "We're, like, ninety miles in the wrong direction."

Todd punched the ceiling of the van. It added a new dent to his collection, and the strike sent a ripple through the Burger King strawberry shakes resting in their cupholders like tom-toms. "Goddamn it, Luke!"

Having little trust in Zach's map-reading abilities, and in equal disbelief that he could have made such a foolish mistake himself, Luke grabbed the paper layout from his friend's crotch, nipping his passenger's left testicle in the process, and held it up to the sun's obdurate glow. "Hmm," he mused, "yeah . . ." The speedometer showed 73 mph as his left elbow steered. "I guess I *was* supposed to get on US-93N. My bad, guys." He then dropped the map back in between his seat and the center console.

"If my balls are any gauge," Bart complained from the most remote corner of the van, legs spread-eagled and right hand buried deep into his black athletic shorts that had a hole right where his asshole was, "I'd say it's hotter than my asshole in here. And now we're ninety miles out of the way? I'm gonna die back here, bro!"

"Bart?" Luke said, and gave Zach a wink with his right eye. "Do you have any ice cubes?" He didn't bother for a response. "If so, could you put some in your mouth and come suck my cock real quick?"

Tensions had already been running high that day after an accounting mishap at a QuikTrip gas station earlier in the morning. Bart was only fanning the flames once more to a previously extinguished problem.

As was customary at the beginning of those early tours, each band member and Todd—all fresh out of college—would pool together as much money as possible from whatever jobs they were working and situate these resources into an envelope labeled "Gas Money." This envelope, always left in the glove compartment and never futzed with for anything other than gas, was considered an entity holier than the Western Wall on Shabbat. Each member of Texas Flip knew the balance of that envelope better than the balance of their own wallets, so when Harry went to fill up the tank that morning somewhere outside of Mesa, he was quick to notice it was $100 lighter than it ought to have been. This brain teaser presented in a cordial fashion to his bandmates as they came back to the van with armfuls of Fritos, Twizzlers, Mr. Pibb, and Pepto-Bismol, not one of them could give an explanation as to how, or why, the money was missing. An inauspicious accounting mishap, perhaps; a kerfuffle that had everyone claiming his innocence, little else could be done besides weave tall tales during long stretches of highway silence—a living game of Clue where you'd rather commit the murder than solve its mystery. As a matter of necessity when thousands of miles away from home, this foul-up—one of the countless that occurred during the band's touring life—was swiftly downgraded to another fabrication and swept under Texas Flip's crusty rug of lies as they carried new suspicions and doubts into the City of Lost Wages.

While wrapping up their third week of a five-week-long North America fall tour, the southwestern heat had done its best to sizzle away most of Texas Flip's audacity and patience. The crisp northern Arizona landscape was sourish in its taste, like a battery to a tongue, and any touchy-feely occurrences among the members that had been simmering to boil were now fixed molds, unfit to be altered. A sidelong glance, a giggle at the wrong joke, even breathing, were all excuses to be angry at someone. The ways of the road: wrath and forgiveness, push and pull with no give. And although in a certain way understandable when you live in a confined space with four other people you hardly know outside of the music you create together and the money you scrape up to eat, bad blood never bodes well with a breakfast of eggs, bananas, and refillable cups of go-fuck-yourself at 6:45 A.M.

With an earnestness in his voice cheaper than a discounted dollar-store item, Luke was talking more to dead air than to living beings. "Dudes, we're fine. Let's all chill out and get lit off this blunt."

Collapsed back onto his designated seat, Todd's bipolarity

changed with the sparks of a lighter. "Thank God someone has more weed!"

A state trooper sped past them heading in the opposite direction, lights blaring, but the five-O didn't faze anyone in the slightest. Neither did their broken taillight.

The van had been holding up well sans the air-conditioning and most of its built-in safety features, but this red rock heat they were now lost in would prove to be its biggest test yet. Still a relatively new purchase, the 1988 Ford E-150—painted black and with no windows except for the two up front—had been the band's largest ever investment and the linchpin to this entire tour that they were currently negotiating in unfavorable conditions. They had purchased the vehicle, with some 187,000 "city miles" placed on its delicate engine, off some dude for $900 after it sat for months in the parking lot of the Blockbuster Harry worked at. With three bashed-in windows and a touch of graffiti during its occupancy, Texas Flip finally bit the bullet once the price on the FOR SALE sign was lowered to the point a homeless person would have been comfortable paying. But months later, with the American-engineered machine broiling past its breaking point in the desert heat and its old engine being put through the most intense audition of its employment on this current detour north toward Flagstaff, nothing ever felt so wrong before.

"Anyone smell that?" Luke asked.

Given the amount of pot smoke wafting through the van, Zach was impressed a second scent could have penetrated such mugginess, and a couple of minutes would pass until Luke spoke again.

"Seriously, do you guys smell that? It smells like somethi —*holy shit the van is on fire!*"

"What?!" Todd screamed. "Pull over! I'm too young to die! I'm not even twenty-seven!"

Thoughtlessly, Luke slammed on the brakes, sending

Todd's un-seat-belted body flying forward into the back of Zach's seat; a discernible crack in his neck was loud enough to be worrisome, although everyone figured maybe he was dead already and would be spared the awful death (and ironic knowledge) of burning alive in a Ford. The van bucked back and forth violently, the vehicle not built to endure such harsh treatment, until it came to a standstill on the side of the highway in a lump; clouds of sand and brake dust rolled through the vehicle's open windows, obscuring the sun above.

Fearful of everything, the band's manager jumped out of the van with a warped gait and started to run around the middle of the road as if he himself were on fire, the bottoms of his bare feet dancing on gravel hot enough to sear a porterhouse. The rest of the band emptied out calmly and orderly as if it were a fire drill, waving away soot from their faces and moseying over to the highway's guardrail, waiting in sick anticipation for either the van to blow up or Todd to be hit by a car, their jaws slack as heaps of heavy smoke poured from all four tires. Moments away from stop, drop, and rolling himself down the mountain, Todd finally found his self-control and took an indecisive step away from the van toward the rest of them.

"Whoa! Okay . . . All right." His tone was much calmer than seconds previous, almost as if nothing had ever happened. "I think we're gonna be fine . . ." He took another deep breath and coughed on the exhale. "It looks like the smoke is coming from the brakes."

"You think?" Bart said with not nearly enough sarcasm, his hand still on his scrotum.

"Goddamn it, Luke!" Harry added. "You drive this van like it's a toy car! The brakes are probably screwed now."

"You're saying this is my fault, bro?"

"Of course this is your fault!" Harry answered back. "You're the one who was driving the van!"

"Well, yeah . . . But you don't have to be such a dick about it."

"Can everyone shut up?" Zach appealed, taking a step back to absorb the heat of the day. "Luke, I'm sorry, but Harry's right. You drive like an idiot . . . We're gonna need to let the brakes cool down for a bit before we can keep driving. We got time. Should be fine to keep going in an hour or so."

Oblivious in their air-conditioned death traps as they sped past at speeds unnatural to this world, not a soul flinched at the five young men stranded on the side of the road next to a van that, on quick glance, looked to be engulfed in flames.

On the search for anything better to do than talk to his bandmates, Zach frisked the infertile, scalding-hot, godforsaken outback they were stuck in for further signs of life, even just a rattlesnake to be bitten by. A mangy coyote circled their position counterclockwise in sixty-second intervals and some jackrabbits appeared among the cacti. There weren't any other life-forms under the 99-degree heat that radiated from the lone star in the brilliant sky. But from their vantage point high up on the vista, he could identify a little sliver of populace off in the distance a couple miles down the road—one part promising, two parts suspect. Focusing his eyes on what looked like a McDonald's sign, the golden arches of saturated fat and cholesterol begging for them to have a share in its delicious offerings, this portent of an oasis brought on an unexpected change in mood and appetite.

Zach pointed into the sun and sneezed. "It looks like there's a town over there. Let's coast down the mountain, get off this road, and find a place to hang out inside that maybe has air-conditioning. I think the van should be fine if we take it easy on the brakes."

The only logical plan proposed to get them out of there, no one else put up an argument, per usual, and so that's what they did. Zach hopped into the driver's seat, while Luke, serving an indefinite suspension from driving duties, sat next to him, shamefaced and low but with hair perfect for the occasion. The engine turned on a dime. Zach spun the wheel left, the E-150's power steering close to the end of its rainbowed life, and inched the van back onto the highway, embarking nice and slow in the manner he had proposed to get them down this misty mountaintop.

The restaurant he had been sure was a McDonald's was an A&W Restaurant.

Spooked at how easily his eyes had played tricks on him in the heat, Zach found this sad stretch of asphalt one finds only off the side of an American interstate evenly spooky. A one-mile-long, two-lane-wide stretch of highway with three banks, a gas station on each end, and road dining staples such as Taco Bell, Carl's Jr., and Boston Market, it was the best *and* worst place possible to have your van turn into a furnace. Parked in a handicap spot, cigarettes lit, Todd got out first and the sun said hello. "I'm gonna go see if Taco Bell is still doing that burrito deal. How's about we meet back here in an hour. Time enough for the brakes to cool down, yeah?"

"I'm gonna come with," Luke announced. "I wanna take a shit in their bathroom. They always have the nicest bathrooms for some reason."

"Bart, want to go to Boston Market with me?" Harry asked.

"Nah, that place sucks. I'm gonna go to Carl's Jr."

"You think Carl's Jr. is better than Boston Market?"

"Bro, you're kidding me, right? Boston Market's corn muffins taste like sandpaper made with butter."

"Your asshole tastes like sandpaper made with butter."

Zach's stomach sat uncomfortable from that morning's breakfast of microwaved White Castle cheeseburgers, and he needed a break from fake meat and the guys in his band, so he decided to play it safe with an ice-cream cone from A&W and what was sure to be the coldest environment of the bunch. The parking lot hotter than point of impact under an atomic bomb, locations agreed upon and questions of weight denied, each of these young men was quick to disperse his own way with the thirst of detachment and the soil of hell thick on their palates. Zach stumbled into the chilled A&W not thirty feet away, and euphoria entered his bloodstream the way embalming fluid does, cheerful to be alone and for an opportunity to take a solid dump in peace. His mouth couldn't help itself from falling agape when he leaned his head back in the restaurant's entranceway, taking in the cooled air and incandescent light bulbs above him like one does after a long, grueling hike or intense workout. Grateful for these technological advancements in climate-controlled buildings, his first step toward a dairy-filled enlightenment and flushed intestines felt secure and full of indulgence. Neil Armstrong on the moon. His second step, not so much.

"Ken you pleeez get da hell out of mahh waaayyyy?!"

Torn from bliss, Zach turned around and regulated his sight to make sure that what he saw was, in fact, what he thought—a woman, and *not* a manatee with legs.

He lost count of the chins on her face after three, and despite the lady's rotundness and overall grotesque figure, there had been plenty of room for her to have easily walked around Zach and avoid this unnecessary increase in blood pressure. But like the walker gripped in her hands, another crutch of opposition was needed to rationalize her piddling existence and government stipend.

Sarcasm tingled his lips. "Of course."

With the least bit of tact, Gilbert Grape's mother hobbled her ass right past and up to the register, rolling her eyes at Zach as if *he* had offended *her*. "Some people—am I right?" she complained to the teenage boy with braces behind the cash machine who wore a black polo shirt three sizes too big.

"Yeah," he agreed, forced to reply because that was his job. "Some people . . ."

"Lemme get fawr cheeeeseburrgs, an order of lawge fries—and not those gotdamn smawwll ones." She lifted her fleshy forearm and drew an uppercase *L* with a puffy index finger. "That gotdamn dumbass in the back always tryyying to gev me smawll fries!" There was solid trust in her steadiness, so she hoisted her other diabetic arm and with this free hand formed a funnel around her blubbery mouth. "*LAWGE!* And one of dem extra-lawge Diet Coca-Colas, and"—pausing for air—"aww hell, it's food stamp day . . . Gev me one dem root burr float thingamajigs too."

Afraid she might decide to eat him instead of the seven thousand calories the federal government had paid for, Zach waited until her food was prepared and placed on a tray and she was seated before he dared to place his own order. Fumbling in his pockets for the spare change he was positive was there, he made his approach, and only an untied shoelace blundered his progression. "Can I get a vanilla ice-cream cone?"

"We're out of vanilla," the cashier responded with a mouthful of metal, junior year of high school optimism still intact. "Sorry . . . We have chocolate, though."

"Whatever."

Zach pulled out the debris from his pocket and handed the cashier the unexamined contents: eighty-two cents in loose change and an unused condom left over from a hard case of blue balls the night before. Short thirteen cents after tax, the cashier let it slide and gave him back the condom in the same hand he delivered the ice-cream cone. Zach tucked around the corner of a wall to evade the Fatty Acid Queen and chose a seat by the window closest to the van, the soft serve's reticulated swirl delightful in the daylight. Dopamine flooded his brain between licks as the restaurant's frigidness cooled his lower back and ass crack. Positioned for fifty-three beautiful minutes of privacy in the most perfect of ways, he stretched his legs, blinked his eyes, and breathed easy, happier than a pig before slaughter. The van within close sight, Zach was posted in perfect position to keep it safe from any buzzards who might have felt inclined to try to steal their gear in broad daylight. It was safe. Had to be safe.

They had been robbed once in Buffalo.

Too poor to afford a trailer, and stupid enough to have left their gear in the van overnight without covering any of it, a couple of punks smashed their window as they slept on the floor of a friend's house after a show, stealing a Gibson Les Paul Studio, a kick drum, and most of their merchandise. This lesson learned in the hardest of ways, the obsession to make sure it never happened again would consume him. Slouched down in his hard plastic bucket seat, Zach let out a lungful of appreciativeness for this immediate instant, for that's all there was to do: breathe and relax.

His eyes soon closed.

"Brakes are starting to look good."

A cat-o'-nine-tails to his solar plexus, Zach was caught from his river of slumber like an unsuspecting salmon by a fisherman without a license. He opened one eye and saw a patchy beard and late-age acne—the telltale signs needed for a quick identification. Opening both eyes to cope with the disappointment he observed from the bottom half of Bart's face, he asked, "Why are you here? Didn't you go to Carl's Jr.?"

"Nice to see you too, asshole," Bart said, and sat down on the bucket seat across from him. The plastic bent in chorus with the nine pounds he'd packed on this tour so far. "Listen, dude, I need to tell you something, but you must *absolutely* promise you won't say anything to the other dudes . . . Can you promise me?"

Zach gave a quick glance over to the van. A couple of teenagers practiced varial flips nearby. Not much to worry about. "What are you talking about?"

Hands flat on the table, Bart's eyes went back and forth with the speed of a peregrine falcon. "I know where the money went."

"Money? What money?"

"Come on, you idiot!" Bart exclaimed, lifting his hands up and then slamming both back down onto the tabletop. "The gas money, dude . . . I know where the gas money went."

Zach had seen this coming for miles measured in the length of the Milky Way. But now that the two of them were sitting together inside an A&W somewhere in Arizona, he was unable to understand why, out of everyone in their band, *he* was the one Bart felt safe in spilling his dirty secret to. Reason being that they didn't like each other. And never had. A snaky dude, greasy in a literal sense, Bart was the kind of person with whom you never knew where you stood. Someone you wouldn't want to leave your dog alone with.

A rough road when left unpaved, individual relationships within a band (an often neglected afterthought) are the most integrated dealings in the rock-and-roll spectrum of psychological malfunctions and best explained in layman's terms: *Just because you're in a band with someone does not mean you have to like them or that they must like you.* And once you figured out who your archnemesis in your own band was, there was an unspoken agreement that this be addressed immediately, lest this relationship turn into a nasty staph infection, a carbuncle of pent-up resentment no amount of success could ever heal.

Too bad no one told that to Texas Flip.

The cold seat against the small of Zach's back felt good. It was all that felt good. "Where did it go?" he asked.

A lonely stool pigeon with a juicy testimony, their pianist confessed without further poking. He might have exploded otherwise. "I took it . . . But I'm gonna replace it!"

"Why are you telling me this?"

"Because I knew you'd be chill about it. If I told Todd, he would have flipped out. And Luke and Harry probably wouldn't have cared that much but would for sure tell Todd."

The kids outside had started practicing frontside 5-0 grinds on the waxed curb next to the van. A Latino boy, the most talented of the bunch, fell backward after his third attempt and sent his Birdhouse skateboard flying in the air, missing the Ford by a couple of feet. Zach's blood pressure rose. "Why did you take it?"

"Remember that bar we went to the other night, in El Paso?"

The skateboarder's close call absorbed most of Zach's attention until he decided to work on his ollies and manuals instead. "Yeah—the sports bar, right?"

"Yeah, that one. Well, after all you dudes went back up to the room, I got to talking to this guy at the bar. A gambling fella."

The bar, Big Tips Grill, was attached to the motel Texas Flip had stayed at that night, a unique opportunity to lodge somewhere with plumbing. A buddy of theirs in another band had also informed them that the chef who worked in the kitchen used to play in a band and loved feeding musicians on tour. When they arrived, there was neither a chef nor a functioning kitchen.

"So, I'm sitting there, talking shit with this old dude," Bart continued, "and there's a football game on. I had no idea who was playing, but the guy goes, 'I'll bet you a hundred dollars he's going to miss this field goal.' Dude's old, at least sixty. It sounded like he was joking around. So I go, 'Sure thing, bro—'"

"Did you actually call him 'bro'?"

"Yeah. Why? What does that have to do with the story?"

"Nothing. Sorry. Continue."

"Like I was saying . . . The kicker goes to kick the ball—and would you believe it, he slips right before impact! Shanks it straight into the bleachers. That never happens! What are the odds?! But I don't care—whatever. *No big deal,* I tell myself. I mean, we didn't shake hands on it or anything. So, I laugh a little and go, 'Crazy, right?'"

The Latino teen, and the only one with any future riding a board on wheels, landed a heelflip. High and tight. Cocky, he made a new attempt at a frontside 5-0 grind, but this time rather than grinding through the wax, his back truck stuck and flung his body down to the pavement, tearing a decent chunk of skin from his knee in the process.

"Are you listening, dude?" Bart asked with desperation.

"Yeah—sorry," Zach lied. "Tired . . . So, this dude misses a kick, and you start laughing?"

"I didn't *laugh* laugh. I was just . . . I don't know—I was being good-humored? I don't know, man, it all happened so fast. But then the old man throws a twenty on the bar, stands up, and says, like, super nonchalantly, 'I'll take that hundred now.' And I'm like, 'What, bro? We didn't shake or anything. I was just kidding around.' And then the dude lifts the bottom of his shirt and shows me the butt of a pistol in his pants and says, 'Did I stutter, boy?'"

"Holy shit . . ."

"Yeah, man. Holy shit . . . And even worse, there was no one else in the place. So, I look at the bartender, and—would you believe it?—guy turns his head and starts trying to change the channel on the TV!"

"What did you do then?"

"I started to empty out my pockets to show him I had no

money. But he's not having it. Goes, 'You're gonna have to do better than that, boy.'"

"He kept calling you 'boy'?"

"Please stop interrupting me."

"Sorry."

"All I can think about is the pistol. Almost shit myself. I was positive the guy was going to pull his gun out and shoot me in the dick right there. And I knew we had that cash in the glove compartment. So, I panicked . . . I told him I had money in the van, and he's like, 'Move it,' and follows me out. When I give him the money, he counts it quick, and then looks at me and goes, 'No one fucks with Texas, boy!' and then"—he lifted his pants leg to display a welt the size of a golf ball—"kicks me straight in the shin."

"Holy shit!"

"Yeah, man, holy shit . . . Before I could recover, the guy got in his pickup truck and drove off."

"Whoa."

"So, listen, I got, like, seventeen dollars in my checking account. My plan is, when we get to Vegas, I'm gonna turn it into $170. And when I do, I'm just gonna put the hundred back in the envelope and nobody will know any better. They'll just be relieved it's back."

"Sounds like a good plan," Zach said. The ice cream in his stomach gurgled uncomfortably, and he just didn't care about anything Bart was telling him. "Listen, man, I'm gonna go the bathroom. And when I come back, we can keep talking about this."

The cleanest bathroom he'd seen for weeks, for eleven continuous minutes Zach read a copy of *Reader's Digest* that someone had left behind and forced out a poop the size of a grape. His thighs went numb from his forearms. After washing his face with hand soap, he smelled his armpits, popped a zit in the mirror, wiped his ass one extra time, and exited the bathroom with indifference. Rounding the corner back into the dining area, he spied with his little eye all his bandmates now sitting at his booth.

Bart, facing his direction, mouthed, *No one.*

Forced to stand as there were no more seats available, Zach said, "I think we can hit the road now. I'll drive."

This assembled mass dragged their bodies full of caloric value outside and back into the van again. Not a word was spoken about the stench of smoke throughout their cramped quarters. Zach's zip-up hoodie, left behind to bake in the rankness, smelled as if it had been used to put out a burning animal. The Ford starting back up with a medium amount of effort, he adjusted the rearview mirror, pushed Dinosaur Jr.'s *Green Mind* into the tape deck, reversed out, and put them on the correct track back to the wrong kind of town, and himself in the middle of a lie.

The venue they were playing that night was called the Exit Sign, a dive bar that was a couple of miles away from the Vegas Strip: close enough to attract the young rock crowd that dwelled in this city, but far enough away to help them forget they had to live in a metropolis that aligned itself with the human inclinations to gamble, screw hookers, and drink twenty-four hours a day. The Exit Sign was "their" place, with free entry, cheap beer, and decent sound. It was the best spot in Las Vegas to forget you were there.

The Exit Sign, in the most generous of ways, paid bands fifty dollars cash and doled out two drink tokens for each member upon arrival: a pot of gold delivered in a white envelope before a note was even played and enough to get drunk off tall doubles of well whiskey hours before your set. Every show there started at 10:00 P.M., ended at 3:00 A.M., and never had a set lineup. Instead, bands picked numbers out of a hat when they arrived, and this was what determined who would play when. Didn't matter if you were the first band to arrive for load-in or the last; you picked out of the same hat and drew the number you drew. That was it.

The Exit Sign wasn't a "headliners" club. It was a club for bands of a smaller measure. A club to bang your funny bone on before you reached that next step. A club that needed to be, in a rapidly changing world of corporate-sponsored music venues and condominium expansions.

After one more detour so Todd could piss on a cactus, Texas Flip arrived in Las Vegas two hours early, and the club's owner, Billy, met them outside to deliver their envelope and have them pull a number out of the hat; they drew 5. This meant they wouldn't be playing till at least 1:00 A.M. Too broke to gamble and too wakeful to sleep, their fate for the night was sealed. They were about to listen to a lot of bad music.

If there's one constant that rings forever true, it's that sitting through shitty bands is always that. Shitty.

Another bad drummer playing another bad drum fill in another bad band made you begin to question why you ever wanted to play live music in the first place. All that death metal, lo-fi hip-hop, acid jazz, and baroque chamber pop eventually sounded like one big hot pile of garbage in due course and further accelerated any preexisting hearing loss—the equivalent of sleeping next to a jackhammer or someone with sleep apnea—made easier only with earplugs.

You suffer because you have nothing else to do.

You suffer because you're on tour in a band nobody knows.

Three beers deep and sipping on a two-finger scotch as he walked onstage, Zach was sober enough to remember their songs but not drunk enough to disregard the emptiness of the room. With a bird's-eye view from the four-foot-high stage, he could make out a total of nineteen people in the entire place, including the two bartenders. Six of them looked to be Vietnam War vets: the gang congregated around a pool table that none of them were playing on, two of them missing hands, the table missing a leg. There were also four prostitutes either looking to score drugs or having already scored drugs, spending their hard-earned cash on three-dollar shot-and-beer combos and waiting for the right drunk dunce to stumble past, the offering of a cheap toothy blow job too good to pass up.

The lights above twinkled with high voltage.

They were out of Miller Lite.

Billy sat outside the entrance on a stool with no back the entire night, his eyes never leaving the copy of *Dianetics* he'd been reading since Texas Flip arrived, and seemed to be apathetic to all the things that might have been (and never would be) in his life or in his club. The Exit Sign, living in the shadows of a city more corrupt than professional boxing, was exactly what it needed to be and not an iota more: a cargo hold for the musical misfits, outcasts, and refugees of modern times, it was a place to forget *about*, not one to try to remember. Zach wouldn't recall what they played or if it was performed well, but to tell the truth, it didn't matter a whole lot, because this gig, like most every gig on a young band's touring schedule, had chalked itself up to another one of *those* shows the moment they got there. The moment they woke up that morning. The moment they booked it thinking, *Playing in Vegas is gonna be dope!* All this show was was another due to pay. Another promise that, without doubt, there will have been something worth fighting for at the end of this dark tunnel they chose to travel down. A positive balance to the heavily weighted negatives of being a young band on the road. Something savory and sweet to munch on. A guarantee.

But unlike the guaranteed delights of refined sugars and the beginnings of a one-night stand, the only guarantees of being on tour in a van was that nothing was ever guaranteed.

Not an audience, a well-paid gig, or a full six hours of sleep. The reason you're a band on tour is to build the audience, the community, and the life that, at age twenty-four, you thought you'd want forever, the dream too good to be true when you're blasting your asshole out in the bathroom of a Jersey City coffeehouse forty-five minutes before your set, asking yourself, *Why did I order tacos in Jersey City from a coffeehouse?* The beauty of this life lies in the eye of its beholder.

Jackson Pollock painted more symmetrical landscapes.

Texas Flip finished their set at 2:10 A.M., had all their gear loaded by 2:14 A.M., and were checked into their smoking room with two twin beds and a cot at the Down and Outer Motel shortly after 2:29 A.M. The room reminiscent of the one in *The Shining* but more morbid, Luke and Harry flopped their bodies down onto the same bed, landing awkwardly next to each other, and were down for the count before all the lights turned on. Suffering from a bout of food poisoning ever since a gas station microwave burrito got the best of him, Harry had been out of commission for the past couple of days and also held no interest in any possible mischief. All Luke wanted to do was watch TV.

"I'm gonna head back to the Strip. Anybody else wanna come?" Bart asked as predicted.

Gulping down a Budweiser can and shaking out his hair in the room's vanity mirror, Zach caught a glimpse of three deep wrinkles on his forehead that he had never noticed before and assimilated himself to the process of aging. "Me," he replied, intent on making the most of his youth and this night.

"If you dudes want, you can take a couple of bucks from tonight for a taxi," Todd offered in a charitable manner uncharacteristic of him. "I'm gonna chill here too."

The envelope on the nightstand glowed with possibility. Heavy with an unused drink token somehow, Bart poured out the remainder of its contents onto the mirrored table and watched five wrinkled ten-dollar bills tumble out along with two small baggies filled with either flour or enough cocaine to kill the 1986 New York Mets. Todd grabbed one of them and examined it under the light like a crime scene forensics unit.

"Is this—"

"Let me see that!" Bart ordered, and grabbed the baggie away. His excitement exciting everyone, he poured out a dime-sized amount of the mystery powder onto the dirty glass tabletop, licked his pinkie finger, pressed it into the little white mountain, and then proceeded to rub his entire gumline with it. A smile wide as the sky, he spoke with rapture and emptied out the rest of the dusty substance: "Oh yeah, boys, this is good shit!" Cutting up five small lines with a ShopRite Price Plus card, one for each of them, he rolled a two-dollar bill cross-wise, snorted a quick inhale through his right nostril, bent his head back, sniffed hard once more, and then offered the trundled green paper to whoever chose to go next.

The look of inquisitiveness on their faces took him by surprise.

"Wait a second," he said. "Am I the only one here that's ever done this stuff?"

Luke and Todd both shrugged their shoulders in a *maybe we have but nah we've definitely haven't* kind of way.

"Too funny . . . Okay, let me show you how it's done then." The ShopRite Price Plus card back in his grips, he explained, "You need to chop it up first; most of this stuff is cut with gasoline and baby laxatives."

"They put gasoline in there, and you're still gonna snort it?" asked Zach.

Bart looked at him almost bothered. "Yes," he said, "these are drugs. They wouldn't be illegal if there *wasn't* a possibility they could kill you." And moving forward with the experience of a trained archaeologist in the field, he began to hack away at the remaining four lines till they became even more powdery, finer and finer, and what had looked like a good amount of cocaine appeared three times its original volume.

"I guess I'll go next," Luke spoke up apprehensively.

And so it went till everyone had snorted a line.

Dubious of the powder's effect as it rushed through his nasal cavity and straight to a still-developing frontal cortex, it would be fair to say that Zach felt little to no effects of the drug, but rather a strange new drip in the back of his throat that stuck to his uvula like gold dust.

Licking away at his teeth like they were Tootsie Pops, hardly a minute had passed before Bart asked, "Who wants to do another one?"

Rapid advances made in the frequency of which they ingested the drug, most of that first baggie was finished within twenty minutes of it being opened. The right side of his jaw already sore and the molars ground down to sand, Zach was frying harder than an egg, although it was difficult for him to know that then. At some point Donna Summer came on the radio and nothing ever felt so right before. Lying down next to Harry on the bed, Luke started to flip through the channels on the surprisingly nice television set, landing on an episode of *Three's Company* before muting the TV, grabbing an acoustic guitar from out of the van, and strumming the foundations of a shaky G chord without a pick before yelling, "*Why is John Ritter so orange?!*" a half step out of key. Bart's eyes beamed with promise and psycho activity. "Zach, you still down to hit the Strip?"

His heart was beating harder than it had ever beaten before, and he felt an enhanced connectivity with the world. "Definitely. Can we take that other bag with us?"

"Do you care if we take that other bag with us?" Bart asked the room, the second virgin baggie of drugs already between his fingers.

"Go for it!" Luke shouted, his head nodding in a risky up-down motion.

"Bring your room key," Bart told Zach. "We're gonna need it to do bumps with. I'll call the taxi."

If he could tell you what happened between the time Bart called the cab and when they made it to the Strip, he would have, but he didn't remember. Drugs make things hard to remember. Almost impossible. Money, though. Money makes you remember everything.

Twenty minutes later, hearts thumping at a steady 130 bpm, they walked through the entrance of the Tropicana, per the taxi driver's recommendation, infused with certainty and void of appetite. Both felt the need to talk but had nothing to say. They also couldn't wait to dip into the first bathroom they saw and dig that room key inside their baggie. Zach hocked up a loogie so the lovely numbness he'd come to enjoy would continue to soak the back of his throat and lit a cigarette, relishing himself, his choices, and altogether missing the misfortune and lapse suffusing the lobby. The smoke-stained carpet and slot machines reported all the sporadic dreams and lonely nights spent here, the fish stories told and done. But Zach felt as if he was in the exact place he always needed to be and wished to never leave. "Bart!" he cried out, his blood fast through an already cramped heart. "This is gnarly, dude, I think I'm having a heart attack. Let's find a bathroom."

The casino lights flickered in his bandmate's eyes. "Right?" Bart agreed. "All right—shit, okay . . . Let's find a bathroom and do another rip from this bag. Then, yeah . . . then I'm gonna—I'm gonna hit up one of those roulette tables."

"Is that the one with the ball and numbers?"

"I think I see a bathroom over there."

"Great. I think it's wearing off anyways."

Through a small hallway off the casino floor was a white marble-tiled bathroom. They both entered the same stall in haste, the three older men from Niagara Falls with hands under faucets paying them no mind. This bag barely bigger than Zach's thumbnail made opening it an almost impossible task, and the anxiousness with which they wanted it unlocked felt more and more pressing with each futile attempt and the air lacked oxygen, the stall small enough to feel crowded but large enough to have sex. He was extra cautious dipping the room key into the teeny plastic sack once opened—careful not to tear a hole through the side of it and lose the entire evening's incentive in the toilet or on the floor. Two quick snaps up the blowhole for each of them, a quick piss, and it was back out to the casino floor with fresh ciggies and fresher sinus cavities. Dean Martin played on the speakers. A little person dressed like Marilyn Monroe walked past. A woman won $250. The lights and sounds of a Las Vegas casino overwhelmed them to the point of queasiness, influential in its declarations. All sound reason was repelled as these two bandmates flowed back into the gambling halls of the Tropicana, past the blackjack and pai gow poker tables, through a maze of baccarat, craps, and video poker machines, and finally to the roulette section of the casino, both young men burning with purpose and prospect.

"I only got seventeen bucks on me," Bart said. "So, I gotta make this money work. Let me know if you see any five-dollar tables."

Zach's central nervous system stood jacked, taking in the sights and sounds of wholesome depravity as scantily dressed cocktail waitresses who looked like they had walked inside this place one day, got a job, and then never bothered to venture back outside again in twenty years sashayed to and from tables in perfect motion, serving free beer to middle-aged red-faced men in Hoover Dam T-shirts and elderly women dressed in their Sunday best, out to destroy whatever posture they had left with each rheumatic pull of the slot lever.

His cigarette never tasted so good.

"Found it!" Bart yelled, sprinting over to a terminal of fifteen different ways to lose your money. Bart had located the cheapest table the casino could legally offer. He delved into his pockets with a fidgety hand, a brush of excitement basting his chances. He shared this space with one other man and a lonely-looking dealer. Saddling up next to his fellow gambler, Bart put all seventeen of his dollars—a collection of singles and three two-dollar bills—onto the table.

The gentleman's guise, off-putting and harsh, held an aura as though he'd done nothing but drain his entire emergency fund for the last hour and was proud of it. He stood well over six feet tall and was costumed (or, in his humble opinion, clothed) in a red bow tie, off-yellow dress shirt, white vest, and khakis. The flushed redness of his spud-Irish face indicated he was half in the bag, which was confirmed by the four empty Guinness bottles lined by his feet. He glanced down musingly at Bart as the dealer, the name Regina printed on her identification badge, cashed his seventeen dollars and pushed over seventeen one-dollar chips. Zach stood off to the side, put his hand into his own pocket, and pinched their little baggie for good luck. Regina coughed without covering her mouth and announced, "Place your bets," to which Bart, the blue clay disks piled flawlessly in front of him, readily pushed all his chips into the black diamond box that stood outside the numbers on the felt board and cracked his knuckles civilly. With a weariness, she grabbed the game's little metal ball and flung it with a sharp snap of her wrist, waving her hand over the table and barking in a voice cold as iron, "No more bets."

"Why did you bet all of your money on one spin?" Zach asked doubtfully from his bandmate's shoulder.

"Because if I hit, then I'll double my money. If I don't . . . Well, then I'm fucked."

"Sounds fun."

The ball spurted up and over the little slots of this wheel of fortune with an increasing savagery, and the drunk potato monkey next to them breathed harder with each tumble of the orb that brought him closer to potential riches; his pile of chips was held captive on the number 32.

"Thirty-three," Regina said. "Thirty-three."

"Come on!" yelled the gentleman, and slammed his fifth free bottle of Guinness down on the fake wood, drops of the beer soaking into the red fabric of the number 32.

Bart looked back at Zach. "And just like that . . . thirty-four big ones, baby!"

Regina pushed over the winnings to his waiting hands.

"Screw it—let's see what happens." He kept his original stack of chips on the black box and put the new stack on the number 6. "My mom was born on the sixth."

Mr. Guinness uttered something to himself in what sounded like Gaelic.

With another rheumy flick of the wrist, Regina sent the metallic sphere whirling around the wheel once again, quicker in its rotation this time as it went slot by slot, tick by tack, and found its home eventually on the number 6.

"Six," she called. "Six."

"*Holy shit!*" Bart yelled out, his hands gripping the table's edge tight. "*I hit!*"

With calculations quicker than any Stanford math PhD, Regina shoved $595 into his waiting grasp.

"Lucky bastard," the man mumbled, unable to stomach the taste of a $200 beer before placing another $300 on the number 5.

"Should I cash out or make another bet?" Bart asked Zach.

"I mean, you only stole a hundred dollars."

"Bro! I told you . . . I didn't *steal* it. I had to borrow it. And I already made it all back—plus more." He lit a cigarette. "I'm making another go at it . . . *Vegas, baby!*"

The number 6 glowed in his eyes, so he left all his previous bets the same.

Another snap, more tumbles, and the ball landed once again on his chosen digit.

"Six," Regina called. "Six."

The Irishman blew like a volcano: "Mallacht na baintrí ort!" His face was red enough to intimidate a tomato, and more than a few people nearby turned around at this threat of violence, the embarrassment of which affected them more than him.

Regina doubled the wall of chips built like a fortress in front of Bart. "Let's get out of here," he said with a conscientious gusto, and stuffed his pockets to the brim with chips, wished good luck to his trounced comrade, and darted to the cashier window, the weight of chips pulling his pants down by inches with each stride.

Zach listened to Regina suggest, in the most appropriate manner, that the drunken gentleman might "want to take a break," and then listened as he told her to "go fuck" herself.

A multitude of crisp hundred-dollar bills spread out in his hand like a fan, Bart returned a couple pounds lighter and a couple of ideas heavier. "You hungry?" he asked, and slapped his gut with the wad of cash.

"Not really," Zach said, rubbing his crusty nostril, "but I'd be down to hit that bag again."

3

Swamps
New York City, NY
7/18/95

Capacity: 500
Tickets Sold: 294

On that barren plot of land west of Manhattan, where the funky smells of marshland, two-day-old tuna salad, and dead bodies afloat in the Hudson River are as effluviant as the scent of a regifted candle, a young Zach Long grew into adolescence, transitioning cumbersomely from childhood pureness to teenage deceit. The perfect place for bored kids to smoke weed, skateboard, and drink forties of Olde English 800 in the woods, life as a middle-class suburban youth in the Garden State was virtuous in all the ways of rascality and disruption and finding out the amount of people who could get high off one can of Reddi-wip. The monolithic steel structures of New York City within eternal sight—giant buildings piercing the sky to infinity and beyond, beaming toward the perpetually hidden sun—the boroughs of the Big Apple appeared almost unsolvable to the innocent who grew up on upkept tennis courts surrounded by manicured trees and not tenement bricks; places only the native and inaugurated could set foot in. The "big city," where crackheads shared side-walk space with the financiers and stoned-out kids easing their way through liberal art degrees at Hunter College: undisrupted and unrefined, commixing with the rumbles of subway cars and old men grunting, "Baconannndegggg salpeppakechupp on an evrrrythinggg." New York City was that place you needed to be if you ever wanted to be something else.

It was also anywhere but New Jersey.

In the summer of 1995, the members of Texas Flip were living together in a two-story house in the college town of Montclair. Rent was cheap, and they rehearsed in the base-ment and printed their own T-shirts in the garage and breathed their own music as if Jesus himself helped in its creation. Close enough to the nonstop action of NYC but far enough away to keep their communal cost of living low, they were conscious in their decision of locale, positive that playing a persistent onslaught of dive bar gigs and café shows in the city would be their chance at some sort of "break" and an introduction to the bigger stages and promoters uninterested in a band that couldn't sell hundreds of tickets any given night of the week.

The tristate area was a blessing in disguise for any band that was looking to play shows in an ongoing nature, the atti-tudes and personalities changing only by degrees as the well-funded interstates took you from rough city to rough city. A local act could play out every night of the week if it chose to.

The list of who did is too long to name here, for these were musicians of another time, but they helped create a wave that bands of later generations, like Texas Flip, could catch on a good day and ride with a milder forecast. Before cell phone photos held more memory of the actual show itself. Before tapers were obsolete. Before posters got framed. Before it lost meaning.

Brooklyn and Queens just as important as the Bronx and Long Island, if there was a venue willing to book them with a 212, 917, or 718 area code, then it didn't matter what neighborhood, date, or venue it was at. What it meant was that they got to drive their van over the George Washington Bridge again to play a show. It was "pay to play" in the sense that the money spent to get to and from the gig was usually more than what was earned playing it, but the rush of excitement when the Empire State Building was in their windshield helped flush down the rotting smell of a city that couldn't give two shits about them, or their dreams, or anything to do with failure. All in this together, their draw was strong, with pockets of friendly folks in places near and reasonably far, and the idea of booking their own headlining show at Swamps—a four-hundred-plus-capacity club in the West Village—didn't seem as far-fetched as maybe it should have, although the traffic light should have turned red, their car of positivism shifted into reverse. The train should have changed tracks. A meteor sent to obliterate them to fine particles lost in the winds of retrospection. Anything but what they were about to do. Anything.

A chocolate chip granola bar crumbled to bits in Todd's mouth, and he spoke with a persuasion adopted only recently. "I think we can pull it off . . . The last time we played at Jerry's Shrinking Eye, we brought, like, two hundred people. And that was without Harry's six or whatever cousins from Bensonhurst."

"I can definitely get them to come this time," Harry said. "They have friends too."

"I like the idea of it," Zach said. "But if we don't fill that place, it's going to look really bad on our end. We're betting on margin here."

"On what?" Luke asked.

Zach ignored him. To explain the concept of "margin" to Luke would be impossible. "If we don't get rid of all the tickets, we might fuck ourselves over big time." The thought of even one pissed-off promoter was nothing they needed to be a part of. "If we book it, we have to sell it out."

Three months out from their biggest tour yet, one that would bring Texas Flip around the country almost twice, they had learned from the tough lessons of previous failures that if you're about to hit the road for any amount of time for over two weeks, you should always book your "hometown" show at the beginning of the tour, not at the end of it. That is, if a band wants to give itself a better chance to start off on the right foot, and an opportunity for those generous friends and family members to help send you off with fat pockets from that merch they bought but will never wear or listen to. Gathering this money up front was an essential add-on feature, because, like almost everything else in life, touring is expensive: the inexorable costs of having to fix something on the van, along with all the fast food you'd eat but promised yourself you wouldn't. Any carefully constructed budget thrown out the window by day four of bending to the wills of your bandmates for another Grand Slam breakfast at Denny's, money on the road liquified quicker than the shit taken after that day's second gas station breakfast sandwich or Ethiopian pour-over.

And good luck not buying more beers after you run out of drink tickets too.

Veterans of the road, no longer was Texas Flip booking a show in Fort Collins and then driving eleven hours straight through the night to play to twelve people the next evening in Dallas. Saving themselves the time and unnecessary expense, they stuck mostly with East Coast tours, and learned early on that the best form of travel was the one that paid the most, not the one with the most scenic views.

What they also learned was that *traveling* and *touring* were two very different things.

Traveling was late lunches, glasses of Malbec overlooking Chilean vineyards, and dirty sex in hostel bunk beds.

Touring was living in a smelly van, eating like a feral child, drinking every night, and doing all the drugs that people were willing to give you for free. And never any sex.

Having built up over a college career a decent following throughout New York, New Jersey, and even Vermont, they continued to walk further down the wire of triviality and did what every band should do once those student loan payments come due: focus your bookings in college towns and nowhere else. New York City had always treated them well, and Bergen County had plenty of firehouses and VFW halls, but they knew drowning in a pool of listlessness would prove to be no sanctum and that their dreams couldn't be achieved in only one place, and so they started playing more and more shows in the places that were guaranteed to pay them well, venues with a budget: large, highly subsidized academic establishments.

Hofstra University, Dartmouth College, Rhode Island School of Design—these gigs would soon become the band's bread and butter. Always put on by the schools themselves, free to students and organized by a student council usually consisting of some stoners, an uptight girl, and an Asian boy who would be delivering all their future lung cancer diagnoses, Texas Flip's bank account relied heavily on these kush gigs that paid way more money than any bar or club ever would. Depending on the school (and tuition), they could pull out of town with $400 to $500 in their pockets—a small fortune to a musician living on an eight-dollar-a-day budget and a pack-a-day habit, gas envelope off-limits.

Todd crunched up the granola bar wrapper and put it into his jean pocket. "Let's book it," he said. "We have three months to promote. How hard can it be to sell five hundred tickets?"

"Dope!" Luke agreed enthusiastically.

"That's the spirit! Zach, Harry, Bart—what do you guys think?"

"I don't really care," came from their pianist's lips.

"My cousins will definitely come," Harry ensured.

Zach said nothing.

"Fantastic! I'll call Paulie and book it. He's probably going to give us a Tuesday night, though, FYI."

And like most things with the band, that was that.

Two and a half months later, Texas Flip hung out in their basement smoking weed and picking their asses, having done close to nothing in preparation for their tour or their Swamps show, or any forward progress of any kind. Todd's fart hardly soured the mood.

"We've sold half the tickets."

"How many is *half*?"

"Are you that dumb, Luke?"

"Maybe?"

From the communal bong, Todd took a massive inhale and coughed up a lungful of cashed herb roughly into his elbow. The smoke escalated the suspense. "What are we gonna do? Has everyone already asked all their family to buy tickets? I knew this was a mistake . . . We should have never booked this show."

"You're the one who told us to book it!" Bart snapped.

"How are we going to sell two hundred tickets in two weeks? How many cousins do you have again, Harry?"

"I'm only a quarter Mexican."

"I have an idea," Zach said. It had been in his head for a day or so and had thus had time to coagulate and combust and froth and melt and solidify, and yet it was still undercooked. Leftovers in a broken oven. "How much money do we have in the band account right now?"

Ahh, yes . . . the consecrated "band account." A pot of funds dedicated to all things your band (and separate from the gas envelope). The band account's sole purpose was for the spending of money on stuff that you never want to spend money on in the first place: T-shirts, tires, brake pads, lighting rigs that would break after the third show—you name it, that's how it got paid for. Any money made from shows was deposited straight into this fund; it was dough saved so that a band could continue to make more dough and not be screwed when the inevitable happened. A world of difference when you're broken down on the highway in San Antonio and holding some cash to fix the problem as compared with no cash and no alternative, this fund had saved their ass more times than Zach could recall or be comfortable with. It didn't pay for those three thousand stickers robbed in Buffalo, though.

An impish glance in his direction, Todd snatched a notepad from his blue JanSport backpack, then looked more worried than before. In fact, he looked sad. "We have $1,694.20," he said. "But we still owe UVM two hundred for that window Luke broke."

Luke had taken possession of the bong, packing a fresh bowl of dry herb, the seeds crackling under the flame of his Zippo lighter. "Oh my god!" he said, slurping up bong water and light petroleum distillate with his inhalation. "I forgot about that!"

"Well, they didn't."

"We sold half the tickets, yeah?" Zach said. "We can definitely sell fifty more before the show. And then I was thinking we can get rid of the other half in a different way."

"Huh?" Todd asked.

"If the tickets are seven bucks each, then two hundred more tickets equals $1,400," Zach penciled in the air. "Almost exactly what's left in the band account after cutting a check to UVM."

"Huh?" Todd asked again, increasingly confused.

Zach backed up. "Okay, but before you all scream no, hear me out first. We need to sell two hundred tickets in two weeks, right?"

"Right," Todd answered.

"Okay. Since that's virtually impossible, why don't we just buy all the tickets ourselves? If we do that, we—"

"What?" Todd interrupted, the look on his face as if he'd swallowed a wasp. "You want to take all of the money we have and buy tickets for our own show? Why the hell would we do that? What are we gonna do with them?"

"Well, that's the thing. If we sell out the club, then we'll get our guarantee, right? We put that right back into the band account. And if we sell it out, we'll also be in Paulie's good graces and can look at this as an investment into our future with the club."

"Okay," Todd said. "I hear you, even though what you're saying makes absolutely no sense. If there's an empty club, and all the tickets are sold, Paulie's gonna want to know what's up . . . Plus nobody is gonna go even if it is free. It's summer, and that means there's no college kids. The city is empty. And on top of all that, the show is on a Tuesday night. And why would we spend that money anyways?"

"That's the thing," Zach said.

"What's the thing? What the fuck are you talking about?"

"Will you shut up and let me finish?"

"Sorry."

"Like I was saying. And again, before you say no, think about it first. What if we take all those tickets and we give them away to a bunch of homeless people?"

Taking another long, meditative rip from the bong, Todd let out a cloud of cynicism and hacked up a seedless reservation. "Homeless people? You mean like the bums we chill with? They're already coming to the show."

"No. I mean like *actual* homeless people."

"Homeless people . . ." Todd echoed. "What are you talking about, dude? Does anybody have any idea what he is talking about? Am I that high?"

"Exactly what I said. We'll give the tickets out to a bunch of homeless people on the streets. What do we care who comes to the show, so long as the room is packed and we can take photos of it? Again—investment in our future, guys. It's not always about money."

The rest of his band stared at him with the same blank face as if being forced to hand over their familial fief and then commit seppuku.

"It's our best shot to get out of this mess," Zach continued. "It will also be much easier to get two hundred hobos to go to the show than two hundred people who have jobs and responsibilities." He paused to allow the idea to float in the air and party with the smoke from the bong.

"It's actually not that bad of an idea," mumbled Luke.

"It actually really is," Todd disagreed. "Let me get this straight. What you're saying is you want to have two hundred vagrants, off the streets of New York City, come to our show for free?"

"Of course not!" Zach argued. "I'm not an idiot. But here's the thing . . . We've got hundreds of T-shirts left over from the last tour, right? We give them a shirt and a ticket, and not only do we fill the room, but we'll also get years of free promo."

A homeless man named Forest had been living outside of their house for the better part of a year. Weather permitting, he'd wear the same Megadeth T-shirt every day. And god be damned if Zach didn't start to see Megadeth-related paraphernalia all over town soon after. The Baader-Meinhof phenomenon in full tilt: a Megadeth cassette tape smashed on the sidewalk, a party with a band whose bass player said his brother's second wife gave their bass player a blow job—so much so were the frequency of these occurrences that it was enough to get Zach's ass into a Sam Goody and buy a copy of *Rust in Peace* just because.

If such easy and free promo could work on him, then why wouldn't it work on the nomadic inhabitants of Manhattan too?

"We do have a fuck ton of those shirts left," Todd spoke, lighting up a nickel-wide joint and unbuckling his skinny jeans. "But who is gonna go into the city on a weekday morning to hang out with a bunch of bums?" His pronunciation assured it would not be him.

The joint came his way, and Zach took a deep drag before passing it to Bart and then stealing a cigarette from his soft pack. "I'll do it," he said. "I can head into the city the afternoon before the show and buy the tickets. Meet up with my dad for dinner."

"Damn . . ." Todd said, defeated in a conflict he had originally begun. He handed Zach a wrinkly checkbook, "Texas Flip Inc." printed in the upper left corner. "Let it be known I'm not in agreement with any of this. But at least we can use it as a tax write-off."

"I never knew we were incorporated," Luke said.

"That's because you don't pay your taxes."

Two weeks later, Zach boarded a NJ Transit train with a cardboard box full of his own band's T-shirts and an unsteady stomach, looking forward to all the unpleasantries coming his way like a bout of diarrhea. He transferred to the PATH train in Hoboken, took the quick trip to Christopher Street, exited the vestibule with arms full of crap nobody wanted to buy in the first place, and was hit in the face with the smell of hot shit, just another boiling New York summer morning and another slice of life in the big city. He choked on his own upchuck, a naive appetite compared with that of the pigeons eating the leptospirosis-infested rat carcass by his feet, and shook his stiff upper back in dramatic fashion. It was a mile walk from the PATH station to the club, enough of a distance to snag a slice of pizza, but not far enough away that he would give up this foolhardy idea and head back home with a tail between his legs.

After two zucchini slices and four garlic knots from a pizzeria run by Mexicans but owned by Greeks and named Luigi's, Zach discovered the club's entrance between a video rental store and a head shop that sold weed in a back room. He threw the T-shirt box on the ground, where it joined the mishmash of promo flyers once plastered to the entrance but were now part of the flowing stream of garbage that constitutes most any NYC sidewalk, and panted in relief.

As out of shape as he was, his passion for success wasn't.

Texas Flip's own flyer hung on Swamps's front door by one thumbtack, ripped apart by wind and rodents and life that passed by. An awful publicity shot showcased their smiling acne-covered faces, along with a giant penis drawn on Zach's forehead with a pink Sharpie. He coughed loud enough to grab the attention of the girl working in the box office and disrupt her from the copy of *Slaughterhouse-Five* she held between chipped, black-painted nails. Her consideration was harder to catch.

"Hey," he interrupted. "Sorry to bug you. But can I buy some tickets for the Texas Flip show tomorrow night?"

Her eyes drifted back down to the page. "How many?" she asked in a slow drawl.

The lights above her head, dimmed by the otherwise black room, hummed.

A moth fell onto the page.

She turned it.

"Two hundred."

"Huh? What? Why?"

"Does it matter?"

"I mean, no. But why would anyone buy two hundred tickets for the same show?"

"Do you take checks?"

This situation Zach had introduced was outside her wheel-house of ordinary, everyday interactions, and thus required her to put down Kurt and now do her job. A sacrilegious sin. "I think," she said, flustered and uninformed, "I should probably ask my manager if we can even sell you that many tickets."

"Sounds good. Mind if I wait inside in the meantime? It's pretty hot out here."

"Sure. But it's probably hotter in here."

She was right.

Upon entry through the lobby door, the smell of flat beer and reverberates of busted eardrums encased Zach in a muggy heater of audiophilic exultation. It was difficult to wrap his head around the fact that *his* band was going to be playing here within twenty-four hours. He sat down on the plastic chair meant for the doorman and laughed out loud at what was about to happen.

By anyone's standards, Swamps was a mecca for live rock and roll in NYC. Far beyond a stepping-stone or forgettable shanty, any band that had ever become anything considered a success had played Swamps on its way up and its way back down.

Open for a little over a decade by the time Texas Flip would grace its stage, the club had originally been operated by a nonprofit to help benefit various Earth-driven charities well before it ever was a music venue. The cozy space, painted dark green, purple, and blue, was owned by a goodhearted lesbian couple, Mary and Kary Chatham; their socialistic ideals would fall fast to the wayside once they saw how much money they could make by booking bands who spoke their message louder, and with better pitch, than they ever could. Capacity for close to five hundred people when packed to the gills, with a stage at chest level and a PA system meant for the Gorge Amphitheatre, any person lucky enough to have seen a show there will tell you what it was like.

Life-changing.

Mary and Kary would divorce once the former voiced her identification as a man and began injecting testosterone.

As part of their settlement, they agreed to sell the ground-level music venue, which was located at the bottom of a four-story mixed-use building—an attractive buy for any deep-pocketed investor—to a Chinese billionaire in desperate need of a way to launder his dirty money with real estate and a safe place for his daughter to sleep between classes at Columbia. Mary and Kary both ended up buying separate town houses in Providence, Rhode Island, on the same dead-end street with their returns.

Plans were immediately made by the building's new owner to shut down the club and make way for a Dunkin' Donuts. The local community of musicians, famous and unfamous, as well as the city's thousands of music fans would go as far as to march to the steps of city hall and shut down traffic during a heavy-commute time in protest. And so much so was the enthusiasm behind saving the club by a bunch of people who apparently didn't have to be at work at 9:30 A.M. on a Tuesday that there were even rumors the Talking Heads would reunite and play a show to raise more awareness. That, obviously, didn't happen, but with such heavy resistance and the need for another fast-food restaurant in NYC like the need for a herpes outbreak, these plans were stymied, and Swamps would live on to fight another day. This large battle won with absolutely no help from Texas Flip, Zach's efforts of the afternoon were focused on winning his own encounter with Swamps for the undetermined amount of time it still had left to operate.

She met him in the lobby ten minutes later. A manila envelope stuffed to the brim was tucked under her armpit. Kurt was under the other.

"My manager said this is some weird shit but doesn't care so long as your check doesn't bounce. You said two hundred tickets, right?"

"Right."

"Here you go. The total comes out to $1,400. She said don't worry about the fees since you're buying so many. Figured we were gonna eat it on this show anyways."

Zach hadn't even thought about the fees. "You have a pen?" he asked.

"Gotta admit," she said, giving him a pencil, "I've been working here for three years, and I've never seen anyone buy this many tickets for one show. One time some dude bought seventy-four tickets for Blues Traveler and then flushed them down the toilet. Literally flushed them. I had to call the plumber."

"That's crazy." He checked his watch; he had thirty minutes till he was to meet his dad at Les Halles for an early dinner he would be splitting the bill for. "Anyways, I gotta get going. Should be a fun show. You gonna be there?"

"No."

She found it too difficult to help him open the door and watched in sick delight as Zach struggled to make his exit with one foot, arms full with the manila envelope and a box filled with over a thousand dollars' worth of nothing. The toe of his Adidas the only prop holding the heavy wooden door open, a need to be a dick on his way out was also unavoidable.

"Maybe shelve the Vonnegut and give Roth a twirl instead."

Tucking his toe back to let the door slam shut behind him before she could argue the merits of Kurt and his ways of helping the twenty-two-year-old female psyche relate to the obstacles of upper-middle-class life through descriptions of firebombings in Dresden during World War II, he hailed down a taxi with his elbow and was uptown in record time to meet his old man for some steaks, martinis, and an hour's worth of pestering questions such as "Why are you spending so much time with this band of yours?" and "Have you called your sister?" and other fatherly ambushes like "You could have been a dentist. Do you have any idea how much money they make?" and "How's your mother?"

Their meal ended in hushed tones.

The two of them were unsure why they had even bothered and were both eager to leave. Father and son swapped niceties and went their separate ways in equal hurry—the elder back to Westchester and Zach up to East Harlem, where he spent the night sleeping on the floor of a pot dealer the band knew, too drunk and too tired to go home on the train all so he could head right back into the city the following afternoon to give away two hundred tickets to people who lived in bushes.

Load-in was at 4:00 P.M., which gave him, after sleeping in till noon, roughly three hours to hand out all the tickets, eat a toasted sesame seed bagel with butter, and find another bathroom to shit in. He headed back downtown, seeing as it made more sense to dispose of the ticket stubs closer to the club (wishful thinking to expect hundreds of homeless people to migrate like wounded geese down the avenues of Manhattan) and intuitively set his broken compass to the dankest, most densely populated, drug-dealing, acceptably decrepit neighborhood that modern media could have painted a portrait for.

Alphabet City.

The subway ride over provided the rhythm of a Lou Reed tune.

Zach readied himself for all possibilities and the high probability of catching a disease while simultaneously being mugged. One could never be too sure about NYC and its infinite availabilities to put you in a bad spot (especially when dealing with people whose home address was under a bridge). He paid even less mind to the likely deceased man in the subway vestibule than he did about hopping over two piles of human feces on the sidewalk.

The sky was cloudless and the sun taxing as he turned the corner toward Tompkins Square Park with most of Texas Flip's liquid assets gripped between his skinny arms. He wished for the best, assumed the worst, and, with the innocence of a frightened kitten, ventured into territories far unknown.

A small sweat formed, and his eyebrows allowed it. Quicker than it could evaporate or be erased, he spotted two gentlemen and an older woman crowded around a shopping cart, all three dressed in a similar getup of soiled sweatpants and puffy jackets, the July heat no match for their reptilian skin.

He approached the way you would an angry elephant.

"Hey, everyone," Zach said. "Sorry to bother you, but I was wondering if—"

"You have any money?" the woman asked.

"Um, sorry. No, I don't."

"Motherfucker, why you talking to us then?" the larger of the two men protested, a shit stain clear as day in the ass of his pants. "Get on with it!"

The smaller man, a piddle of saliva in the corner of his mouth and an even bigger shit stain on his ass, groused. "Yeah, move it! Unless you got a cigarette?" He looked like Willem Dafoe if the actor's growth had stunted at twelve years old but his body continued to age into an elderly state.

"Listen," Zach said. "I don't have any money or cigarettes. But . . . well, this might sound odd, but I have a bunch of free concert tickets. And I was wondering if—"

"A concert?" The woman coughed up a purple mass of phlegm and spit onto her own foot. "Is it Barbra Streisand? Oh my, I just loved her in *Gone with the Wind.*"

"Bitch, she wasn't in *Gone with the Wind*," the larger man said, the superior male making his stand. "And what we gonna do with concert tickets anyways?" he asked Zach. "Can we sell 'em?"

"I doubt it. They're for my band and we're playing at Swamps tonight. I've got two hundred. If you want them, they're yours. If anything, it'll be a chance to get off the street for a couple of hours." The smell emanating from the three hobos was as if Zach had fallen asleep in a Staten Island dump truck and then remained there after he woke up.

"Two hundred tickets? There's only three of us."

"Yeah, I see that . . ." A glance around the park showed at least thirty to forty more homeless people billowing about their location, many of whom were smoking crack, nursing babies, or both. "But if I gave all of them to you, could you hand them out to your friends, you know, out here? The shirts too."

"I'll do it!" the smaller man shrilled. "But only if you get me two packs of Marlboro Lights and, uhhhh, shit . . . What's that soda stuff called? Not Coke, but the other one. Oh yeah . . . Payepsi!"

"Pepsi?" Zach asked to make sure.

"Yeah, Payepsi. It's green, right?"

"No. It's black. And it's called Pepsi. Maybe you're thinking of Mountain Dew?"

"Mountain Dew? Nah, that stuff kills your sperm. Whatever, man. Just get me my stuff and I'll hand out your tickets and crappy shirts."

"Are you going to sing any songs from *Gone with the Wind* at your concert?" the woman asked. "I just love Barbra!"

"We are," Zach said. "Let me go get your soda and smokes, and I'll give you the tickets and shirts when I get back. Is there a bodega around here?"

"There's one on Ninth Street. And tell Mohammed he still owes me seven cents!"

Zach didn't ask Mohammed for the money, but he did grab cigarettes, Pepsi, and a Mountain Dew, just in case he had been mistaken, and tossed the items into the box of shirts and tickets.

The smell of excrement was stronger on his return.

"Ah, man, you got me Payepsi! And Mountain Dew! I love this stuff! All right, man, you da man. So, all I gotta do is just hand these tickets out to whoever, right?"

His intuition told him he needed to get out of there. Soon.

His watch made sure of it.

"Exactly," Zach said. "And thanks again for everything. I gotta go to the club now and help my band load in our gear, but I'll see you all at the show tonight. Get excited. Gonna be fun."

A misjudgment of his geographical location and miscalculation of the rate at which his legs moved, Zach arrived at Swamps thirty-five minutes late; all of Texas Flip's gear had already been loaded in by his bandmates, including his own.

An unamused Harry waited for him in the green room.

The A/C was broken.

"What were you doing all day? Giving out tickets or blow jobs?"

"I didn't see *your* ass down there," Zach said. "It's gonna be a full house tonight because of me."

"Sure hope so, because Paulie is here. Todd's talking to him right now."

"He is? Shit . . . Okay. Damn. Let me go see what's up."

Spread out like people at a party inside of a small studio apartment with no windows and cheap wine, Paulie, Todd, and the box-office girl from the previous day stood in a triangle inside the club's main entrance, all three unsure of the persons next to them. A crooked poster of shirtless Frank Zappa smoking a cigarette with a white owl on his shoulder hung on the wall behind them. A New York Public Library copy of *Cat's Cradle* clutched in her hands like the nuclear football, box-office girl, upon seeing Zach enter the fray, said with a loud spirit, "That's the dude who bought the tickets!"

Pointing at Zach with his pinkie finger and his thumb at himself, Paulie asked, "He's the one who bought all those tickets?"

"That's him."

Todd stood silent. In fact, he even bit his lip as Paulie asked the obvious question: "Why did you buy two hundred tickets to your own show?"

Zach lied like a dirty rug. "Wanted to make sure it was a full house for you tonight! And as a thank-you gift to all of our fans who might not have been able to afford a ticket."

To most everyone's knowledge, Paulie was a "connected" guy. Not directly involved with organized crime (he wasn't even Italian, he was Croatian), but he did know some dudes who probably knew some dudes in the underworld of North Jersey and thus conducted himself like a guy you didn't want to mess around with. His masquerade was aggressive, with a mop top haircut and a black jumpsuit no matter the weather. Paulie was a businessman through and through and also scary as death. The owner of two strip clubs in Lodi and another small bar in Fort Lee that they played frequently called the Sloth Taproom, the band had gotten to know him well over their exchanges, which helped explain how they had even gotten their feet into the door at Swamps to begin with.

"If they can't afford to buy tickets, how are they going to afford to buy alcohol?" the boss asked.

"I'm sure the joint will be hopping," Zach lied again, and punched the air with a gosh-golly uppercut. "Don't you worry about it."

"Let's hope so. I gave Todd your drink tickets. The opener starts at eight and you guys hit at nine. Hopefully there's no other questions, cuz I gotta run over to the Sloth now. One of the sound engineers had his girlfriend hanging out behind the board with him last night and she spilled her drink all over the mixing console. Whole thing's fucked."

A woman not seen previously came and joined them, turning their square into a pentagon.

"Perfect timing!" Paulie said. "Guys, let me introduce you to Swamps's newest stage manager, Adriane."

Standing over six feet tall with thick black hair, thicker black-rimmed glasses, and an even thicker black Misfits T-shirt, Adriane effused stubbornness, obduracy, and female emancipation.

"Tonight is her first show here, so make sure you take it easy on her. Now if you'll excuse me."

"I got it from here, Paulie," Adriane assured.

Her boss gone, she cut to the chase: "If you guys are ready, you can start sound check. Jesse is running FOH tonight. He'll help with anything you need up there. Doors are at seven."

Swamps boasted the most legit sound system Texas Flip had ever worked on up till this point, and the band would mistakenly spend their entire sound check futzing with the mix of the four giant wedge monitors placed at their feet in a long exercise of what would prove to be a total waste of time. Anyone who has ever played a show with decent monitors will know that once the gig starts, the first thing to be thrown out the window is that mix you forced the sound guy to spend twenty minutes adjusting. The classic duel between artist and audio professional as faders pretend to be moved up and down, and musicians pretend to hear the difference, this stint could be better spent rehearsing a new tune, adjusting amp settings, reorganizing your merch table, or completing one of the million other tasks that can be accomplished during a crappy band's pointless sound check.

But then again, this is live music we're talking about.

Ask someone inside a rock club how to spell "efficiency."

With a perfect blend of sonic goodness amplified in front of Zach's face, his guitar giving off the right amount of midrange from a dedicated wedge speaker and Harry's snare drum clear as day, the band was as happy with their monitor mixes and newly heard harmonious balances as could be. Except for their lead singer, of course. His vocals louder than anything else in the whole room—and the whole block—Luke had to have been deaf to ask for more of them in his monitors. But he did. And the rest of the guys waited. And then his microphone shocked him.

"Fuck!" he yelled out to Swamps's FOH engineer. "This thing shocked me!"

"Yeah, sorry about that," Jesse spoke back to him via the stage monitors with an unmodulated voice. "Had to flip a ground switch. Should be good now."

"Maybe let me know next time you're gonna do that?"

"For sure."

Their pedal boards and set lists were perfectly arranged around the bottom of their microphone stands, the pages taped down to the stage next to opened bottles of beer and unopened bottles of water. Their monitor charade over (one of thousands this young band would endure and lose their hearing to), Zach was now free to spend the next hour before doors opened playing his guitar in the green room and eating Swamps's infamous Fire Nachos. He ran his fingers through the CAGED system on a white Fender Stratocaster with three-week-old strings, its intricate web around the thin fretboard breathing new life into a stale loaf of a habit. A pungent odor soon scratched his nostrils mere minutes following the click of 7:00 P.M. An odor not of the dairy kind.

Zach ordered a second plate of nachos from one of the waitresses (because why not) and wondered if maybe it was the kitchen that was stinking up the place. Monterey Jack and Todd's joint helped to mask the odor, but he was still unable to place a finger on it. Worries then began to turn more toward the high likelihood he would have to go to the bathroom during their set than the likely reintroduction of the bubonic plague his plan might have conjured up.

Outside the green room doorway, a nervous Adriane stood, tapping a pen to her upper arm, its cap tight between her molars, her brow tight between her eyes. "Hey, guys," she said. "Sorry to bother you, but I have a quick question"—she took a long, uncomfortable pause—"and let me state that in no way, shape, or form am I one to judge . . . But, well, there's a *lot* of people here already."

"That's great!"

"It's Todd, right?" She swallowed her honor before she continued with her next polarizing sentence. "Thing is"—a briefer pause—"well, if I'm off the mark here, then please inform me, but"—waiting, sensing—"everyone that is here so far looks like they're homeless. And they're all wearing your band's shirt."

"Homeless?" Todd went down the righteous path. "Weird."

"Should I expect"—swallowing harder—"more of them?"

"Who's *them*? I don't know who you're referring to."

A rubber band ball of stink built onto itself quickly in the club, and the odor soon became unavoidable, its aroma only picking up steam the longer Adriane and Todd talked in circles. Political correctness stashed deep in her bones, Swamps's stage manager dropped this topic too hot for even the NAACP button on her sleeve and decided to go ahead and let one more occupational dilemma pass with no ramifications. Taking a Reese's Peanut Butter Cup from the complimentary bowl meant for the band, she pulled out the small saucer of sugar and threw the wrapper on the floor. "Since it's going to be a full house tonight, I'm gonna have the openers push their start time back fifteen minutes." Chocolate and peanut butter basted her teeth. "Doesn't seem like the people here now are spending a lot of money at the bar. Get a couple more bar sales in before they hit."

"Sounds great," Todd agreed.

Picking at the second plate of nachos with the Stratocaster still in his lap, Zach left the scraps for the rest of the band to munch on and followed Adriane out of the green room, guitar attached, and took a right at the end of the hall for the bathroom, the nacho cheese having curdled a little too quick for comfort in his stomach. A bird flew by, but it was actually a member of the opening band. The bathroom was covered in stickers from every act that had ever played there ever. There were even stickers for a holistic pet food store. Zach reminded himself to grab a Texas Flip sticker to put up but would forget while flipping through a copy of *Guitar Player* magazine left behind by another band's guitar player. The club's culinary offerings blasted through his digestive system like spears at a bucket of fish. Not even the bowl was prepared. And it was during this time of reflection that he also began to prepare himself for the repercussions that were most certain to come their way, seeing as there was no way in hell one of those loafers would be buying a drop of booze at the bar.

They couldn't even buy a paper clip.

They were homeless.

At 8:25 P.M., with the show already starting late, Swamps found itself packed to the brim with an intermixture of Texas Flip fans and more panhandling than Venice Beach saw on a weekday morning. The openers, a band from the city the club insisted on booking called Tied Eye, took the stage looking as if they'd seen Teen Wolf break-dancing right in front them; their saxophonist gave a *what the fuck?* glance at the audience, who stank worse than an old sponge. The two hundred bums—spun out, murky, and impossibly stinky—would move not an inch to this band's generic brand of accented third-beat reggae-rock and predictably gave even less love to the bar. How to explain any of this to anyone who worked at the venue, let alone Adriane or Paulie, would not have been possible.

A lifetime of Tied Eye's music caught in only a couple minutes, Zach headed back to the green room to take one more dump and hang out with some of his family and friends backstage before it was time for their moment in the moonlight. Music Bob Marley would never have let be created faded away from range.

"I need you guys on the stage as soon as they're finished," Adriane barked at them from her position in the doorway. "I also need to speak with you, Todd."

The band felt rushed clambering up the three dementedly high steps that led to the uncomfortably small stage what felt like minutes later. Luke almost tripped on his bass cable and into the audience of homeless people taking up most of the venue's space, confused that a different band was about to play.

"Ladies and, um, gentlemen," Jesse announced from behind the mixing board before they had even plugged in and turned their amps off standby, "please welcome to the stage tonight's headliner, Texas Flip!"

The club darker than a coffin, colorful lights suddenly

lambasted them with red, green, and blue circles; the response to their appearance onstage was soft enough to hear a feather fall onto a pillow made of feathers. Zach's Boss tuner pedal was on the fritz, and he tried tuning his D string but it was stuck at 440Hz. Luke whispered into his ear: "It smells like my grundle in here."

As though Moses had divided the Red Sea, an invisible barrier shaped within the audience between the paying patrons and the vagabonds, a clear five-foot gap separating the closest of the two clans. The smell of patchouli oil and unwiped ass combined to form a thin layer of ozone analogous to what the atmosphere of Venus must be like: something that should kill you if ever breathed indirectly.

"What's up, New York City?" Luke spoke to the crowd, and no one responded. "Let's give it up for Tied Eye. What a dope band!"

"*They suck.*"

Luke couldn't see who heckled, but they sounded homeless. "Anyways, we're gonna take a quick moment to get ourselves tuned up and for you to relax, maybe get a quick drink."

Over it, Zach turned off his Boss pedal and tuned by ear to Bart's keyboard. Harry put a sizzler on his ride. Luke's amp was still on standby. The set lists that they had written out earlier were committed. It was showtime.

In patient form despite the evening's evolution, Texas Flip started their set with a wobbly cover of "Roadhouse Blues," by the Doors, and the homeless drunks screamed, "*Got myself a beer!*" louder than any monitor or Jim ever could, and an uneven surface wave promptly fluttered in the blur. One needed to be in a vegetative state to not sense the confusion among the audience members who had bought a ticket and the venue staff. The band, short of announcing the literal sticky situation they were all in, finished the song to little applause and tuned again.

"Thank you so much, New York City and its fine inhabitants!" Luke thundered before they did, ignoring the aromatic elephant in the room.

Mr. Payepsi screamed, "Fuck yeah, mang!" from somewhere near the front.

Texas Flip kept doing their thing to the best of their ability. Zach's monitor ceased to provide a balanced blend after the set's third song, so he bit his tongue and prayed for it all to be over before someone got shanked or he passed out from the stink. Time moving thicker than cold gravy, with half the crowd pinching their noses at the other half of the crowd, they got through their fifty-five-minute set with minor incident and sprinted off the stage like a hit-and-run suspect knowing they'd be caught after the first eye-witness report. A performance in the books and done.

The backstage area somehow felt less sanitary than before. Luke sprayed the air with a can of Lysol from the bathroom, the disinfectant trail of which Paulie walked right into, and the elements clung to the owner's beard while his anger clung to the air. Nothing felt good and everything smelled worse.

"What kind of stunt did you guys just pull?!"

In a fright, Luke yelped, "I'm sorry, Paulie!"

"You gave away two hundred tickets to the fucking homeless of New York City? I'm gonna be cleaning the smell of shit out of this place for the next three weeks!" He grabbed a slice of pizza from the complimentary box meant for the band. "And I just caught two of them screwing in the ladies' bathroom!" He ate the entire cheese portion of the slice in three bites and threw the crust onto the ground next to Adriane's two-hour-old Reese's wrapper. "Whose idea was this anyways?!"

Todd chucked his compatriot under the bus like a used rubber in the Castro. "It was Zach's."

"Well, thanks to Zach here, the bar sold a total of sixty-eight beers tonight. There were over four hundred people in that room, and we sold less than seventy beers. What the hell, guys?" The air curdled with his unanswered question. "I gotta make a phone call right now about this goddamn soundboard, but consider yourselves lucky, because I don't know what else to say other than you ain't ever playing here again."

He walked out as Adriane walked in, but there was no sign of confusion on her face.

"Some stunt you guys pulled tonight," she said with an odd measure to her tone. "Here's your check." The sympathy in her eyes deepened with the truth. "Safe to assume this is the last show I'll ever work with y'all, so I guess I'll say it now." She searched behind her to make sure her boss was gone. "That was some of the ballsiest shit I have ever seen in my eleven years managing clubs . . . Kudos."

Texas Flip took the compliment and the clue and left Swamps (and a small portion of Manhattan's homeless population) in their wake. Todd was quick to deposit Swamps's check of $555.55 before Paulie decided to cancel it.

Recalling this evening with warm remembrance a few nights later in a motel room with no hot water following their tour's fourth show at the Ocelot Music Lodge in Poughkeepsie, Zach was reminded to make a call to his answering machine back home; he was expecting a reply from a potential purchaser of a Carvin amplifier he'd been trying to sell for months.

The first message was from a debt collection agency.

The second message was from a girl named Amanda.

"*Hey, Zach, this is Amanda Garcia from the* Village Voice. *I wanted to see if you had some time to talk with me soon. Happened to catch your show at Swamps the other night, and I gotta say . . . Whoa. I was completely blown away at your guys' community outreach capabilities! I have a great idea for an article that I think the* Village Voice *would love to run. My number is 212-327-5555. Hope the tour is going great. Thanks!"*

You've got to be kidding me was the message he left for himself.

The rest of the band was playing beer pong on a makeshift table constructed with the now detached bathroom door, and Zach had to speak loudly over Steven Tyler's stereo voice warning them about Janie and her gun. "Guys, you're not gonna believe this. A girl from the *Village Voice* left me a message. She wants to do a piece about our community outreach capabilities.'"

"Community what?" Luke asked, tossing Zach a beer way left; the can flew over his shoulder and into the window.

"I think she thinks that all those homeless people at Swamps were there because of some Good Samaritan act on our end."

With a misjudgment in his own surprise, Todd knocked over four cups of beer onto the carpeted floor. "Christ! That's fantastic news! Are you going to call her back?"

"Should I?"

"Yes!"

Zach picked up the motel room's phone at 2:34 A.M. on a weeknight and dialed the number Amanda had given him.

She answered after the sixth ring.

"Hello?"

"Hey, Amanda? This is Zach Long from the band Texas Flip. You left me a message about a possible interview?"

R.E.M. played in the background and Michael Stipe lost his religion with each spin of her vinyl record. She sounded as fresh as if it were 2:34 P.M.

"Hey, Zach! Interesting time to call me back, ha-ha, but yeah! Gotta say . . . the other night at Swamps—wow . . . I can't believe that's what your band is all about! And it's even crazier because, well, bear with me, but I've had this idea kicking around forever about an article on local musicians helping their local communities. And by my measure the other night, it seems like that's a big part of Texas Flip's identity. Am I right?"

"I appreciate that, Amanda. To be honest, though—"

"Oh! And your singer! The way he serenaded those women in the front row."

Zach almost laughed out loud.

"Women who looked like they have seen and been through so much in their lives. Your music able to provide them an evening away from what must be a series of constant miseries. That is exactly what this article should be about. Female empowerment!"

"Yeah, about that—"

"You guys formed in Oneonta, right?"

"Well, kinda. We ac—"

"And how long have you been a band for?"

"Oh, I don't know. A couple of years. But, Amanda, there's somethi—"

"And your newest album is called *Cool Hair, Bro* . . . ?"

"Yeah. Bu—"

"Perfect! That's all I need. Thanks for taking the time to talk to me. I know how busy you guys can get out on the road. My phone is probably going to disconnect any second because I'm a little late on my bill. Life of a writer, right? I'll be in touch if the paper decides to run the article. Take care!"

Click.

Luke lobbed Zach another beer, this one missing far right, another casualty of the night, and the MGD can disappeared into obscurity underneath the bed along with any possible excuses. "What'd she say?" he asked.

"I . . . don't know? It was so quick. She asked some generic questions about the band and then hung up. Wouldn't give me a chance to speak. I can't imagine there's enough for her to write a whole article. There's nothing to even write about."

"Yeah, I wouldn't sweat it," Luke said. "On a more urgent note, though, whoever is the least drunk needs to go make a beer run in the next fifteen minutes before that liquor store closes." He touched his finger to the tip of the nose. "Shotty not it!"

After stops in Philadelphia, State College, and Cleveland, the charming city of Akron was next on Texas Flip's calendar.

The first couple shows of their tour were well attended for a young band not many knew, but something felt off about the chain of older gentlemen hanging outside the rear load-in door of the Bakers Dozen Bar & Grill as the band arrived seven hours before showtime, parking near the venue's rear entrance with two tires that needed air and a check engine light blazing bright.

In a rush for privacy and a nicotine fix, Zach ran across the street to a convenience store/rib joint, hoping the $6.33 in his pocket would get him far enough for a pack of smokes, some pork, or an ashy combination of the two. He combed his pockets for an extra thirty-three cents and realized then that his lighter was missing—surely in Todd's pocket. Then the display rack of local newspapers and magazines to the side caught his attention more than the handgun sitting on the table behind the cashier.

Between issues of the *Akron Beacon Journal* and *People* magazine stuck out two copies of the newest edition of the *Village Voice*. The occurrence too uncanny, Zach picked up one and energetically thumbed through it, on the search for he didn't know what.

From beyond the barrier of supposedly impermeable glass, the cashier, a woman in her forties who was missing most of her teeth and hair, smiled a grin containing mostly gum. "It's the owner's favorite paper," she said. "No one ever buys it. Not sure why we even stock it."

Wondering how many times this business had to have been robbed before that barricade went up, Zach moved his head in a motion that indicated he'd heard her and began to peruse the paper's contents. The name Amanda Garcia stood out like a zit on your wedding day. Next to her byline and printed in a bold font was the title of her newest article: "Can One Band Change the Way We See the Homeless?" His eyes stung as if coated in chili pepper and garlic powder.

"If you want the paper, it'll be an extra buck."

He forewent the BBQ and paid for the publication and read with determination the three-page article that Amanda Garcia had penned in a matter of days and published within the week. The first third of the piece focused on a string of lies about how deeply the NYPD and Mayor Giuliani cared for the displaced population's well-being. The meat of the report started with a more formative composition:

It really can come down to one band, though. And why not a band from the same state as the greatest city in the world? Maybe they can be the ones who show us how tranquil it is to be ardent and amorous to a popu-lace of beleaguered, persecuted, and trodden entities.

Her writing made Zach want to eat a cigarette.

Fortunate to have witnessed the boldness and lengths at which the band Texas Flip displayed such generosity throughout their show at Swamps last week—scouring the streets of Gotham and handing out two hundred free tickets, to make no mention of the T-shirts, to various factions of people with no place to call home—they not only offered the comfort of their music but also a safe place to step off the neon avenues and venture inside to a functioning restroom and artificially heated environment.

Zach was back across the street before he could finish.

He might have puked otherwise.

"You guys aren't going to believe this . . ."

"You're not going to believe *this*," Todd answered back.

In a side alleyway on the same street as the venue were approximately one hundred homeless people of all shapes, sizes, genders, and ethnicities. Some even had tents set up.

"The stage manager told me they started showing up last night and he has no idea why."

Zach stretched the *Village Voice* article up to his manager's schnozzle. "Might be because of *this*."

"Oh shit! She actually wrote the article? How is that even possible?"

A short Latino man with an eye patch that held a syringe to the side of his face tugged at the back of Zach's T-shirt. "You got a light, ese?" he asked through three black teeth and a fake gold implant.

Worried about infection by some rare drifter disease, Zach stepped back fast with a rude instinctiveness. "Nah, man, someone stole mine."

"Damn, you too? Shit always happens to me."

"Quick question for you, my man. What's bringing you and all of your friends here today?" Zach asked sympathetically.

"*Amigos?* You think these putos are my friends? I don't know any of these fools! But word on the street is some band is giving out free shirts and food."

"Did you read that in the *Village Voice*?"

"Nah, man. I read it in this!" He held up a newspaper entitled the *Peace Piece*. "I sell these rags on the street . . . But shit— you look like the hombre on the front cover!"

He was right. In a picture plain as the nose on Zach's face was the same publicity shot from their Swamps show. Texas Flip was front-page news on a periodical for the homeless, pilfered from another article that was based on a lie. A penis was doodled on the same spot of his forehead. "You draw this?"

"If I say no, will you give me a cigarette?"

4

Foggy Bridge Studios
Sausalito, CA
6/1/97

After spending over \$300,000 and a month in the studio, Texas Flip had five tracks to show for it.

Their first full-length record, *DERP!*, was cut in two weeks and cost \$1,500.

It was also recorded in the living room of the guy who sold them mushrooms.

Self-released to little fanfare in the fall of '93, *DERP!* was the product of four guys who had been playing the same songs in the same band for way too many years.

Tracked live, with no overdubs and their neighbor's beagle bleeding through, *DERP!* was that unavoidable step all creatives must take, a recording to look back on and cringe with mortification that you had once written such poor lyrics and shoddy chorus structures and had attempted to sing in falsetto. Flash points of time created with the best intent and under the worst of circumstances, and with only three songs on it that would ever be played again live, *DERP!* served its purpose to the best extent possible: providing a prelude to the band's sound and a catalyst to tour.

The earlier part of that decade had seen most of them graduate from college and all of them avoid the procurement of any serious career-minded employment. An unwonted break in that predictable medium of collegiate afterlife—get an internship, get a job, get a girlfriend, get an apartment, get a dog, get married, have kids, die inside for the next forty years— the members of Texas Flip instead chose an alternate route to that same, predictable dead-end street.

None of them wanted "real" jobs, Todd included. They wanted to live forever in the delusion that was fed to them daily through band logos, music videos, and magazine covers. Planes and drugs. Mansions and cars. Babes and blow. Playing those limited cities in the middle of the week when en route to what- ever boundless city you were playing that weekend—why not? Wichita, Redding, Lubbock, Tacoma—the places and faces all blending into a rank stew of free drink tickets, gas station snacks, and regretful sex—no town could ever be too small if sixty people were willing to see your band on a Wednesday night instead of watching another episode of *Seinfeld*.

This is what life on the road is.

This is what being in a touring band is.

Ask Dr. Dog.

But like the slow gains after a long year in the gym, Texas Flip was too closely involved to notice the measured, steady growth of their audience. And before they knew it, their second full-length record, *Cool Hair, Bro . . .* , was out. And then their third record, *Cherry Eye*, was out. And then, comfortably filling venues in the two- to four-hundred-seat range, they had ballooned one more human in size with the part-time procurement of a roadie, Rusty.

A man twenty years their senior, Rusty met the band while they were still doing their thing around the bars and clubs of Upstate New York and the only people who knew them were the drunks who were forced to sit through their set during MLB highlights on the TV. Helping them load in and out their gear, never asking if he could but rather taking the dreadful task upon himself for no reason other than what looked like pure boredom and probable divorce, he started that day and, like the music, never stopped. Only speaking when spoken to, Rusty was a theorizer and wonderer. Someone content with the hand dealt him. A man society set the burner on low for. A man whose last name Zach was still unsure of.

Todd would come on full-time too, quitting his father's accounting firm to join the circus of ever-changing misfortune.

Everyone's shitty full-time day jobs felt no longer needed. Now they were shitty part-time day jobs.

Cool Hair, Bro . . . and *Cherry Eye*, self-released like all their other previous releases (as no other option had been made available to them, every record label in the country having turned them down multiple times), would force Texas Flip to go back to work with what they had: nothing. Doubtful anyone in the band would have thought of himself as a "professional" musician, being as they bordered the poverty line and hadn't spent a second gaining any musical education within an academic or structuralized setting, they were still making enough money to pay for all their expenses and feed themselves daily, which, at the age of twenty-six, was pretty hard for both Zach and his parents to believe, so why question it?

And it was somewhere in between Portland, Maine, and Portland, Oregon, when the band started to think these proverbial thoughts, as one does when success on an even higher level might be achievable. They started to think with greed. They started to think ahead.

Truth be told, there had never been a real conversation among any members of the band about signing with a major label, same as there had never been a serious conversation about Bart's depression or Luke's sex addiction; it wasn't on their radar. Texas Flip had cultivated and ran within their niche, created solely by them, since the band started: a killer live show and hard work. And now they were playing in rooms bigger than they had ever fantasized, all from word of mouth.

On a good tour, they might have sold two thousand copies of their catalog. Poster and T-shirt sales treated them well too. And in retrospect, it would have been easier (and a much better idea) to have kept this train rolling as it was, building up their crowd year by year, and continue to make a semicomfortable living for themselves as the rooms expanded in combination with the expenses. And even given the amount of shows they played, it never felt like work anyways. It was too much fun to be work. At times, it was hard to take it all that seriously. They'd get press in local papers and weeklies wherever they were playing thanks to Todd. Maybe an interview for some college radio station. But MTV and FM radio sure as hell had no clue who Texas Flip were. And neither did their audiences.

Which was exactly how they *thought* they wanted it to be.

Ahhhh, musicians.

Back on the road again, the band sound-checked among chaos and muddle on the second night of their two-night run at the Musical Box in Louisville, Kentucky, a 550-capacity theater Harry Houdini had once performed in. The labor onstage quick and tolerable, so was the luxury of ignoring some of the industry-looking folks roaming around the empty venue well before doors opened and catering was served.

Tours of a certain scale are a congress of bendable pieces built for flex and durability. Fast moving and slow developing, the quicker they run, the slower time seems to move. And when thick in the middle of living your life on top of tires and engine exhaust, the litany of strangers (and stranger things) that enter your life on the daily can, and will, become mind-numbing.

No special occasion for some fresh character to shake your hand, offer a hug, or pay you an empty compliment about your mediocre guitar playing; this was all another part of the gig, mostly forgettable and undoubtedly irksome. Someone telling you something you lost interest in long ago, the attention left to pay them dwindles into nothingness as time becomes limited in your world of *Next city. Next show. Next bag of drugs.* Playing video games and finding moments to masturbate occupy more of your imagination than day trips to Navajo reservations or tours of Mount Vernon ever could. These were the sacrifices made to gain a little semblance of normalcy in your skull. Or normalcy in anything.

With most of the tickets for both nights of their occupancy sold, the band, Todd, and even the stage manager were all in good spirits seeing that money was being made. An enjoyable first set in the books on that second night, with one debut and a new cover performed, the crowd radiated a heat of encourage-ment between sets of eager and misguided improvisational rock and roll while Texas Flip and crew hung out backstage, smoking cigarettes, eating salty cold cuts, and taking snips from a complimentary bottle of Stolichnaya provided by the venue and not requested by the band. Zach sat on a couch with a ring finger two knuckles deep in his ass crack, his mind on the following items, in order: another bump of cocaine, what songs they hadn't played yet, and who the figure standing before him looking like she had just walked out of a copy of *Vogue* was.

"You guys are fantastic," she said to them all, yet to no one at the same time.

Smelling his finger, Zach replied, "Thanks. Who are you?"

The pretty woman introduced herself to the band with the energy of a hospice patient. "My name is Melissa Vaughn, and I'm the senior vice president of A&R at Mountain View Records." Held in her pink-manicured nails scented with a lotion that made Luke's dick inch upward were copies of a business card printed on thick paper and thicker meaning. "If you gentlemen have a moment, I would like to speak with you."

The texture of her card on the tips of Zach's fingers felt rugged, which meant it wasn't a cheap print job and that maybe she hadn't bullshitted her way back here like most women who looked as fashionable and attractive as her are able to do with the littlest of effort. His attention was piqued, testosterone forcing an undeniable keenness, and he flipped the business card over in the hopes it would reveal the famed Mountain View Records logo—three loud letters in a V shape, two gold wreaths laid behind—and was not disappointed when he felt the raised characters, solidifying her claims and credentials.

In control of the room and them, Melissa commenced like Germany at the beginning of the war. "We at Mountain View Records have noticed an increasing trend in the last few quarters of what our industry has dubbed 'DIY bands.'" Her throat was parched, not for lack of liquid but lack of air. "If anyone is unfamiliar, this would stand for 'do-it-yourself.'"

Harry laughed out loud.

Sensing she might lose them before she could even begin her pitch, Melissa backed up her verbal assail. She was a professional, and she knew they were stupid. "Or maybe you'd all prefer the term 'grassroots'? Either way, I am here tonight to speak to you on behalf of the label and tell you that we believe Texas Flip has what it takes to make it to the next level. Some of our A&R people have had their eyes on your band for a while and believe the iron is hot."

Zach's groin started to hurt.

Todd felt the thinness of his wallet through his jeans.

Bart came back from the bathroom.

Luke kept his eyes on her ass.

Turning her back to them, Melissa pushed away a fold-out chair with three of their leather jackets on it and made room for herself against the cement wall nearest the exit. The room suddenly smelled like peaches from a can. "Our studies show that fifteen- to forty-year-old single Caucasian men particularly enjoy the style of music that your band produces. And seeing as they are one of our largest customer demographics, and the fact that you play as many concerts a year as you do, has all produced a positive upward slope on our forecasted gross revenue graph."

"Gross what?" Todd asked, undecided what a graph might have to do with rock-and-roll music, and undecided if he was too high for this conversation. "I'm sorry, but who the hell are you again?"

"Ahhh, you must be the band's manager?" It took just nine syllables for her to belittle Todd.

"Yeah . . . I am."

"Her name is Melissa Vaughn," Harry informed him. "And she is the senior vice president of A&R at Mountain View Records."

"I *know* that!" Todd yelled.

From her large purple Louis Vuitton handbag, Melissa pulled out a folded piece of paper and pinned it flat against the wall for the whole gang to see the lines and angles scribbled in bright colors in directions that looked neither favorable nor disapproving. Her index finger traced the paper up and down while the band's squiggly eyes did their best to follow along.

They'd have a better chance of following a fly in a sandstorm. "The fine folks in our analytics department have constructed this graph to illustrate how we at Mountain View Records predict the success of a band like Texas Flip in the musical environs of today. The orange line *here* tracks the release of your debut record—"

"*Debut* record? We have, like, three records out already."

"And you are Luke, the singer and bassist, correct?"

"Yeah." Luke checked himself, the harshness of his previous outburst replaced with confusion at his own name.

"Good to know . . ." She started to speak quickly like a play-by-play announcer to maintain their diminishing attention spans. "Now, as I was saying, the blue line *here* showcases that Texas Flip should have a sustainable, up-trending career arc of three to five years. The green line *here* is projected album sales, along with touring revenue. You'll see how each line affects the others in a corresponding relationship."

Bart looked as if he was sleeping, and Todd looked like he was ready to hit a child.

Melissa backpedaled yet again. "I can see by the expressions on your faces that this might be a lot to take in at once. Let me start over. The reason I'm here, and what this boils down to, is that Mountain View Records is interested in signing Texas Flip to a deal." A thick, multipage document emerged from her black hole of a purse and made a thud loud as a Georges St-Pierre head kick on the table. "Your contract would be for three full-length releases, with an option to pick up a fourth record, as well as a greatest hits."

Zach knew he had heard the term "trend" used more than once, plus "career arc." Something about single white dudes liking their music too.

Todd, frustrated by each click of the second hand on Melissa's Cartier watch, and with more of an education than the whole band combined with regard to discussing such financial obligations, felt the need to chime in. "Listen, lady, we appreciate you taking the time to stop by—"

"Mountain View Records is willing to offer Texas Flip a $300,000 recording budget for your debut record," Melissa interrupted, "and a $50,000 advance—against any future profits—for all band members. We can discuss the terms of your contract, and any other particulars you might have, at a later date."

"—but I just wanted to say that I love how professional you are. And did I compliment your nails yet? They look magnificent."

Like a grenade detonated beside him, the air sucked out from Zach's lungs. He began to feel faint, his heart fluttering. Grabbing the rear of Harry's chair, he inhaled deep through his nose and steady out his mouth, his breath hitting the back of Harry's neck in triplet beats, and found a sliver of space to compose himself just in case Melissa's sentiments were, in fact, real.

Luke took the cue before he took a dive. "That's fucking awesome!" He sat apart from the rest of the band, his spine stiff against the impractical love seat he occupied, and looked like a dummy without its ventriloquist. "But this is, like, a lot to digest during a set break. We should probably sit down and, like, talk it over before we make any commitments . . . Ya know?"

Melissa spoke not a word, mute as a mouse.

"Cool if we get back to you in a couple of days?" Todd tacked on top of Luke's suggestion.

"I'm boarding a plane back to Los Angeles at one P.M. tomorrow," she said, her eyes progressing backward toward her scalp. "If I haven't heard from you by then, you can consider the offer no longer on the table."

The words clawed through them worse than her nails ever could have, and the room sat flat for a couple of seconds that felt like three lifetimes. The word "advance" rang continually in Zach's skull. He looked at Todd, who was looking at Bart, who was looking at Luke, who was looking at Melissa's legs.

"Where do we sign?" came from the chorus of musicians.

With a smile as wide as the Ohio River, pleased with another sucker sold, Melissa said, "That's what I like to hear. There's a couple of little things that need to be done on my end first, so I'll be in touch tomorrow morning to begin ironing out all the details then. I will also have copies of your contract sent over for you to review as well. But in the meantime, you guys go on back out there and give those fans more of what they want! There's going to be a lot more of them soon."

His face expressionless as a chalkboard, Todd stood dumbfounded as he watched Melissa walk out the door of another workday, the only items left on her agenda consisting of a kale salad, a double martini, and half a Xanax. Breathing reality into the room and himself, Todd said, "Second set starts in four minutes. I don't know what the fuck just happened, but—"

"Holy shit, guys!" Luke shouted. "Did we just sign a record deal?"

"I'm not sure what's going on," Zach said, trying harder to remember where he stashed his bag of blow than figuring out the implications of a four-record contractual obligation. "I don't *think* we did?"

"All right, guys," Todd interceded, somehow more overwhelmed than anyone in the band. "We're all kinda fucked up. This is kinda fucked up. It's the middle of a show. And we didn't actually sign anything." He looked at Luke for reassurance to make sure he hadn't actually signed anything. "Tomorrow morning . . . That will be a good time to talk about this . . . As in *after* tonight. Tomorrow. Morning."

"Yeah," Luke responded. "Tomorrow morning."

"Yes. Tomorrow. Morning."

It was 10:57 A.M. when the phone rang in the hotel room Zach and Todd shared. The receiver on his side of the queen-sized bed, the guitarist answered snappishly, and the stick of phlegm that stuck to the walls of his throat got stuck to the wall of the room.

"Ughhh, hello?"

"Good morning! It's Melissa Vaughn from Mountain View Records. Is this one of the members of the band Texas Flip?"

Her sunniness was too cheerful for the hangover/cocaine comedown he was sporting. "Yeah," he said, the phlegm puddling in the shape of bologna slices. "This is Zach. I'm the g—"

"Great! I've had four copies of your Mountain View Records contract sent over to your hotel for review. They are waiting for you at the concierge desk. There are also four plane tickets to Los Angeles for all band members. Your manager will need to buy his own ticket if he would like to join you."

"Melissa—that's great," Zach said, nudging his sleeping partner awake, "thank you so much. But, uh, I don't think we can fly to Los Angeles right now. We're on tour."

Todd rolled over and blinked, in a state between the paralysis of slumber and wakefulness.

"Your tour schedule tells me you have a day off after your show in Houston. Am I mistaken?"

"Todd, do we have a day off after Houston?"

"Give me the phone!" he barked. Pinching the receiver between his ear and shoulder, he lit up a roach and coughed into Melissa's telephonic ear, ash covering the white bedspread in drab shavings. "This is Todd Shift, Texas Flip's manager. What's up?" The small joint burned his fingertips before he could inhale a hit that could get him high, and he gave Zach a look that said, *I already know whatever it is this lady is going to tell me,* and disposed of the useless joint into an empty beer can; the singe of it was heard all the way in the security office. "Houston? Yeah, we have a day off . . . Well, okay, but . . . Okay . . . I have to buy my *own* ticket?!"

"Give *me* the phone!" Zach shot out his hand and snatched the phone from Todd's face. "Hey, Melissa, Zach again. Whatever we need to do, we'll figure it out. Thanks again for everything."

"Sure thing."

She hung up before he could.

"The hell?" Zach said, aggravated but amused. "I'm gonna go wake up the other dudes and tell them what's up."

"Nah, not yet," Todd argued. "Let's you and I go downstairs and see what the story is first."

They nabbed croissants, bananas, granola bars, Pop-Tarts, and extra glasses of apple juice on their way to the concierge desk. None of what was currently happening, or might happen, wanted to register itself in Zach's fried egg of a head or Todd's smudged sense of himself. Zach's left nostril was roasted from perpetual cocaine abuse and his heel bruised from a jump onstage a couple of nights prior; he had yet to even smoke a cigarette and heal his morning ailments before a lavender Hermès bag was delivered to them by a bubbly desk clerk.

Back in their room, sitting at the end of the bed that still smelled like all four of their feet, the thirty-page agreement lay before them on the floor, untouched and unread like the majority of *Infinite Jest*s you find on people's bookshelves. Baffled at the sheer size of the legal document, Zach lit a cigarette and blew out smoke along with a question:

"What is this thing?"

"I . . . I didn't think it was gonna be this big," Todd stuttered.

"That's what she said."

"This is crazy. The biggest contract we've ever had was two pages. This thing is"—he picked up the hefty bundle and looking underneath it—"like a hundred pages."

"Should we read it?"

"I don't know . . . I still can't believe I have to buy my own plane ticket."

"Houston is two nights from now, right?"

"Yeah."

"All right . . . That'll give us plenty of time to read it then, yeah? Let's go wake up the guys."

Not one member of Texas Flip had read past the first page of their record contract as they boarded a 3:15 A.M. flight from Houston to LAX (with a layover in Sacramento) two days later. It was a pleasant journey thirty-seven thousand feet in the air across the American Southwest and into the City of Angels, where a measureless smog screened the Hollywood sign and the Capitol Records Building with flakes of gold. Sunny Southern California's warmth and shattered dreams broiled their insides before their first cigarettes could. Outside of their gate, a goombah-looking fella straight out of a reject pile from the *Goodfellas* casting call held a sign that read TEXAS WHIP. His suspenders did little to hold up his pants—his ill-fitted suit the physical embodiment for his and every other failed acting career in this town. He drove with his knees and talked for twenty minutes about how he had recently been an extra on an episode of *Law & Order*. The stench of show business was in his voice, in the Lincoln Town Car, in the air, and everywhere else the eye could see, inexorable. Easier to choke on than a whole chicken with brussels sprouts.

What an awful city, Zach thought.

Dead souls hauled their hindrances and miscarriages off to

one more failed audition, inching through traffic on the foul-smelling and apocalyptic 405, which stunk worse and worse the longer traffic sustained. A steady rhythm built, and the car's engine fell flat in line. They drifted in time as they drove past the Troubadour and Whisky a Go Go; past grown men in Spider-Man costumes and grown women in She-Hulk makeup playing the roles no one cared to give them the first time around; past Pink's Hot Dogs and the Hollywood Forever Cemetery. The luminous sky weighed heavily on the whole crew. The smoothness of a chauffeured ride on someone else's dime didn't. The gates of Mountain View Records manifested before them like the kingdom of heaven, the believability of the moment absent.

Their driver parked and turned around in his seat, and with his best B-level delivery, he said, "This is as far as they told me to take you. Call in on the buzzer, and someone will open the gate."

"Seriously?" Todd asked, offended.

"Dead serious," he replied impassively.

Driving off—aiming on a cheeseburger lunch with garlic fries and a frozen yogurt afterward—he left behind the four members of Texas Flip (and their manager) to loiter on Sunset Boulevard like the jackasses they were, decked out in jeans, hoodies, and jackets on an 83-degree morning. A collective gathering of chickens with their heads cut off, they were directionless.

Zach felt flustered trying to find his lighter so they all could smoke a cigarette, but then the big metal gate behind them slowly slid open before he could procure a flame, and then he felt more flustered. No sound came in its smooth-running course, and no one was waiting for them on the other side of it. The band (plus Todd) made their way through the parking lot of Mercedes-Benzes, BMWs, Jaguars, and Range Rovers and up to the twelve-foot-tall wooden doors of the eight-story-high glass building that was the headquarters of one of the largest record labels in the country. Walking into a brilliantly lit lobby of Constantin Brâncuși sculptures and Mark Rothko paintings, the band remained patient as a puppy on a leash while Todd marched up to an impressively impenetrable receptionist's desk.

No one belonged there. Not even the janitor.

"Hi," he said to the receptionist, a girl Zach was positive had been in a recent issue of *Hustler*. "We're here for our appointment with Melissa Vaughn. The band is Texas Flip."

Nothing on this planet could stop her from the rigorous filing of her nails. She spoke into the small metal box fixed an arm's length away, not an eyelash raised to the person in front of her. "Melissa, your ten forty-five is here." She indicated with a head tilt that they station themselves in the middle of the lobby's $4 million art collection. "You guys can go sit over there."

"Thanks."

Before anyone could guess why somebody would pay that much money for a *Multiform* painting, Melissa appeared before them with a face that held more makeup than Nordstrom. She looked rushed, as if someone more important and richer were over all their shoulders. A real Angeleno. And there probably was.

"Hey, guys, happy you could get here on such short notice. Hope the first-class lounge at United treated you well. They can be pretty lackluster with the catering spread sometimes."

"W-wow," Todd stammered, "that was quick. Were you waiting around the corner?"

"I see there was an extra seat on the plane."

"There wasn't. I was on standby. Got lucky after some lady missed the flight because her service dog took a shit at security."

The receptionist coughed.

A Rothko shook.

"That's fun," Melissa said. "Anyways, now that you are all here, let's head upstairs, shall we? They're waiting for us."

The elevator had small, piercing lights meant to intimidate; it shot up to the eighth floor fast enough to shoot Zach's nuts into his feet. Stationary within seconds of take-off, its doors opened to lime-green walls lined with gold and platinum records and an entire floor filled with over-paid youths throwing footballs and blasting music their own label released—basically doing anything other than what looked like their jobs. Guiding Texas Flip hurriedly through, Melissa grabbed a couple of memos from an intern and took a twenty-second phone call about an impending lawsuit before leading them into a corner conference area hidden away like the Situation Room in the West Wing.

This room, in comparison to everything else in the building, was small, but the enormous table—made from some wood likely found deep in the Amazon, but now stained with mug rings and occupied by half a dozen suits—did a good job adding levity to what was, up till then, the most important meeting of their lives.

Melissa broke ground first.

"Everyone, this is Texas Flip. Texas Flip, this is the Mountain View Records executive staff."

None of them said anything.

"Gentlemen, please take a seat."

An assortment of tea bags and pastries and their record contract were the only items inhabiting any of the table's vast space. One could sense this was a group of people that was not about wasting time. Or money.

"Let me first start by saying that we're sorry that Gary couldn't make it today," Melissa continued, still standing. "He had a tee time with Donald Trump and Irving Azoff at seven forty-five, and Mr. Trump likes to be first in line at the club-house buffet when they open."

Munching on a heavy almond croissant, Luke asked, "Who's Gary?"

"Gary Katzka," one of the suits broke in, "is the *owner, president*, and *CEO* of Mountain View Records."

"Gary is a legend in our business," Melissa explained further. "And I believe I can speak on behalf of everyone in this room when I say that Gary, well, he's a special man. And a man we all owe so much too."

A grown woman seconds away from breaking into tears picked up Melissa's confused adulation and toasted, "To Gary!" with a champagne glass full of sparkling water.

"To Gary!" hailed the rest of the suits.

Standing more erect than before, Melissa took back control of the room—something she did very well. Something she was paid handsomely to do very well. "Let's get down to brass tacks, shall we? Your contract—are there any questions?"

Todd spilled some of his beverage onto the table. "Urm-mm"—he sponged up the mess with his jacket sleeve—"in all honesty, we haven't had the chance to read it yet. By the size of it, I imagine it's very detailed. And this is all happening quite fast. I have a buddy who is a lawyer. Racial injustice law, specifically. But I'd like to hand it off to him first before we go ahead and sign anything."

Melissa giggled and looked around at the table of suits who made the decisions in this business. She cracked her neck. And then her knuckles. And then her neck again. "Look outside that window behind you."

"*That* one?" Luke pointed at the floor-to-ceiling window behind him.

"Do you see what I see?"

"I see seven homeless people."

"Out there is a line of twenty thousand wannabes

dreaming about sitting where you are, right now." She towered behind a seated Luke and rubbed his shoulders roughly with a fresh set of orange nails, their middles fingers painted white. "This is the best contract *any* record label is ever going to offer you. I know this because all the people you see in this room, they are the ones who make the rules and write the deals. You can either sign our agreement as is or walk out the same door you came in through. The choice is yours." She handed a pen to Luke and came close to his ear, her violet lipsticked lips next to his lobe. "Initial wherever you see a red circle."

Pen in hand, Luke asked his bandmates with a timorous look, "What should I do?"

Zach looked over Luke's head at Melissa. "You said $50,000 advance for all of us, right?"

"For all *band* members," she said, spying Todd's reaction. "Correct."

"Sign it."

In less than four minutes, every *t* was crossed and every *i* was dotted by each member of Texas Flip. Zach would have had his mother sign it had she been there. Having a pedicure appointment, Melissa kept the rest of the proceedings going with much less attachment than ten minutes previous. A cat tired of play. "Great! Now on to the next order of business . . . Here is a list of producers we would like Texas Flip to work with on your debut album." She handed out sheets of paper to everyone in the room; the title at the top of each page was printed in bold block font: "Top 5 Rock/Alternative Producers of the Year—1996." "An answer now would be greatly appreciated, as these producers are typically booked out months in advance."

No one in the band knew a single name on the list, so in the spirit of the meeting, they picked the first one on it: Alexandre Leblanc.

"Perfect choice," Melissa reported back. "Alexandre is a doll and real professional."

If record labels are good at one thing (besides screwing over their artists), it's lying.

So Melissa told Texas Flip they would have free rein in the studio. That there wouldn't be any interference with the creative process. That they were the label's number one priority. Like a lover with a bad track record, she said the things that needed to be heard—fluffy bits of backing and support—and would continue doing so so no one put a gun in his mouth and blew his brains out in Grand Rapids after two bad reviews.

"We will reach out to Mr. Leblanc first thing this afternoon," Melissa said assertively, as if she already knew all the answers to their questions unforetold. "Apart from that, your contract is signed, all parties involved have agreed on logistics of said contract, and a producer has been chosen . . . Am I correct in saying this?"

More silence.

"Happy to hear . . . I think that then wraps up all of today's business. And let me say again how happy we are to have Texas Flip as the newest member of the Mountain View Records family!"

A bird flew into the window behind Luke, knocking itself unconscious and falling to its death below.

At the farthest end of the table sat a gentleman who looked to be one cough away from his own passing. Dressed in an understated Brioni suit and hand-painted tie that sat atop a belly filled with rapacity, his voice was soft like a child's when he asked, "Where did you guys get the name Texas Flip, anyways?"

"You don't want to know," Zach said.

"You're probably right."

Contracts signed and smiles worn out, the band left faster than they arrived before they could second-guess what had transpired in less than thirty minutes, their goodbyes stuttered with rashness to strangers they had just initialed their lives and master recordings away to. A new receptionist was helming the switchboard as they exited and were given a ride right back to LAX to board another flight (with a layover in Albuquerque) and resume their tour in Houston the next day. Shell-shocked and light-headed, with much of nothing to be said about everything, Todd violated the car's awkward silence, asking the question they were all too afraid to solicit: "Did we just make a huge mistake?"

His head hanging out the window of the Lincoln Town Car (driven by a failing stand-up comedian three bad sets away from jumping off the roof of the Hyatt West Hollywood), tongue wagging like a dog in heat, Luke farted out the almond pastry and shouted his own lifelike translation. "So, this is what Los Angeles smells like!"

A package awaited them at the Houston Theater.

Covered in plain wrapping and heavier than a waterlogged stiff, this parcel contained four copies of their signed contract, various Mountain View Records apparel, and a handwritten correspondence from Melissa:

Alexandre Leblanc has signed on for the project. His schedule holds availability three months from now. Preproduction will begin two weeks prior to the first scheduled day of recording. Foggy Bridge Studios in Sausalito, California, has been chosen for the recording of Texas Flip's debut album.

Please send over all pertinent bank information so the agreed-upon advance may be deposited into your accounts no later than three weeks and not less than one week *from this date.*

Gary, I, and everyone else here at Mountain View Records are excited to hear what Texas Flip has to offer the world and look forward to all future success.

Melissa Vaughn
Senior Vice President of A&R
Mountain View Records

"Bank info . . . Does she mean, like, what bank I have?"

"No, Luke," Todd ground out, words tougher than cold leather. "She's asking for all those numbers that are on the bottom of your checks. Guy is getting $50,000 and doesn't even know what the fuck his bank info is!"

Weeks left till the end of their current tour meant the band would have a little under a month until they began preproduction with Alexandre Leblanc. Having more than enough material to make two double albums, and having spent years on the road playing these tunes only to a live audience, they found little point in putting more pressure on themselves than there already was by coming up with new material. Instead they made the wise choice of the nouveau riche and immediately set about buying cars and drugs upon their return home from tour. Days were pissed away getting high and watching TV for the most part.

They rented a five-bedroom house in the Berkeley Hills for two weeks with more money borrowed from the label—not much was done during this time meant for preproduction except half the Bay Area's cocaine supply—and arrived at Foggy Bridge Studios with a spirit of openness and a shovelful of thoughts.

A six-thousand-square-foot gargantuan luxuriance hidden among the house boats and afternoon wine-tasting rooms north of San Francisco, the recording complex was as inspirational a place to make a record as Headley Grange, Electric Lady, Abbey Road, or the multitudes of other famous studios with even more famous clientele. That said, it was also more expensive than a hedge fund hooker.

The value of money lost when time becomes unaccounted for, Alexandre Leblanc would dedicate that whole first week in the studio working on drum sounds and not a damn thing else: an entire seven days of only snare hits, drumhead changes, drumhead tunings, microphone adjustments, cymbal swaps, high-pass filter alterations, low-pass filter deviations, compressor settings, stick modifications, EQ bypasses, limiter variations, mic-preamp settings, X/Y stereo configurations, and rack-mounted gated reverbs. If there was a piece of equipment (or hour of time) that Alexandre could use to make the drums sound "better," then that's what happened. No questions asked.

Like the worm in a frozen margarita, Texas Flip's producer was wearisome and languid in all that he did. The man's body looked consistent with his ravenous consumption of narcotics, and like the gods who had run the boards before him in the '60s, '70s, and '80s, he also encouraged their use in the studio.

But only while bands were tracking. And only if they shared with him.

Cocaine, by the time he could finally afford it, had quietly become Zach's newest occupation (and still the only Eric Clapton song he ever liked), the habitual dependence a house of cards that everyone else in his band and his life had noticed. He was rapidly slithering down a hole of irreversibility that only a drug costing upward of $100 a gram can dig. The lackadaisical consumption by his bandmates of any and everything that could also get them high helped little in the ways of his own moderation.

Todd couldn't get out of bed without smoking weed.

Luke popped Percocets like Pez candy.

Harry drank two bottles of wine a night.

Bart smoked opium.

And they were all still broke.

Insights gained early on were that recording a big-budget album was not the same as recording a four-track EP in your friend's basement, that people and things needed to be paid for: producers, engineers, equipment rentals, takeout for breakfast/lunch/dinner, plus the expense of occupying an entire studio for a month. These expenditures added up like Double Stuf Oreos eaten on a Sunday night: no one the wiser for when the red light was *not* on.

Their album half finished and not a cent of their recording budget left, it was in the thick of a particularly rough vocal tracking session one early afternoon when Melissa popped in out of the blue, maintaining quite the mood and intolerant of excuses. "Gary would like for some rough mixes to be sent to him by the end of this week. And also an explanation as to how you've already maxed out your entire recording budget."

Gary Katzka.

An eighty-one-year-old entertainment lawyer born and raised inside the plastic teepees and drug deals of Co-op City in the Bronx, he had purchased Mountain View Records back in the late '80s as an investment opportunity and a way to launder his clients' illegal money before Bitcoin was a thing. The label had fallen on hard times after sticking with the disco sound well past its prime—ignoring the rise of Madonna, Duran Duran, and hair metal from only pure ignorance—and was put up for sale at a significant loss by its previous owners, Brian and Robert Frippeno, two brothers as shady as Mr. Katzka.

Heirs to the Frippeno family fortune, their great-grandfather was one of the very first prospectors of the California Gold Rush and one of the country's first real estate moguls, buying up plots of land worth more than any amount of gold. The brothers played with their inherited money like pigs play with shit and had initially started the label for fun, losing no sleep over the loss of their initial investment and retiring to one of the family's estates in Palm Desert. A steal for a rich, no-bullshit kind of guy like Gary, he acquired the label for a fraction of what he would turn it into, firing the entire staff and replacing them with a slew of stolen talent from Epic and Geffen Records, and watched the price of CDs rise to an average of fifteen dollars and the price of his stock bubble up to a level Warren Buffett would have been pleased with.

From behind an SSL 9000 J console, suffering from too little sleep and too many substances, Alexandre Leblanc spouted from his red face the sad, honest truth: "Wey weehl send 'im ze trahcks when zey ahre fuckeeng ready!"

"What do you mean, 'when they're ready'?" Melissa asked. "How are they not ready? You've been in this studio for over a month and have blown through your entire budget. Surely there is *something* that Gary can listen to?"

"What do you whant me to sai? Ai can't mak magic, oot of shite, Melissa. Please . . . Just tell Gary to cut anothair chek. He's got ze money!"

They had all agreed, Alexandre included, that their song "Fake News" would be the lead single off their Mountain View Records "debut." It was also the first song they had cut for the record and the only tune that clocked in under four minutes, and if they were aiming for anything that could be a "hit" or considered "commercially acceptable," this song would be their best bet and something they could deliver to Gary pronto.

"Wey can send 'im a song," Alexandre said. "On-lee one, though. Eet eez not complete-lee finished yet, but eet eez good."

"Great. When can I tell him to expect it?"

"Well, if you would stop talking and leeave us alone, zen I'd sai by ze end of ze dai."

The sound of her Longines watch clicked in a fixed bpm, and she shot back ahead of the beat, not the least thrown off by its pulse. "Gambling only pays when you're winning, Alexandre," she said, before backing out of the control room. "Gentlemen, have a great rest of your day. And I look forward to listening to what it is you will be delivering."

Before the door had had the chance to fully close behind her, Alexandre launched into a profane denunciation of all things Mountain View Records. "Zat cheap fuk Gary! Guy washes 'is asshule wiv ze money that's been spent on zis recaird. La fukeng nairvé! And Melissa . . . To 'ave ze audac-itay to come een haire, unannouncéd, and tell me 'ow to do mon job? Ai feel bad you signed a contract wiv thos crooks! Fuk 'em all . . . Luke, let's finish zese background vocals zo ai can mixdown zumtheng to send zat slimeball."

Inside the vocal booth this whole time, Luke adjusted his Sony MDR-7506 headphones that were on backward and spoke into the Neumann U-87 microphone with the voice of a child. The SSL's preamps smoothed over his concern. The pop filter did its job. "Melissa can't be that bad, right? I mean . . . she did sign us."

His accent thicker than a slice of quiche, Alexandre yelled, "Who geevs a merde!" through the talk-back microphone in the control room, spittle spattering onto the mixing board from his watery mouth. "We 'ave six songs finished. Ze label whants at least eleven faire zis recaird. If we 'urry zis along, we can get trakeng done faire la rest of le recaird een deux weeks. And zen ai, and you, can move la fuk on to zumtheng else!"

Fortunately for some, advancements in digital technology had caught up to the recorded music realm and the music was now being captured on alternative media. Having held the throne for forty-odd years, physical audio tape in its inch-by-inch form was becoming obsolete by the end of the millen-nium, and Foggy Bridge Studios (one of the first in the country to do so) had overhauled all three of its rooms to be outfitted with the then brand-new recording software Pro Tools. Guinea pigs in a slaughterhouse, Texas Flip would experiment with this foreign machinery (and a foreign producer) and record their entire album "inside the box," as there was simply no other option available to them, expensively learning that like most 1.0 software versions, there were still some bugs that needed ironing out.

Error codes, unsaved sessions, and perpetual digital clipping only a few of the sufferings that would cost both time and large sums of money for hours-long solutions, what was much worse was the mechanism's audible counterpart. The 1s and 0s like harsh digital pricks to your eardrums—the recording's warmth, its quintessence, stripped away by hidden computations—most listeners' ears felt exhausted after only a couple of spins of their compact disc, a technology initially created to usher in the highest-quality audio possible. Bands of this generation were stuck hearing their thinned-out recordings played in public spaces on even thinner speakers forevermore, wishful that an alternate universe existed where they had waited two more years to cut that album instead, pondering, *Why was it us in the right place at the wrong time?*

An unreasonably quick release date given to them in an unreasonable manner, Texas Flip not only had to finish the rest of basic tracking for their record but also mix and master it. Blasting through basic tracking with Alexandre like they did bags of drugs to meet yet one more deadline, the band also hurried their decision-making and made the fatal mistake of rushing through the album's other processes with equal stupidity.

Alexandre, along with his engineer Thomas, had done a superb job recording their raw tracks at Foggy Bridge Studios with pristine clarity, despite all digital impediments. Too bad that's all they did. Mixing and mastering: arguably the most significant components of a professional-sounding album. Even the highest-end recordings can be victim to an audio engineer's dynamic, covetous knob-turning hands. Dozens of Telefunken and other German-made microphones sent through Neve 1073 mic preamps, transferred into an SSL 4000 E console, and tracked on sixty-four channels of 24-bit/192kHz HD digital goodness—all capturing the slightest infractions of the hundred-plus Cleveland Orchestra—can just as easily be ruined by someone who paid for a ten-month audio engineering degree and served tea and biscuits to Tom Hanks as an intern during an ADR session once.

A poorly mixed record is like bad sex with a hot chick.

Pointless.

On the firm recommendation of some no-name suit at the label, the tracks were sent to Guthrie Klein at Title Recorders to be mixed down for a "radio-friendly" sound. A small studio east of San Jose, and a holdout from the earlier disco days of Mountain View Records, the studio still held connections that were as strong as graphene and worthless as an anthropology degree and was now a dumping ground for the label's newest artists and contemporary jazz roster. Texas Flip's record was mixed by Mr. Klein out of adherence to some moribund clause; his ears were more shot than a nightclub DJ's, producing mixes scooped of all their midrange frequencies and a low end that sounded like it had been recorded inside a hippopotamus's asshole. The band hogtied by nonnegotiable contractual obligations, they took this aural blow on the chin like Michael Spinks and figured Mr. Klein's garbage mix could be saved in the mastering process.

Another big mistake.

A great recording ruined by an awful mix won't ever be rescued by even the most blessed mastering engineer, theirs included. The mixes were sent to Los Angeles to be mastered at No Man's Land Mastering by the über-talented Nala Walsh, but not even her Grammy-winning touch was enough to bring back Texas Flip's mixed mush from its auditory necropolis.

But at least it was loud enough for radio.

Although the band's first time at bat in the majors, they also weren't *that* dumb. They were aware the label's only concern regarding them was a single it could push to help its bottom line, not another *Graceland* or *Dark Side of the Moon*. The band was insulted at how awful their record sounded, but they still delivered to their new bosses sixty minutes of garbage and one finely crafted song they had spent eight full days tirelessly perfecting.

The shock of everything happening so fast allowed the band little time to be upset over the many lies they'd been forced to eat and would continue to eat throughout their tenancy at Mountain View Records. This album the start to the race—and thus cuffed, bound, and with the taste of someone else's chewed gum stuck in their mouths—their debut record for Mountain View Records, *Friday Night Friends*, was released to the world without a wisp of promotion or publicity or advertisement of any sort. No subway billboards, no posters in record stores, no radio interviews, not even a cheaply made music video for their single "Fake News," which would also never be given the wings it needed to get off the ground. The album was another recorded artifact that would be quickly forgotten, a scratch-off lottery ticket already scratched and presented a loser.

At the end of its first year out, sales were 31,829 copies, half of those purchased at their merch booths after shows.

Zach's end-of-the-year royalty disbursement was $6,383.91 before taxes.

Provided with only one option to save themselves from bankruptcy and an even more insolvent mentality, Texas Flip went back to the one thing they could always count on and the one thing that would pay for their drugs.

The road.

5

Montreal Coliseum
Montreal, Canada
1/21/2000

Capacity: 5,500
Tickets Sold: 5,500

T he RGM watch adorning Todd's wrist worked well with his Prince PURPLE RAIN TOUR '84 AT THE COW PALACE T-shirt.

A reminder that money looks good on anyone.

"Is everyone here?" he asked, the weight of the day thicker than the smoke that drifted aimlessly from his hashish cigarette. "It feels like someone is missing. And where's my Pellegrino?"

Their dressing room was crammed with people who

weren't in their band or made money for them, but these commonplace misunderstandings felt comfortable, nonetheless.

"Sound check is at three, dinner at five thirty," he continued, "but I'm gonna need the whole band in the dressing room foyer at seven sharp. Some of the fine people from Mountain View Records are going to be gracing us with their presence this evening." Unsure about being sure, his watch helped to do most of the talking. "Lord knows why they insisted on scheduling a meeting before your set, but I imagine it's to blow a little smoke up our ass, schmooze us. I do like the idea of discussing a budget for the next music video. Pull some of our weight around, ya know?"

Another bus ride, another city, another show, another reduced night's sleep.

Through chance and circumstance, whether you could believe it or not, this is it: the life of a "rock-and-roll star" in a new era.

That forest for the trees clear-cut, exhibiting a paved pathway rid of any labors or hardships. A flash of a dream when you plugged in that Epiphone starter guitar for the first time—the posters of Jimi Hendrix and Black Sabbath sharing space with the lava lamps, glow-in-the-dark psychedelic mushroom prints, and Christmas lights that hung from ceilings and bottoms of loft beds—closing your eyes and developing photos of all the chicks in the front row while you played those out-of-tune, out-of-sync Led Zeppelin riffs to all the dudes in the back row, a dream that couldn't have felt more real, a dream for dreamers—that dream is now, with the beginnings of a premature middle age circulating along your veins, that Les Paul slung low enough to slip a disk in your back every time you put it on. You still pretend to be Jimmy Page in *The Song Remains the Same*, albeit absent the sexual prowess and charm and charisma and talent, and heavier in weight and in mind. Monday and Tuesday your weekend, the years of living in the abstract have abstracted you from the ways of a normal life, a life without making a living from your music: functioning in a society where most people's wage is dependent upon an actual skill—a thought scarier than taking a header off the Golden Gate Bridge.

The same imbecile you were when not a person on this Earth concerned themselves with your existence, here you are now—years, records, and tours later—and wouldn't you know it? People have become concerned. Very concerned.

Concerned with what they're owed from *you* and with what you owe to *them*.

That Porsche your keyboardist bought, or that out-of-court settlement your singer paid some B-list porn star? Everyone's divorce? These breaking developments become part of a greater news story. Amenities and satiation paid for by the effort your band put into writing and practicing and performing and caring and interviewing and photo-shooting and filming and touring and demoing and recording and lying and cheating and dealing and fucking and losing appreciation for anything worth valuing—all these forfeitures become another brick in the wall of eventuality. Welcome to the machine: write, record, go on tour, sell records, repeat.

The time for pissing off club promoters and banging cocktail waitresses well in the past, the present of a "successful" band in the modern day and age will find itself filled with a much different kind of anxiety from that of unwanted pregnancies and chlamydia when questions like "What were the ratings this week in Pittsburgh and Tampa?" take the place of "Do I have enough money to eat?"

That one-person crew you used to have. Now it's three to five people whose names you still can't remember.

How about the small trailer that barely stayed attached to the back of your old van? The one that took out a couple of fast-food drive-through kiosks with a quick burst in reverse?

Good thing for you that that little wagon train has been replaced by a semitruck stuffed with all kinds of expensive lights, sound equipment, grand pianos, needless amplifier cabinets, and more merchandise than your band could possibly sell on one tour. And someone needs to drive that truck too. And unload it. And get paid.

What about those CDs you hawked yourself after each show?

Sayonara!

Those face-to-face interactions after the gig you played following a full day of travel are now no longer needed. If people want to buy your albums, they can find them in the shelves of every single record store across the country. Or at the merch booth. A merch booth run by a merch person, a person whom you're paying to do something you used to do yourself.

Or they can listen to it online for free.

Remember those mornings waking up with debilitating pain in your right hip from sleeping on the wooden floor of a friend's house? Or better yet, sleeping with all your bandmates in two twin beds with Marvel Comics blankets, or lying feet-to-face in another bug-ridden motel thirty miles outside of whatever shithole city you played that night? With vast amounts of effort on your part (the hip pain persistent), those one-story ranch houses and motels have bloomed into five-star hotels with fancy lettering on their marquees, concierge service, and never a question about complimentary breakfast in the morning.

Was that Stevie Wonder hanging out in the lobby?

Yes, yes, it was.

And how does all this happen? How do you go from a band with a niche, loyal fan base who sold well in the clubs after years playing them to selling out every minor-league hockey arena you pull up to? Even more, how does this all happen within the span of eighteen months? Sadly, the answer to all these pertinent questions is rather as simplistic as 1+1. Your band, your ultimate musical creation, writes, records, and releases a *modestly* successful single.

Then your band writes, records, and releases a *massively* successful single.

Most bands have never set out to write a hit song. How could they? Recordings are a snapshot of time, a period piece for who you were as an artist, not who you thought you *would be* as an artist. When Texas Flip recorded *Friday Night Friends*, they were doing what they always did, except with a much bigger budget, in a much bigger studio, and on much better equipment than they even knew existed. Four dudes playing songs that were polished, road-worn and tested for years. Recording these tunes was a breeze. Finding success with them, however? Well, not so much . . .

In total, the band played 291 shows in 1998. Yet after performing almost every night for over a year and selling a quarter of a million records (and enough merch to clothe a small Cambodian city), they were still flat broke. Strange hints sifted around Mountain View Records that it was "make or break" for them after only one outing with no help for their troubles either, the iron lukewarm after a good end to a tough year. The label demanded Texas Flip's second record come out ASAP, for their employers were in the business of turnaround, not headway. Tough shit for the band; this meant they were forced to write their whole next record, *You're on the Back of the Worm!*, while still touring for their last record.

Texas Flip was able to piece together enough guitar riffs, hi-hat grooves, bass lines, and chorus melodies in hotel rooms, airplanes, cars, trucks, and buses that when the time came to begin preproduction for their new album, they had the amateurish sketches of seven decent tunes and at least one hidden bonus track. The little candle flame of popularity they'd scrounged up with their previous effort close to extinguishing itself out with each anxious breath and new gold record presentation, this latest effort would unearth a kindling powerful enough to light any uncertainties into an incandescent fireball of optimistic opinions.

In a practice of frugality and a throwback to their roots, they decided to forgo the big-name producers, lavish studios, and expensive engineers and instead locked themselves inside the quaint H&W Studios up in the Catskill Mountains of New York State. The studio was named after the husband-and-wife owners, Henry and Wynonna, who were some of the best talents working in the field, the duo having produced a successful record for their buddies in the band Horrible Stars; the sounds and tonalities of that band's album right on point with what Texas Flip thought was needed for a record made at the turn of the millennium: tight drums, bright guitars, up-front vocals, and a mastering job so thin and compressed it made Larry David's hair look thick.

With years of wisdom and a century's worth of patience, Henry and Wynonna put their best feet forward to provide Texas Flip the tremendous help they so desperately needed to sculpt the small amount of material they had into a cohesive and releasable collection of music worthy of a sticker price. And with the band firing on all cylinders, and not a whole lot to lose (except everything), it felt as if they were swimming through a dream that they'd fallen into anyways. Something never asked for. Playing with house money.

It's only too bad that what Zach was playing with cost real money.

Lots of it.

About this time, Texas Flip's guitarist was, with little effort, shoving an eight ball of cocaine up his nose on the daily. Everyone aware he had a problem, including his girlfriend, Kristina—who had asked for a break in their relationship and left him to go live with her folks back in New Hampshire weeks before they started recording what would become the biggest record of their career—the blow he was snorting made the road bearable, while the music he depended on to keep him out there hit less and less. Basic tracking for *You're on the Back of the Worm!* wrapped up in three weeks' time, and the tapes were overnighted to Nashville to be mixed by Milton Walter at Sugar Shack Studios. A mixing engineer in high demand who was coming off not one but two back-to-back platinum records —the breakthrough album *Get Dirty*, by the nu metal band Pool of Dirt, which then led to his mixing *I Offered My Love, You Offered Your Blood*, an album that would sell three million copies in its first year alone, by the country's biggest emo band, Our Toxic Affair—there were no back-and-forth exchanges necessary with Texas Flip, and he sent over his final mix to Splendid Sound in NYC to be mastered by Alice Xia, another legend in the business.

You're on the Back of the Worm! tracked on a Studer A827 twenty-four-track two-inch tape machine, Alice insisted the record be mastered in a digital format rather than to half-inch tape—an idea no one was stoked on, afraid the "analog" sound would be lost in the transfer of system. This naive sentiment washed away like broken glass at Rockaway Beach as soon as she pressed play inside her cramped mastering suite for the record's final playback. The band listened to the album's lead track, "Speechless," come at them in a flurry from the pair of Bower & Wilkins speakers installed high up in the sound-insulated wall, and the song's title described exactly the feel of the room. A/Bing between the massive loudspeakers and her Yamaha NS-10 monitors to ensure that Texas Flip did, indeed, have a solid record on their hands, the mood was strangely similar to when they had been in the Mountain View Records offices.

No time to waste when money is time, the label would

release the album's first single, "Sight Glass," barely a month after the band handed over the masters. And to keep the little momentum they still had from their last record going, Mountain View also offered to shell out some serious dough for a professional music video at a time when budgets were more bloated than a peripheral edema sufferer, hiring Mikael Antoni, the biggest and most expensive music video director in the game, and approving his $400,000 financial envelope and the rental of an LAPD helicopter in order to film a mini-movie up in Griffith Park for three full days and a workforce fifteen strong of makeup people, hair people, assistants, and stuntmen.

In the end, 85 percent of the footage Mikael shot would be taken out of the final cut, the remaining scraps edited down to a generic-looking music video complete with nonexistent story line and scenes of Texas Flip playing in front of a crowd of onlookers outside some cabin in the woods at night, their instruments not even plugged in. The at-home viewer was never given an explanation as to why they were in the woods playing with no amps and surrounded by a bunch of strangers who looked as if they had never even heard of the band before. Likewise, most people at home would be left to scratch their heads at this huge waste of money for a video that could have been shot by the band itself or, better yet, not at all. But who cares when your label has grown revenue by 19 percent year over year and sells twenty-five million units in a quarter?

A slow start to a fast end, little would occur in the first couple weeks of the video's release.

But then something strange happened.

Through sly maneuvers behind the scenes that they didn't even know existed, their distended music video was pushed into rotation on the music television show *Your Score Live!* (*YSL!*), a spectacle broadcasted on the Canadian network MBC (Melodic Broadcast Corporation). Hosted by two ex-rocker dimwits, Brad Krowger and April Lavin—married at one time but now divorced and contractually paired to work together—their joint venture was taped in front of a live audience with viewers at home calling in to vote on their favorite videos every week and would run for only two seasons before audiences realized they preferred Carson Daly instead. Someone at Mountain View Records, by whatever means possible (and with a lifetime of favors), got Texas Flip's video for "Sight Glass" on the playlist, as even the show's hosts seemed surprised when it debuted at number nine.

By the end of the first week, the video rose to number four.

The following week it was number one.

They officially had a "hit" in Canada.

By the measures of rock critics, rock musicians, and even the dudes who wrote it, "Sight Glass" was, at best, an all right song. It sure as hell wasn't the greatest song they ever wrote. But it was by no means their worst. So why, then, would a little song like this, with a crappy video like that, be so successful in a foreign country? Well, that's because everything else out at the time sucked ass.

Before the White Stripes and the Strokes, the musical landscape of the late '90s was a harbor of bubblegum pop, hybrid rap/metal, and bands from New Jersey that people would start caring about in five years. A sliver of space left open on the gearwheel of popular awareness, one quirky guitar band was graciously allowed the tiniest amount of room to weasel in and remind people that bands like Blind Melon once existed. And with the bizarre success of their music video and the power of a major label behind them, radio stations all across Canada soon started to play "Sight Glass" ad nauseum, which in turn boosted record sales, so much so that *You're on the Back of the Worm!* reached number two on *Billboard*'s Canadian Hot 100 chart.

This fruition pouring into the already oversaturated American market, the video would continue to have an impact on

MTV and VH1 and spawn more record sales and radio spins. Even Zach's father was proud. Victory blowing a favorable wind into their sails, that first tour for *You're on the Back of the Worm!* would also see their room capacity amp up considerably. Depending on the market, they were suddenly playing venues ranging from 1,200-seat theaters to 3,000-seat ballrooms to, in some cities in Canada, small hockey arenas, and all to fans who had never even heard of them six months prior. The demand there and the supply ample, and with a decade spent slogging away in bars and clubs paying those dues, if Texas Flip was ever going to be ready for a level of stupid success like this, it would need to have been at that very moment. There weren't going to be any second chances.

Overnight, they went from a band your friend's friend knew to a band your mother heard of, and this newfound celebrity was full of all kinds of perks and advantages. People, for no good reason, began to listen to every word they said, no matter what they said. Rules bent and broke in their favor. And the drugs. Holy shit, the drugs . . . Penthouse apartments, actresses, and Princeton doctors who spent their weekends moving kilos of the best cocaine ever sniffed—this hidden underworld revealed itself to them through the darkest of lights and the lightest of powders.

It would also reveal a band circling down a shadowy drain of individuality.

Gas surfed out of Zach's asshole courtesy of an al pastor taco with extra sour cream, drowned out by the sound of the opening band, Flawed Algorithm, playing to a third-full house. The locker room/converted dressing room stocked four strung-out musicians and that dude they paid to do everything for them. Cheap thrills for high times, here he was, backstage at a hockey arena before his band's show, and still all the man could entertain was the recurring need to shove more stimulant up his nose. Disturbing photos of past glory on the concrete walls —piglets on the wing of self-reflection—it was all too much to handle, but not too much to worry about, and so with a lazy yawn he brought himself back to, scratched his ear, and applied a fuzzy focus to the current happenings of the room: his bandmates, Todd, Melissa, Gary Katzka, and some other guy he'd never met before, holding court around a table of concessions not one person had eaten from.

A soggy cigar settled in the corner of his mouth like a spoiled Italian sausage, cancerous snowflakes tumbled onto the boss's gut in a holiday fashion. His hair was the color of his ash. "Gentlemen," Gary said before choking on a hot puff, "thanks for taking the time to meet on such short notice. I know how busy you all are these days." He stretched himself erect on the leather couch. "I'll be brief. I speak for everyone at the label—and not just because I own it, but because it's true— that we are beyond pleased with the response to your last record . . . err . . ." Gary adjusted his glasses to read from the prepared notes that sat next to untouched bananas on the table in front of him. "Yes . . . *You're on the Back of the Worm!*" He pushed his glasses back up the bridge of his nose with a ruby-ringed finger. "Clever title, if I say so myself." He coughed up a tobacco leaf and more felicitations. "It looks like we will have sold close to a million copies by the end of Q4. Great news! Melissa, when is the platinum record presentation party for these guys?"

The senior vice president of A&R at Mountain View Records slouched awkwardly away from her boss. The couch they occupied was the same, but their understandings of this meeting were far different. "We haven't scheduled one," she said. "I was told that money needed to be allocated toward your fundraiser next month for President Bush."

"Oh," Gary said, clenching his teeth, "yeah . . . anyhow . . . great stuff! Melissa has also informed me"—he peered down at his notes again—"that your single 'Sight Glass' has been a big hit. Especially in Canada. Great folks up there. Great people. The best." He grabbed two croissants. With a mouthful of butter and sugar, he swallowed with difficultly and strangled on a rushed bite. "But yeah—super stuff. I'll have Melissa take it from here."

Melissa stood up and smoothed her dress pants. Creases perfect, hair trimmed, and nails painted aqua blue, her presence demanded your attention, and that attention was demanding. "'Sight Glass' has reached number one in Seattle and in a few of the bigger New England markets," she said. "Analytics have also shown a bump in the fifteen- to twenty-five-year-old demographic. I guess we can say all that money we gave to Mikael was worth it."

"Yes, yes," Gary agreed, and pointed at Melissa with his croissant before stealing her summit. "That's very good news for both Mountain View Records and Texas Flip." He spoke as if he'd never heard of their band, as if this meeting was just a hassle penciled in between rounds at TPC Boston and a table at Smith & Wollensky. "And what that means is that we'd like to capitalize on this good fortune and have Texas Flip extend your contract option with Mountain View Records." If he breathed any harder, they were sure his heart would have stopped and they'd out of a job. "Given how wildly success-ful . . ." He again looked in Melissa's direction.

"*You're on the Back of the—*"

"Yes, *You're on the Back of the Worm!* Given the success the record is enjoying, I can only assume your next release will sell twice as many copies." A pointillist painting made of pastry flakes and cold ash formed on his bulbous stomach in the shape of a dollar sign. "People can't seem to get enough of you guys, which means business is good, and as a businessman who does business, I'd like to keep it that way, gentlemen."

The other man next to Gary, who had not been introduced or bothered to introduce himself, coughed.

"But if you don't mind," the boss said, "I must be on my way; the wife's been on my ass about the flooding at our condo in Boca Raton." He extended his hand to Melissa, who shook it with a shy unwillingness. "Great talk, everybody. Great talk."

The owner, president, and CEO of the fourth-largest record label in the country was led out by a lackey through the door and to a waiting town car that would shepherd him off to a private jet destined for southern Florida.

Stepping out of the batter's box and up to home plate, Melissa assumed control of the room again. There was little else in her life she had control of.

"Here is your new contract."

A three-page document held together by a purple paper-clip, Todd's eyes perked with worry. "Why is it so much smaller than our last one?" he asked.

A shrug of her shoulders as if a fly buzzed her ear, she countered with a snap hook of snark and a jab of patience. "If you'd let me speak, then you might learn the answer to your prematurely ejaculated question."

Stumped, embarrassed, and depreciated, Todd had no response. *She's good* is all he could think.

And she was.

"If I'm the only one who can recall, signing you guys the last time was a painful enough experience. So, to save me the headache, and you the money, we've had our internal legal department comb through your contract front and back. If I can be honest, I'd go as far as saying that this is one of the fairest contracts I've ever seen in my career."

Harry sneezed.

"It should also go without saying that Gary is very fond of

you guys. He wanted to make sure I emphasized that sentiment after he left." This pronouncement bounced around the room and lost direction with each precarious hop.

"He didn't even know the name of our album," Luke said.

Melissa laughed like a serial killer. "Gary has a lot on his mind and is a very busy individual. But make no mistake about it, he is a hundred percent on board the train. Choo-choo!"

Todd flipped through the contract and gritted his teeth in fearfulness, his face spelling out *Not good.*

Even Ray Charles could have seen they were fucked.

The only reason Texas Flip was sitting backstage at such a large venue in the first place was because of a throwaway lick Zach had written during a sound check in Virginia Beach. The notion, let alone the gall, to presume that they could re-create such unforeseen success, was a near impossibility. They'd have better odds of winning the Powerball lottery, twice, than writing another hit song.

Fifteen minutes left until they hit the stage, the gravity of the circumstance gnawed at their bones in a termite approach. The skepticism about their sudden good fortune was reflected in Melissa's diamond earrings. Chris Cornell sang over the house PA, and all at once Zach felt woozy, almost sick, by the unsurety this locker room had roused within a flash.

The new sight of an old Rusty allowed him some sense of normality, or at least a direction in which to vomit.

"Guys," their roadie spoke briskly, "openers just finished. Not sure how much time you have left in here, but maybe you should start getting ready? Petey was radioing about some problems with the kick drum mic. Said he's looking into it now."

Rusty lit the cigarette in his mouth with a match, blew it out, and threw the stick on the ground; the burned potassium chlorate flew as easy as dust in the wind, landing on Melissa's Manolo Blahnik pumps. Straightening himself up at the sight of a suit, Rusty hacked respects into his fist and blood. "Hey, Melissa! It's been a while." He checked her up and down with the absence of shame. "And can I say . . . looking magnificent as always."

She ignored him like a hangnail. "No rush with the contract, guys. Just need an answer within the next day or so."

"*No rush?*" Todd exclaimed. "A day or so, in the middle of a tour, isn't a rush?"

"You know Gary . . ."

"No, I don't."

"He would prefer this be wrapped up as quickly as possible. Very exciting stuff, guys. Very exciting. But let me get out of your hair now. It's game time!" On her way out of their unshampooed manes, she remembered to give thanks one more time. "And I appreciate the awesome seats for tonight. I brought my sixteen-year-old niece with me. She loves you guys!"

As she left through a different exit from the one Gary took, the room cleared of the foul odor of record label employees and nail polish, and Todd, ever present to the prospect, began his opening statements like Johnnie Cochran. "Fuck . . . I wasn't expecting this. I'm nervous . . . This is how this stuff always happens. All these bands—they have a big single, sign another awful contract, their next album flops, and then one of them dies."

Astonished at Todd's pessimism, Luke counteracted with confidence. "I don't know, dude," he said. "I mean, we're already *kinda* famous, right? I think it'll be easy street."

"*Easy street?*" Todd asked, having not a clue what in the hell Luke was talking about.

"Yeah."

"What do you think, Zach? You're somewhat rational."

Zach's logic always reverted to cynicism. The guitarist sought a neutral position.

Rusty.

"What do you think?" he deflected to their roadie. "Mountain View wants us to sign a new contract with them. They're pushing it pretty hard."

"You guys have one song that people in Canada like," Rusty said. "What makes you think you can write another one?"

Stubborn like a mule in mud, that query—could they write another hit?—somehow refused to be addressed by anyone other than the person most least involved.

Stuck shin-deep in reservation and questioning his own logic, Zach reacted emotionally. "We *already* did it. Why can't we do it again?" he asked, more to himself than the people in his presence. His nose felt runny, and he felt like running from the room.

"Fuck yeah, we did!" shouted Luke.

"Then why are you asking me?" Rusty asked rightfully. "Sign it. Who cares? But right now, you dudes need to play a show. I'd wait till maybe afterward to flesh this all out."

Rusty was right. They did have to play a show. And Zach also hadn't touched his guitar all day. Come to think of it, unless he was onstage, his guitar was hardly ever in his hands. The high living and inflated optimism left little time for nonsense such as practicing and improving the craft that had made this all possible in the first place.

The man was a *rock star.*

This was his time. His window of opportunity. His moment to snort all the drugs and write an episode of *Behind the Music* to be proud of. Why would he waste that time practicing the guitar?

Seeing as Texas Flip played close to the same set each night, Zach's fingers were now alleviated from their younger two-set grudge matches and left to relax in a quiet slumber of inflammation and rheumatism before each gig, a welcomed ease on his joints and once callused fingertips. Their machine rolled along smoother than butter on a hot roll onto the stage each night with a seventy-five-minute set and two-song encore —*Goodbye, so long, nice to know ya*—and were out of your city before you were out of the venue.

Steady as she goes, the repetitiousness of this routine night in and night out was one of the few things that helped alleviate the stress of this dark new corner of the world the band had herded themselves into like sheep outside their pen for the first time, and Zach held on to its support for dear life. One mediocre song had changed their whole lives forever, without warning, for better or for worse, and the pretty hippie girls in the front row had somehow turned into dads with their daughters and drunk thirty-somethings who hadn't been laid since Texas Flip's second record: the anticlimax of a briefly popular band up front and center for all to witness, 3-D glasses not needed. Like someone seasick at the beginning of a morning fishing trip, Zach felt only queasier with each new wave of stimulation.

That night's show was at the Boston Palladium, a 3,100-seat multiuse venue that looked (and sounded) like a deserted airplane hangar. The performance finished and forgotten with the interchangeability of socks, the band went straight onto their bus as soon as the last notes of the set had been played to continue their trek north past Newbury Comics, Fenway Park, and that Coca-Cola sign and up to the nefarious city of Montreal for the next show of their elephantine-length tour. Booked for a host of Canadian dates, in addition to this show, they were also scheduled for stops in Quebec City, Ottawa, and Toronto before channeling back to the States via Detroit.

Their draw equal in strength on both sides of the border, this route of travel would also allow them to stay on their bus rather than fly, which, as drug addicts, was always preferable. Flying with narcotics is illegal and a giant hassle. The safety of a rolling drug den was the best option for someone who, at this stage of the game, thought his problem was well hidden but was more obvious than a genital wart. Stupidity on a level like this was only to be expected from such a sloppy addict as Zach. On a normal day, he'd wake up in the early afternoon with some blow left over from the previous night—quick bump, cup of coffee, and cigarette to clear the cobwebs—and would be flowing smooth as a Cessna 208 Caravan thereafter.

But following a night of relatively light consumption in Beantown, his brain screws were loosened, and he was much more primed for the darkness of sleep instead of the weak party happening in the back of the bus, crashing on the couch before midnight, his eyes closing quick after the opening credits of *Ace Ventura: Pet Detective* rolled on the TV screen.

When his eyes opened next, the bus was no longer moving, but bodies were.

After sprinting to the toilet at a squirrel's pace, Todd gave the crapper a quick flush and a spritz of air freshener, like a kid hiding the scent of cigarettes or weed from his parents.

Bart looked like he was about to puke. And then he did.

Before Zach knew what was happening or could open his eyes fully, he was prodded stiffly in the chest with the butt end of a flashlight. The bruise would last for weeks.

"Looks like it was quite a night," the uniformed man towering above him, who looked incapable of spelling the word "fun," said. "My name is Officer Pender, and I am with the Canada Border Services Agency. Please state your reason for entering our beautiful country this morning."

"Hello, officer," Todd said from the other side of the bus, his hand waving in the air to dispel any stable fumes. "We're the band Texas Flip. My name is Todd Shift. I'm their manager."

His heels the anchor for a rotation of power, the officer turned around in a manner pasty as glue, slow as nectar. "Can I please have all your passports, as well as work visas for whatever business you'll be conducting in Canada?"

"Su-sure," Todd stuttered. "They're, um . . . all together, in an envelope"—he pointed at a spot next to Zach on the couch—"that was right there." He flipped over a cushion, some porn magazines, and three different Arby's bags before Luke saved them all.

"Is this it?" the singer asked, his hand conducting an unchained melody with the papers. "It was on top of the Dreamcast."

In the briefest amount of time legally reasonable, the officer peeked through their documents with one eye, all the while continuing to survey the scene on the bus with the other. He didn't like anything that he saw. "Thank you. Now, if you could please pull your vehicle over there"—he motioned to the farthest corner of the rather large parking lot—"we can continue."

"Uh, sure," Todd said, concerned. "Is everything all right?"

The officer stepped down off the bus, dismissing Todd's query like a cat its owner. His restrictive blue uniform made it difficult to manage the three steep steps, but he stopped to raise a stiff finger for them to get a move on. "Please pull to the location I am pointing to," he directed again, and then entered his still-running police cruiser, fiddling with the knobs on his police radio and taking a sip from his iced coffee.

Todd closed the door to the bus. He was sweating. It was 14 degrees outside. "What in the hell does he want us to pull over for?"

His head pounding from lack of sleep, nutrients, and rips from the little baggie tucked safely in the pocket of his green athletic shorts, Zach tried to relax. "Who knows? It's Canada. They're super chill here," he said, and laid his head back down with a gelatin effort onto the couch he had yet to leave.

Todd stared through him like a radiological exam. "Everyone is clean, right? Nobody has any shit on them?"

"Yes," they all denied.

Their bus driver, Chet, rolled them into the designated space and then turned off the engine a little quicker than needed. Dog-tired from thousands of miles driven, the motor released itself like a seal taking a nap in the heat, and Chet tucked the brim of his hat over his eyes, ready for what looked to be a long rest.

He'd last slept twenty hours previously.

The sun had yet to rise. The officer approached their bus once more, his Maglite turned on before entering their domain once again. Lips flat like pancakes, he talked through flour and melted butter. "Given your band's business here and a recent rash of narcotics violations along our border by American entrants, I have been instructed to proceed with an inspection of the inside of your vehicle. Let me state that now would be the time to let me know if there is anything inside the vehicle that I should be made aware of. Such items would include firearms, plants, as well as any illegal narcotics." He stretched his neck to the left, and it popped with a turn to the right. "Need I remind you that Canada adheres to a strict drug policy and does not take such matters lightly. Ever since the passing of our glorious Opium and Narcotic Drug Act of 1929, this beautiful land, my beautiful country, has worked its hardest to smudge out this hideous stain. And let me assure you that my sole purpose on this earth is to make sure it stays that way. With the help of God —blessed Jesus, our mighty creator—I can be a small part of ridding the planet of the evil sins destroying our neighborhoods and youth." He bowed his head in prayer, moving his hand from forehead to chest and shoulder to shoulder in the sign of a cross.

The perspiration from Zach's balls ferocious as a waterfall, he brushed the outside of his pocket to make sure his baggie of cocaine was still there and felt the familiar lump on top of his thigh with a viscous relief, enclosing his doubts with assuredness.

"If everyone can kindly vacate the vehicle while I perform my search," the officer said.

The lot of them, still clad in sleepwear and slippers, walked off their bus to let the man do his job while they waited to do theirs. The Canuck morning was as cold-blooded as their Canada Border Services agent.

It would be three cigarettes later before rays of light narrowly peeked through thin clouds and the gurgles of intestinal tracts, heard only up till then by birds, were being detected through other antennas. The officer exited the bus with a quenched look but indifferent attitude in his march, breath flat, posture firm. "Gentlemen, thank you for your patience as I performed the mandatory search through the inside of the vehicle."

Snooping a glance at his watch in bad taste, Todd dismissed the earnestness of their present climate and severed it like a true American. "Thanks for being so courteous," he said disingenuously, "but if you wouldn't mind, we do need to be on our way. Got a show to get to."

The officer snickered. "My apologies. How foolish of me to be holding you up. I'm sure there's a big night ahead of you! But please, before you head on your way, do humor me with one more question." He lifted a red-gloved hand to shoulder height and jiggled his wrist. "Might I ask whom *this* belongs to?"

Zach felt the lump.

He knew he felt the lump.

He reached into his athletic shorts pocket, and his heart

sank to his heels as the lump he had felt was not a bag of drugs but instead a used piece of tissue paper.

"I will allow up to five seconds for a response before I am forced to arrest all members of your party."

With his baggie dangling in the spry Canadian air, the balloon of anxiety in Zach's stomach burst from too much pressure, spraying gastric acid over all the entangled. "It's mine," he admitted, for that was all he could do.

The officer snapped into action. "Please turn around and place your hands behind your back as I administer my handcuffs on to your wrists. This is for my safety as well as your safety and the safety of everyone around."

Zach could see Todd's handprint impressed into his forehead. The coldness of the cuffs against his skin was unreal. He farted.

"I have placed handcuffs on the criminal," the officer spoke aloud and with force, continuing to recite the text from his Officer's Handbook the way his sergeant would have liked. "If the arrested person would please follow my motions and sit himself down inside the back of my patrol cruiser . . ." With a quick jerk, he pulled Zach away, his feet slow behind so he could whisper into his ear, *"How dare you bring this filth into my land? The Lord shall smite you and all that you love for this heinous act. God have mercy on your soul, you wretched beast,"* before shoving him headfirst into the back of the running police car.

The heat was not on.

Through a back window coated in morning frost, Texas Flip's guitarist could see the rest of his band standing around in disbelief. He hadn't the faintest idea of what they were thinking or the faintest idea of what he should be thinking, non-thoughts pacing in dumb unison. Prompt as ever, the officer got in the front seat and put the cruiser in D, driving them a distance less than two hundred feet away from the scene of the crime and into a PERSONNEL ONLY parking spot in

front of the glistening Canada Border Services Agency building. Exiting with an intent that could only be read as aggressive, he opened the back door and screamed, "Let's get
moving!" his exhalation the hottest thing in the foreseeable
future.

Zach maneuvered as best he could with his cuffed hands
out the door and tripped on his shoelace. "Whoa, dude," he
said, "where'd the good guy/Christian act go?"

An elbow to his lower back quickened the pace.

"Listen, you piece of shit. I'm sick and tired of having to
deal with all you 'rock stars' thinking you're above the law in a
foreign country. You play the devil's music. That's what it is—
music for Satan. And with all that devil music comes your
drugs and loose women and sin. It is my civic and God-given
duty to make sure I keep as much of your filth out of Canada
as possible." His accent thicker than frozen maple syrup, all the
officer had left to say was even harder to swallow. "I don't
know how you do it down in the U.S. of Ayyyyy, but up here in
Canada, we have laws, and decent human beings doing a
decent day of God's work. But enough wasted oxygen on you.
Get moving! It's time to put your ass in a cell."

His hands held tight to Zach's cuffs, he walked his criminal
into the building like a hunting trophy and up to a glass parti-
tion with three identically dressed officers seated behind it,
everyone with a face of equal seriousness but different salary.
"Possession of what appears to be cocaine. The rest of the
band was clean. Let's book him, get him in lockup, and deal
with the paperwork later."

"Wait, what?" Zach pleaded. "Just like that? You're not
even gonna let me explain myself?"

"What is there to explain?" the officer came back. "You're
scum, and you belong with the rest of the scum. Book him,
people!"

Dressed in the same outfit, but with the addition of yellow

puffy jackets, two more officers appeared and took hold of Zach's restrained arms, grips tighter than their haircuts. Dudley Do-Right, ready for a prayer and jack-off session to God only knew what, faded himself away into the land of cubicles and fax machines that took up the majority of the building's ground level, leaving behind a trail of excellent work and righteous saving behind him like goose shit on a windshield. He would be the main suspect in a triple homicide later that year.

These new border agents—both young, handsome, and promising—promptly led Zach through a small side door, down two flights of concrete stairs with no lights, and into the basement that housed this government-funded complex's holding cell.

A holding cell with no one in it.

By his quick estimation, it appeared to him that the border officers were somewhere in their late twenties, and given their demeanor and professionalism, Zach also was safe in assuming they were probably not fans of his band or any form of distraction, but he figured maybe he could still level with them and flex whatever celebrity he had that might bluff his way out.

"Hey, guys," he began. "So, you know my band Texas Flip, right?"

"Nope," they both replied.

Fuck.

"Over in that corner is your toilet," the taller one informed him, showcasing his promising future in a desk job position. "The other corner holds your bed. In addition to your meals, you are also allowed one phone call while incarcerated. It might be in your best interest to use this opportunity to contact your legal representation and explain to them the situation that you have found yourself in. This phone call can be made after lunch is served."

The cell door closed in front of Zach with a depressing soft clink. He looked toward his bed—a metal bench—and felt the urge to piss on it and sleep in the toilet instead. Through the wall of tall bars, the shorter officer, who after being fired from this job would go on to become an enforcer for the Rizzuto crime family, broke character. He almost laughed. "We're sorry you ended up here, Mr. Long. But this is Canada . . . What did you think would happen when you tried to smuggle drugs over the border?"

They bolted the heavy door behind them, walking back up the flights of stairs, and the air glinted in disgust.

Like a diseased wharf rat, Zach took in his new surroundings with a feverish touch: cold floor, bright overhead lights, and a stainless steel shitter and sink arranged in the style of a Costco bathroom. Left to absorb the infinite emptiness in a solitude of his own making, it was also impossible to not think about the 5,500 people beginning their days and gearing up for his band's concert that night. People who had planned for weeks to leave work early, who had hired a babysitter and rehearsed the next morning's excuse for calling in sick, not to mention the rest of his band, venue staff, security personnel, promoters, and food/beer vendors who would all be losing a substantial chunk of change if he didn't get out of this cell in time. Or at all.

After a solid twenty minutes of scornful considerations—enough time for him to take a dump and contemplate masturbating—both officers were back in action. This time, they looked mad.

"It is now time for your lunch," the taller officer said.

"Lunch?" Zach asked. "It's eight A.M."

"And as was mentioned earlier, this is also the time that you will be permitted to make your phone call."

This hell in a cell putting a wrench in his soul and spine, Zach stretched his body out long and wide, then moseyed over to the pay phone installed on the brick wall in better humor.

"Looks like this thing doesn't get used often," he joked, wiping away dust from the top of the receiver with his forearm. The guards' eyes stuck to him like an ice cube on your tongue. "You guys took my wallet when you booked me," he said. "In there is a business card for my lawyer. If you could please grab it—that would be greatly appreciated."

The last card Zach would have had in his wallet would be a lawyer's.

But he knew the one person who might have a chance of getting him out of this mess was Felicia, their booking agent. And that's whose card he did have in his wallet.

She picked up on the first ring.

"Zach?"

"How'd you know it was me?"

"I just got off the phone with Todd . . . Jesus—what were you thinking smuggling cocaine over the border? It's Canada!"

"Listen, I don't know. What am I gonna do? The cop that arrested me was some Christian weirdo and was spewing all this crap about me going to hell and sinning in his country. Am I in that serious of trouble?"

"Yes, you are. But—and I say this with a capital *B*—but there might be a chance I can get you out of this."

Felicia's deceased husband was Jay Stubborn. A singer-songwriter who had scored three Top 10 hits off his debut album, *Album Name Here*, he would die tragically during a performance at the 1996 Weekapaug Folk Fest in Newport, Rhode Island, a day before his twenty-seventh birthday and ten months after he had met Felicia, she booking him, he proposing to her shortly after.

As was his trademark during the final song of every performance, the entertainer could be relied on to climb the stage's lighting rig with his microphone, singing passionately all the while, before ultimately catapulting himself into the crowd of drunks below not a minute later, freely as one might take a dive into a lake of pillows. But due to an unfortunate chain of uncanny events involving union disputes over rigging and sound equipment and a couple of no-show jobs, Jay's shoelace would get caught that fateful night on what the coroner would later say was an "improperly installed J-bolt"—this product causing him to lose his balance and plummet straight to the ground, his backbone snapping in half on the crowd barrier and the arm of a fan club member in the front row.

As tragic and horrifying an event as it was, his death came as no big shock to a quick life lived. But for the luck of all involved in our tale of death and desire, what Jay also happened to be, and what would hold significant weight in matters of illegality, was Canadian.

In fact, the guy was born and raised in Montreal.

When he died, they even named a street after him.

On top of that, his cousin was also a high-ranking Canadian political figure with ties to the Canadian Police Association.

All of this was explained to Zach in rapid succession. "I've put in some calls," Felicia said, hungry for a solution, an upbeat in her down-pattern rhythm of diction, "but I can't promise anything." Her French bulldog barked in the background. "Are they treating you all right at least?"

He looked at his cold cheese sandwich and plastic cup of hot water. "I've had worse on tour."

"Okay. Well, if things go well, you'll know soon enough. If they don't, then we're all screwed big time. Think about that in the meanwhile."

Click.

For the next three hours, Zach lay sweating, a little dope sick and with the urge to masturbate stronger than ever. Yet before his body could finally fall asleep on the metal bench, a man and woman, both dressed in black suits and wearing sunglasses, knocked on the door of his cell, the sound it made like a singing bowl.

"Zach Long?" the woman asked, pushing her sunglasses up and taking a sweeping glance around the cell to make sure he was still the only person there, her straight dark hair swinging.

"That's me," Zach answered, assuring her that he was, in fact, the only person in there.

"Mr. Long, I am Michelle Sun. And this is my partner, Daniel Moon."

Picking the wedgie out of his ass, he said, "Your last name is Sun, and his last name is Moon?"

"Yes."

"Weird."

"Any more questions?"

"Nah."

"Great." She eyed her partner with concern, like she'd eaten a bad tomato. "As associates of Police Chief Perlman, we have given the proper authorities here notice that you are to be released and have this matter wiped clean from your record. Now, if you'll please follow us, we will be taking you to the Montreal Coliseum."

A cakey dungeonous residue had formed on the back of Zach's throat and made it hard for him to speak, but not hard to cooperate. "Um, sure . . . Whatever you say."

With the tiniest key he'd ever seen, Mr. Moon opened his cell door. "This way," he said.

Escorted back up the stairwell (this time without handcuffs) and out into the building's main lobby, Canada suddenly felt like a new country.

Officer Dudley was leaning against the receptionist's desk and peering at her cleavage in a way Jesus might not have been proud of. When he saw Zach, he was naturally livid. "You've got to be kidding me! Where are you taking this lowlife? I *just* arrested him!"

"To the Montreal Coliseum," Ms. Sun sniped back. "His presence is needed there tonight. That will be all."

The receptionist's breasts bounced in rhythm with his frustrated fist on the desk. "What do you mean 'his presence is needed there tonight'? I arrested him with cocaine! Emma, call Chief Perlman immediately! I can't believe this shit . . . No way he is leaving my jail."

"I assure you this won't be necessary," Mr. Moon said.

Emma passed the phone to the officer. "It's Chief Perlman. He said he's busy and to make it quick."

"Chief Perlman, this is Staff Superintendent Pender. Well, yes . . . Okay, but . . . Sir, I . . . Sir . . . Yes, sir . . . No, that's fine. Thank you."

"Will there be any more questions?" Mr. Moon asked.

Castrated of what little power he might have possessed, Staff Superintendent Pender gave the phone back to Emma and plopped his body low onto a swivel chair, an apostate on the verge of collapse. "No," he said, and rotated his body away toward the building's rear-facing window, sighing a dejected sigh. He stared past the white exhausts above, a denouncement of God and one final prayer for humanity all there was left in the smoldering heap of his purpose.

Zach was happy the Lincoln Town Car was warm.

"What just happened back there?" he asked, buckling himself in.

"Your work associate, Felicia Kluger, really pulled off a miracle," Mr. Moon said from the passenger seat. "Turns out that Officer Pender had a couple of skeletons hidden in his closet."

"You don't say."

"On your behalf, Ms. Kluger reached out to Nathan Farr."

"Nathan Fart?"

"Mr. Farr is the former regional director general of the Quebec region and a dear friend of Felix Gagnon, the minister of border security and organized crime reduction. Mr. Gagnon, in conversation with Mr. Farr, was briefed that Officer Pender is a real hard-ass and universally disliked by all others in his department. A grudge held from who knows when. We were then instructed to have you released, and so we did. That's all we know.

"It must be reiterated that Mr. Farr and Mr. Gagnon are in no way condoning the behavior you have demonstrated in our country this morning, but it was understood that if tonight's show was canceled, he would have had a very angry Mayor Brute calling his office, demanding an explanation as to why over five thousand people were floating around downtown Montreal in an angry riot. And since Mr. Farr knew that Officer Pender has a bit of a drinking probl—"

"Wait a second," Zach interrupted, this paperback thriller keeping him on the edge of his seat. "That stuck-up asshole has a *drinking* problem?"

"That's correct."

"Unbelievable! That dude was spewing holier-than-thou shit to me this whole time, talking about how much of a sinner I was. Satan fucking me in the ass. Rotting in hell . . ."

"He's also been known to beat on his wife from time to time too," Ms. Sun added.

Shaking his head left to right in a disbelief that was believable, Zach said, "Wow, I guess Billy Joel *was* right."

"Huh?" Mr. Moon asked.

"His song 'The Stranger'"

"Great song," Mr. Moon agreed. "Saw him on his *An Innocent Man* tour at the Providence Civic Center back in 'eighty-four. But there you have it—an explanation as to how we all ended up here, in this car, talking about Billy Joel."

"It really is a good song, isn't it?" Ms. Sun quipped.

Speaking to Zach and not her, Mr. Moon agreed: "It is. I

wouldn't call it the best song on *The Stranger*, though. That would obviously be 'Vienna.'"

"Not a chance," Zach disagreed. "The best song on that record is 'Scenes from an Italian Restaurant.' No question. Billy sings it just the way—"

"You are?"

Zach's head filled with heat and interest. "We're heading to the arena, right?" he asked, no longer exhausted. "It's still early. Should be able to make sound check."

"Correct," Mr. Moon said. "We'll be there shortly."

Ms. Sun turned on the radio dial, allowing the voice of an annoying DJ to fill the car's blind spots.

"*—ight at the Montreal Coliseum is Texas Flip! And guess what, listeners?! We have another pair of tickets to give away to one lucky fan! All you need to know is the answer to the following question . . .*

"*Which college did Texas Flip form at?*

"*Be caller number three for your chance to win not only two tickets to tonight's sold-out show but also copies of their newest record,* You're on the Back of the Worm!

"*And look at that—the phone lines are already lighting up! Let's go to Olivia calling in from Saint-Jérôme. Hey, Olivia, welcome to* The Jimmy Lewis Show *on CYXJ—the Rock Clock!*"

"*Oh my god! Oh. My. God. Mom! Mom, they put me on! Oh my god. Oh my god. Oh myyyyy god!!*"

"*Hey, Olivia! Sounds like you're excited there! But I need you to stay focused. For your chance to win a copy of* You're on the Back of the Worm! *and two tickets to tonight's sold-out show at the Montreal Coliseum, can you name the college that Texas Flip formed at?*"

"*Of course I can! I know everything about the band. They're my favorite! They formed right here in Montreal at McGill University! Ahhh, I can't wait for the show! Mom, I won!!*"

"*Ohhhh . . . So sorry, Olivia, but that's incorrect. In fact, you even got the country wrong. Let's go to our next caller!*"

About ready to heave his body from the moving vehicle,

Zach asked Ms. Sun, "Can you please shut that off?" before the pain in his chest became a pain for the road.

Ms. Sun reached back for the dial, her chewed-up finger-nails turning it down but not all the way. "Sorry . . . That must be weird, huh?" she said in an awkward, deadpan manner void of all sentiment or tenderness in her voice. "Hearing people talk about you. Your song playing on the radio all the time."

The white lines on the interstate began to form different shapes in Zach's head, began to form into white lines the likes of which he was searching for. "Did you hear that girl?" he spat at the window, and pushed back hard in his seat. "She thought we were from Canada. That's who's coming to our show tonight . . ."

"Well, the good news is the arena is coming up soon, so no need to worry about any of that now."

A Tim Hortons doughnut the size of a tractor trailer arose on the side of the highway, tall in the sky, signaling the gateway to the venue's parking lot.

"We are going to drop you off in the loading zone."

The town car was soon pulling in front of the garage entrance quicker than Zach thought capable.

"Someone from the venue will escort you inside from here." And it was at that time a stern look entered Ms. Sun's facial structure, its previous blankness now holding a tight perturbation. "Once again, Mr. Long, it should go without saying that we, up here, are good folk. And the stunt you pulled today was not only foolish but of an immeasurable disrespect to the governing laws of our country. By gosh, what were you thinking? This is Canada!"

The car hardly stopped before Zach unbuckled and got out. He stretched his right arm across his body to help ease the discomfort persistent in his shoulder since he'd been put in cuffs and found as much relief as you would in an armbar submission hold. "Thanks for everything, officers? I guess I can take it from here."

"Of course," Mr. Moon spoke through his window. "Happy we were able to be of assistance. And do have a great show tonight." He tapped Ms. Sun's shoulder, a clear indication for her to pull away, which she did.

Dumbfounded and enjoying a headache that pounded his skull like a frying pan, Zach remained motionless as Luke approached him from a doorway next to the closed garage entrance, composed with a triple IPA in one hand and unfiltered Camel in the other. "At least you're back in time for sound check," his best friend said, a security guard keeping him close company. "Todd has been losing his mind."

The two walked inside before the door locked them out.

"Didn't Felicia call him?" Zach asked.

Their manager's nasally voice pinged through the arena hallway: "Well look who the fuck it is . . ."

"Spare me," Zach said. "I'm here. Let's just get this shit over with, okay?"

"'Get this shit over with'?"

There were photos of athletes and celebrities and musicians on the walls.

Texas Flip's would never make it up there.

Todd pointed at a framed Santana poster from the '80s. "There's 5,500 Canadians in this building here to see your band. This isn't *just* about you. And I won't even go into detail as to what would have happened if Felicia hadn't pried your ass from jail and we had to cancel the show. What were you thinking, man? This is Canada!"

"If one more person says that to me, I'm going to kill them." Grabbing a bottle of water from the table next to him, he threw it against the wall, and the still-sealed plastic carafe bounced back and hit him in his sore shoulder.

A youngish blond girl wearing a green staff shirt appeared

suddenly and picked up the plastic bottle from the floor. "Did you want this, Mr. Long?"

"I'm sorry," Zach said. "You can, um . . . yeah, I'll take it. Thanks."

"Sure," she said, and approached him nervously.

"What's your name?" he asked, unsure why.

The young woman, taken aback as if no one had ever asked her that question before in her life, stammered, "I'm, um —I'm Sara. I work in the production office for Syrup Entertainment. Is there anything else I can get you guys while I'm here?"

"No thanks. Appreciate it."

"'Kay," she said, and then walked away, passing another framed Santana poster from the '80s but of a different tour and rounding a corner out of sight.

Todd laid back into him. "How messed up are you, man? Your eyes look darker than a cheap whore's in the morning."

Zach felt attacked, like a cornered animal. "I don't need this shit. I'm going to my dressing room. Knock on my door when I'm needed."

He made a hasty exit from this scene of shame and guilt that he was the star of and floated down a damp hall of humiliation until he found a small white sheet of paper attached to a door with ZACH LONG printed on it.

Inside was Sara.

"Mr. Long, I'm sorry!" she apologized. "I was told that you didn't like mangoes and preferred apples instead. I was supposed to replace them before we bumped into each other outside. I wasn't expecting you to be back here so quick. I'll leave and let you be."

He laid himself down on the room's clumsily placed La-Z-Boy chair and silently let loose some gas. The smell spoke louder than he did. "No worries," he said, and kicked off one of his shoes. "You happen to know the time?"

"It's two."

A coarse silence followed before either of them spoke again.

It was Sara who broke first, her smile angelic. "I'm not supposed to say this because Syrup Entertainment has very strict protocols about talking to the talent, but I absolutely love your band. You guys are so freakin' cool! Every time I hear that one song of yours, I can't ever get it out of my head . . . Anyways, just wanted to tell you I'm a big fan, and I hope you have a great show tonight."

"Thanks, I appreciate that."

Before she could leave, though, he had one more question to ask.

"Sara?"

"Yeah?"

"Do you know where I can find some blow?"

6

Happy Hills Recovery
Malibu, CA
5/25/2002

There's not much worse than being forced to talk to someone you don't like about something you don't care about in front of a bunch of people you'd rather not know.

In a room painted in bright aqua blushes, with an inescapable sun seizing hold of your insides, you hear half-baked clichés about "letting go" and how "your energy regulates all" and "the universe is a mystery—it's up to you to solve it" from people too long gone to care about anything other than the pleasure of immediacy.

Waves crashing down on thoughts like a mallet beating ground beef flat, the night ocean is a white noise without pause. Little else is available in the form of a "release," so one becomes addicted to the smiles. Too many smiles. People constantly on edge with their smiles. Addicts in recovery talking about drugs: booze, pills, meth, blow, smack, Vicodin, and Viagra—the fulcrum for tales of death, desire, and multiple botched suicide attempts. These twisted accounts become a disease of their own, too slick to command for the weak of spirit or unapprised.

And so are the smiles.

So many smiles for so many sad people.

But a sad place this wasn't.

A majestic Spanish Colonial estate nestled deep in the mountains of Malibu, Happy Hills Recovery was an area of conservation where the sum of its parts appeared green and sublime, hiding any rot. It was a rehabilitation center built for the people you're not supposed to know, where overprivileged, self-indulgent slobs find themselves after life starts treating them in ways they're not familiar with.

Happy Hills Recovery was a break from the snooping eyes of Hollywood, New York, or Paris, where the gates were meant to keep people out, not from escaping. A place the bulimic, pill-popping starlet went after tabloids printed pictures of her smashing tits with some random chick on top of a bar at Mardi Gras, or where the alcoholic film director goes when his wife leaves him to join a sex cult in Oregon with a twenty-two-year-old actor from one of his own movies. Rock stars and movie producers, actresses and swimsuit models, Happy Hills Recovery was for the *real* 1 percent the rest of society reads about but will never encounter. The people on whom we hang false ideals and dreams like a rickety coat rack.

Still, these luminaries born to powerful lawyers and these daughters with overdeveloped cheek bones and breasts—they were the same jacked-up, insecure blobs of meat as those inhabiting the rest of this planet, floundering conjointly through this ether of emptiness. The sole difference was they had way more money than you ever will.

It would be here, in ways the polar opposite of any Beach Boys song, that Zach Long, a member of one of the most popular bands in the country, would find himself afloat in a life jacket made of cork and a stomach full of vinegar, too afraid to piss in public. His admittance was one of no worry. The tab was paid for.

Exclusivity.

Dumb money.

With a hit record out of the limelight long enough for Texas Flip to be worried about their impending insignificance, the band had been set to begin work on their next album under a brand-new contract with Mountain View Records and with a whole new set of expectations. The unpredicted overnight success of their album *You're on the Back of the Worm!* had sent them on a perpetually jarring trip around the planet for close to two years—long tours with hardly a week off, numerous passport stamps, delayed flights, and innumerable bouts of hotel diarrhea—and the world only became smaller and smaller the more and more they journeyed around it first class, Rome becoming Baltimore becoming Helsinki becoming Paterson (not much of a difference when you're never in town for longer than twenty-four hours). Eat all the food, stay in all the hotels, screw all the back-page prostitutes, Texas Flip, whether they cared to admit it or not, needed a break from not only the road and music and hard drugs but, more important, from one another.

You spend time with your significant other because you *want* to. And because they'll have sex with you.

You spend time with your bandmates because you must.

Conjoined at the hip (and wallet), Texas Flip had trouped city by city, country by country, playing their weathered songs for longer and for more money than ever thought possible—the ultimate cost being their now unsalvageable interrelationships. Yet rather than take a couple months off to recharge and refresh their faulty batteries, they instead wrapped up the *You're on the Back of the Worm!* tour with a headlining festival gig in Barcelona, then flew back to the States for five days before meeting at Newark Airport with suitcases they hadn't bothered to unpack to board a plane for Hawaii.

Flushed by the confidence of a padded checking account and new level of flex with Mountain View Records, the band sprung the well for their next record, *Golden Door*, and went all out: no expenses spared, and no fucks given. Occupying for three weeks one of the most expensive studios the internet could provide a result for, Reel Lyfe Tracking, they had set the nonsensical goal of having their new record written and recorded by the end of their time there, the fools thinking a change of scenery would bring about a change of work ethic.

Depleted of $25,000 from studio/equipment rentals, Ritz-Carlton accommodations, and almost the equivalent on weed, they, in a way only their own, still managed to wrangle up enough music to please a roomful of suits and a theater of people too drunk to care, their goals about as low as the ocean floor, and it would be at the end of this process, with weeks lost to sunken costs and a guaranteed clunker of an album on the Pacific horizon, when Zach decided that rather than face the inevitable music this practice in stupidity had brought upon them, his relationships, and his bank account, he would instead enjoy one last night of decisions based on affluence and maybe kill himself.

On the band's second night in town, Zach had scored two eight balls off a bellhop at their hotel—more than enough for the weekend amateur on a monthlong vacation, but an amount that would hardly last a junkie two days.

This connection dried up after the bellhop was fired for selling peyote to one of the sous-chefs.

Adaptable, Zach then started buying his drugs off the sous-chef's cousin, until that person got arrested for selling bubble hash to an elementary school principal.

So, with recording finished, and a warm ocean breeze fanning him on the kind of night Hemingway could write about in his sleep, Zach, his belly full of lobster tails and Chianti, zeroed in on a busboy at the hotel's restaurant rocking a tattoo of Lois Griffin on the side of his face and a metal bar pierced between his eyes, who looked to be his strongest chance in scoring some weak blow.

He approached him near the restroom.

The crust on his nose said everything.

After a wink of his tatted eyelid and a quick trip to the kitchen, the busboy came back holding a matchbook with a drawing of an older woman in fishnet stockings on its front cover; the lady of the night was bent over and glancing back convincingly over her shoulder. The name of the place was scratched off but not the address. "It's called the Tiki Slut," the teenager told him. "Give the cabbie the address. He'll know."

His ass in a taxi minutes later, Zach arrived in short order at what looked like someone's foreclosed house: a dilapidated two-story condominium set on a residential street with Christmas decorations in the front yard and a lit neon sign in the window blinking TIKI SLUT. Opening the door and careful upon his entrance, he was promptly introduced to a land where time had stopped somewhere between 1970 and the first *Back to the Future* movie. Positive he had walked into a *Deep Throat* reenactment—complete with a rough-looking man getting a hand job on a barstool by an even rougher-looking woman—Zach averted his eyes from what could easily be him in eight minutes, ponied up to an untainted barstool, and ordered a glass of the house red; more concerned with mixing his liquors than he was about buying cut-up powder from a stranger. The framed posters of Donny Osmond and Liza Minnelli behind the bar throwing him off more than the act of prostitution in the entrance, he settled in nicely nonetheless, took a sip of something that tasted like menstrual blood, and only then breathed easy.

This is my kind of place, he thought with an unbreakable confidence.

Drunk enough to strike up a conversation with the person sitting to his left, Zach soon made acquaintances with a gentleman named Kalino, a plumber and member of the local biker gang. A bulldog of a man, thickset and hard of breathing, Kalino spoke with a nasally tone in contrast to his imposing, bald, and muscular build, and the more he talked, the more Zach's spider sense crawled up his back, sending to him undoubtable signals that Kalino was a "coke guy" and that the bellhop hadn't steered him wrong. And then his nose started to bleed.

"Damn, kaikaina! You all right?!" Kalino asked his new compatriot, genuinely concerned.

"Yeah, sorry," Zach said, searching for a napkin but using his shirt instead. "Happens from time to time. My bad."

"Looks like you've been getting after it, if you ask me."

"Ha-ha. Yeah, maybe a little bit. My band is here working on a new album. We've been partying kinda hard the last couple of nights. I should probably take a break when we get back to the mainland."

"A *break?*" Kalino asked, offended. "Nah, you should probably try some of this." He placed a little baggie on the bar; a tiny red devil face was printed on one side.

Zach quickly put his hand down on top of it, scared this

forward display of criminality would arouse unwelcome attention or another jail stint. "What is this?"

"What the fuck you think it is, kaikaina? That's the purest cola you're going to find in this shithole tourist trap."

Thank God. "Can I try a taste?"

"Of course. And if you like it, there's plenty more where that came from."

Zach excused himself from the bar and went into the den of iniquity's sole bathroom. It smelled like a dead body and looked like one too. Licking his left pinkie, he dipped it into the baggie, pulled out a pinhead-sized amount of the funky-smelling batter, and pressed his fingertip onto his upper gums; the immediate numbing of his two front teeth reported back to him that this was some shit one best go easy with, and then he did what any true abuser would do and plunged his hotel room key deep inside it. Producing a sizable bump—nothing his tolerance couldn't handle—Zach sniffed it up like a Hoover vacuum, thanked the heavens for something to be happy about, and closed his eyes.

"Looks like he's coming to . . . Nurse, bring over three milligrams of Lorazepam. Mr. Long, can you hear me?"

A doctor blinked a small flashlight on and off into his right pupil.

The white drop-tile ceiling and four strangers in medical scrubs stared down at him in disgust.

Tubes ran from both of his arms.

He wiggled his left foot.

"Wha . . . Wher . . . Wher'm I?"

"Mr. Long, my name is Dr. Palakiko, and you are in the Queen's Medical Center." He shifted the flashlight's beam to

Zach's left pupil. "You overdosed on a mixture of cocaine and heroin."

Zach scratched his right eye, and one of the tubes connected to his arm came loose in the process. "Hrin? Iv —neverrherrin."

"The paramedics that retrieved you from the restroom of the Tiki Slut"—everyone in the room shuddered with embarrassment—"found you unconscious with a small bag of white powder nearby. After running a lab test on the contents, it showed the substance to be a combination of both drugs. This grouping, outside of a medical terminology, is also known as a 'speedball'. You're very lucky to be alive."

Trying to put the fallen tube back into his arm, Zach asked, "But Kalino . . . ?" as you would for a lost pet.

"Kalino?" Dr. Palakiko asked. "Who's Kalino?"

An outrageous need for liquid seized him, his throat parched like a rock. "Kalino . . . Hewwas dah, uh —whouh . . ."

"Kalino was the gentleman who gave you the drugs?" the doctor asked. "I see." He jotted something down on his clipboard. "I can't speak on the topic of Kalino, but I can speak about the condition of your nervous system." Dr. Palakiko took a breath deeper than Zach could have dreamed of in that moment. "Mr. Long, how long have you been abusing cocaine for?"

Todd and Luke walked into the hospital room before he could lie.

"He's alive!" Luke wailed, and then hugged his best friend, ripping out a tube in Zach's other arm. "I thought you were dead, dude!"

Todd stood cross-armed behind him. "You need help."

Dr. Palakiko stepped in. "That was the next thing I was going to bring up." He motioned for a nurse to place both tubes back into Zach's arms. "Mr. Long, as your current physician, it is my professional duty to strongly recommend that you enter a rehabilitation facility immediately."

Todd groaned.

Luke started to flirt with a nurse.

Zach farted.

"I know this is probably not what you want to hear, but another episode like the one you just experienced might be your last. Some of the staff here has made me aware that you play guitar in a popular rock band. I'm more of a classical music fan myself, so sorry to say I'm not familiar with your work, but if your drug abuse is all a consequence of your career choice, then sobriety will be your only option if you'd like to stay alive. As it so happens, I'm golf buddies with the owner and operator of Happy Hills Recovery in Malibu, California. It's a five-star rehabilitation facility where many high-profile individuals like yourself have found success. If you'd like, I can reach out to him and see if they're currently accepting new patients."

"I already bought him a plane ticket," Todd said. "You leave tomorrow."

"Don't I have a say in any of this?" Zach asked, then coughed up blood onto his hospital gown.

He didn't want to die.

His life was good.

He had all his hair, his dick still worked, and his bank account wasn't empty . . . yet.

But after coming close to death on the floor of a crusty bathroom inside a whorehouse, there was not much further down Zach could actually go other than underground, and therefore he agreed with the consensus of the room that this stint would be obligatory if he wanted to keep his job, his mortality, and his fairly cheap two-bedroom apartment. Anxiety about the unknown pumping through a skull full of bathtub gin, he asked that everyone leave him be for a bit, feeling deadly tired, and shut his eyes for one last narcotic-induced daydream.

He woke up nineteen hours later and was on a plane shortly thereafter.

An ache in his right ear, Zach sat in first class on a 747 crunched up in the fetal position on what seemed to be a flight to Israel and back, landing at LAX seventy-five minutes late all so the plane could taxi on the runway for another forty-five minutes before pulling up to the gate.

Then he vomited.

A quick piss next to one of the *Pete & Pete* brothers later, he was waiting around the luggage carousel in an oversized Title Boxing hoodie and sunglasses, his stomach on fire with antacids and unsalted pretzels and flat ginger ale. After twenty more minutes a professional-looking gentleman in a suit approached him with a cup of coffee and half a blueberry muffin: "Mr. Long, I'm Nicholas from Happy Hills Recovery. If you would please follow me."

Before Zach could snag his luggage from the turnstile, Nicholas had his tiger paw clenched around Zach's biceps.

"Hey, man, I'm not going anywhere. Can you ease up?"

"I'm sorry," Nicholas said. "This is when they usually run. Habit."

A black town car idled at the curb outside, and with a cigarette lit, Zach got inside the back, Nicholas in the front passenger seat, and the driver took off into another stereotypical day of Southern California smog and gridlocked melancholy, a trip that should have taken thirty minutes taking two and a half hours with traffic. They were somewhere along the Pacific Coast Highway, passing the multimillion-dollar views and penniless drifters, when the car pulled into the driveway of a house that had been staged for a couple of movies in the late '70s and then foreclosed on. Complete with windows that substituted for entire walls, an eight-car garage with no cars in it, and foliage greener than jealousy, there was no possible way they could have been at the right place.

This must be a detour.

The car parked.

"We're here," Nicholas said.

A woman stood at the entrance of the main building of the stunning estate, bright orange hair and lips to match, her poise hinting that she had played a supporting role in a film shot here. She walked up to Zach supporting a grin of misery; she smelled like an old Vanillaroma air freshener left in a hot car. "Hello, Mr. Long," she said. "My name is Rebecca, and as general manager here at Happy Hills Recovery, let me be the first to welcome you. Here is your itinerary." A glossy piece of paper was placed in Zach's hands. "The next scheduled meeting today is at three, followed by male enhancement yoga and then acrylic painting. This will be capped off with a dinner prepared by Michelin star chef Antonio Esposito, served on our veranda overlooking some of the most beautiful real estate in all of California. There will be vegetarian and vegan options as well."

"Isn't that the dude from that show?"

"You mean *Vacant Booths with Antonio Esposito?*" Rebecca beamed. "That's him! Chef comes and cooks for us twice a month. Claims to be forever indebted to the hard work and salvation he realized here at Happy Hills Recovery. No complaints from me!"

"Whoa."

Rebecca had yet to stop smiling, but her stare isolated itself to the center of Zach's chest with hollow-tipped bullets of happiness shot through his core.

"If you'll please follow Will," she said, pointing to a short, stocky guy with a buzz cut standing some distance away, "he can show you to your room."

Will waved and Zach sighed.

"And as we like to say here at Happy Hills Recovery: *Your road to a new life has finally begun!*"

Zach coughed up black phlegm and spit it on the lawn. "Sounds good."

Making their way through a garden with exquisite floral beds, up marble staircases straight from *The Godfather*, and past three Olympic-sized swimming pools and an exotic bird sanctuary, the two men eventually came across another building—just as big and just as grand—that Will explained was the living quarters.

"Can we hurry up?" the newest tenant of Happy Hills asked. "I think I'm gonna be sick . . ."

They entered, and at the hallway's eventual end, Will pointed to an auburn-colored wooden door with the number 18 above it. "Here we are," he said. "Once again, my name is Will, and I'll be your personal liaison here at Happy Hills Recovery. Anything you ever need"—wink—"you let me know."

The drapes were closed and the lights off when Zach walked in.

And they stayed that way after he puked in the sink.

For the next fifteen minutes, he lay in bed on top of the comforter doing his best to fall asleep, not die, and forget about life for a while. Soft piano music played in his head like the sounds of an unhinged carnival. The insistence of the sun's beams on all the room's windows would prove to make this essential slumber a near impossibility, and so he forced himself back up with tired limbs, pulled the window shades arms' width apart, and within milliseconds was ravaged by an atomic blast of vitamin D.

His sleepiness crisped to dust, the corpse of which stained the bedding behind him, he knew he was now committed to the act of wakefulness and thus walked onto his private balcony—without sunglasses—to gape at the Pacific Ocean and its infiniteness, at a loss for such accepted beauty. Mother Nature's healthy waves crashed down below his misty disposition. Cloudy thoughts of intestinal gas were soon shredded from his head with the sound of a loud smack on the bedroom door.

A dark-eyed junco flew by and brought with it a sense of remission.

"Zach Long!" the man on the other side of the door yelled with childish enthusiasm. "I know youse in der fukkah! Open up . . . It's Char! Char Komsa!"

Standing a stout five-five and built like an avocado, Char Komsa was a grown man who shined with the sad remnants of a former child star. After a string of starring roles in Mob-themed movies panned by critics but loved by fans, he became a heroin addict once the studios ran out of ideas for mobsters to kill each other and had only recently turned rehab stints into his newest occupation. On his third recovery spell that Zach was aware of—having met the guy only once at Gary Katzka's eighty-first birthday party a month after Texas Flip had signed their first contract with Mountain View Records—his appearance on the other side of the door was welcomed like a split toenail.

"What's up, Char?" Zach called from the balcony and through his closed door.

"Open the damn door at least!"

Capitulating, he went inside and opened his bedroom door a pinkie finger's width. His eyes felt bigger. "Sorry to see you in here too."

"Is wat it is—right, kid?"

Char was only four years older than Zach.

"Dis is my second time here. Great place. Great. Da best. Cleanses da soul. Dat fuggin' Colombian powdah, eh?" he asked with dense humor and through a door still mostly closed.

"Yeah," Zach admitted, dying for a quick end to this exchange, or his life. "How'd you know?"

"Youse just look like a coke dude, is all. Anywayz, here we is now. As one unit. Let us bask in da glory. Light shine upon dee."

Zach had no idea what Char was talking about. And he didn't care to know. He needed to take another shit. Or jump off the balcony. "Hey, man, that's all cool, but I need to go to some meeting they have me scheduled for. Let's maybe catch up another time?"

"Of course. I'll join you."

"I don't think that's necessary, Char. But thanks anyways."

"Is it with Bud?"

"I have no idea. It's on the itinerary they gave me."

"Then youse coming with me—won't hear any different. Capisce?"

Zach couldn't tell if Char was acting or just being an annoying asshole. Both were poor performances. "All right, all right," he surrendered, opening his door wide enough to fit a slender frame through. He noticed his Judas Priest *Hell Bent for Leather* tour T-shirt was looser than normal. "Might as well go now."

Char kept up with the questions as they walked down the muraled hallway toward the lobby (the painting made more sense this way). "Dis your first time in one of dese places, kid?" he asked at the same pace of their progress—fast.

"Char, I'm only a couple years younger than you. Why do you keep calling me 'kid'?"

The former child actor stopped walking and took a backward stride, his hands up toward his shoulders like he dropped something hot. "Ohhhhh!" he said, pinching Zach's left nipple. "Look at Grandpa fuggin' Dick-Tits ovah heeyyaaa . . . Eaze up, will youse? It's nevah good heading into a group meeting with ya pisello allz in a knot."

"I'm sorry. I haven't had a chance to sleep other than in the hospital, and my head feels like it needs to take a shit more than my body. What's this meeting gonna be about anyways?"

Char laughed and his breath made Zach gag. "Youse wait and see, kid . . . Youse wait and see."

Rebecca passed them in the foyer. "Mr. Long, I see you've met Mr. Komsa." She looked at Char with melancholy eyes. "Please make sure to keep tabs on our newest friend here, Char. Don't want him getting slaphappy now, do we?"

"Youse got it, Becks!"

What the fuck is this place?

Traveling back outside and into the overabundant sunshine, the two strolled past the main building of the complex and then into a miniature version of the same building they had left only minutes ago. This one housed a softly lit conference room set off from an industrial-sized kitchen and what looked like a chic Marriott hotel ballroom used for training seminars on sexual harassment and racial sensitivity; there were thirty or so chairs set up in a circle with people seated in each one (and an original Monet on the wall), assuming a much different feel.

An older, bald man in the front of the room greeted them: "Ah yes, Mr. Long and Mr. Komsa! We are just about to get started. Please, grab a chair and come join us." He motioned to his seated congregation and spoke with a sureness that seemed bought, almost fake. "As everyone can see, we have a saucy new spirit joining us today . . . . If you could all please extend a warm welcome to Happy Hills Recovery's freshest ingredient, Zach Long!"

This stranger standing and clapping his hands viciously in front of Zach's face was Bud Spalding, a former air force pilot turned Hollywood actor turned pitiless alcoholic who was also the residential counselor at Happy Hills Recovery.

With an illustrious twenty-year-long military career well

behind him and a pension that would make a senator blush, Bud, while reciting Marlon Brando monologues for friends at a bar in Century City one night drunk off Kahlúa, was "discovered" by a casting director for Twentieth Century Fox—a chance encounter that led to an audition and the supporting role of Colonel Forbin in the film *Vietnam Glory*, a role for which he won an Academy Award. Success lending itself to failure, Bud would turn this gifted life into a burning pile of rubble soon after.

Pursuant to a heap of failed starring roles, domestic violence disputes, and a public intoxication arrest, his "bottom" would come when he drunkenly sideswiped a police motorcycle on his way to a recruiting center in quest of reenlisting himself at the age of fifty-seven in the immediate aftermath of September 11.

He checked into Happy Hills Recovery the following morning.

The spotlight thrown on him and no stage to stand on, Zach sensed he was supposed to say something, but void of words to use, he sputtered out a simple, "Hey, everyone," and aimed his butt straight for the center of his seat.

"Zach, please," Bud said, wiping away sweat from his completely hairless scalp with a hairy forearm, "you're among friends now. There's no need to be so shy. How about we try that one more time?" he appealed in a higher register of voice.

Zach pinched his thigh to repress the urge to scream profanities about Bud's mother. Standing back up, he spoke slowly, like an actor on the wrong audition. "Uh, yeah . . . So, my name is Zach Long, and . . . . Wait, is this where I'm supposed to say I'm an addict?"

"Are you an *addict*, Zach?"

The rock star scanned the room, noting the other souls seated around him for the first time, and was blindsided by their widely known celebrity. Grouped together in this pleasure palace, detoxing and crying as one, were some of the most famous celebrities in the country. And each blank face showed that not one of them knew who the hell he was.

"Maybe?" he asked half jokingly. "I mean, I definitely have a problem."

"What kind of *problem*, Zach?"

He tried his hardest to sound both open and contrite—"A cocaine problem"—but it came off more as a question rather than an admission.

"That shit's crazy!" bellowed a gentleman seated beside him.

"Yeah—crazy," Zach said to his fellow junkie.

"How *crazy*, Zach?"

"I'm here, aren't I?"

This bit received a few chuckles from the audience, but then he took their goodwill too far.

"I overdosed in the bathroom of a whorehouse in Hawaii."

"That must have been some good shit!"

"You OD'd on cocaine?" asked Char. "How much were you snorting?"

"Um, it was actually cocaine and heroin."

"Damn, son!"

"Thank you," Bud said, "you are in a safe place now," then cupped his ear. "But wait!" he shouted at the heavens. "Can everyone hear that?"

The gathered mass extended their heads forward along with him, flamingos on strings.

"That, my friends, is the sound of waves breaking. That is Mother Earth beginning to nourish Zach's energy. Yes . . . I can feel it. Can everyone else feel it?"

Like members of a Jonestown meeting on November 18, 1978, the personalities abided their dear leader for fear of ex-communication. *"Yes, we can hear it!"* spouted an array of devoted vocal timbres.

"That is healing," Bud continued. "Don't forget that. We are here to heal. Thank you for sharing, Zach."

Feeling it appropriate, the cocaine addict sat down, a small drip of sweat forming on his lower back, and let out a sigh of repugnance. *Just kill me now.*

Char whispered into his ear: "I blew that guy, like, three days ago. He tryze to act all tough, but it's bullshit."

"*What?*" Zach bent away from him. "You what?"

"All dose military guys. Dey're around sweaty, hunky men all day." He poked Zach in the ribs where he felt most sensitive. "How can dey not get curious, am I right?"

"Jesus, Char . . ."

"Is there something you would like to share with the group, Mr. Komsa?" Bud asked apprehensively.

"Oh no," Char replied. "Please, keep going."

Bud tweaked the collar of his blue polo shirt and a muscle in his neck.

"Today's group exercise will center around 'dialogue.' 'Dialogue' is what we use to open our soul. Our chakra. Our inner light. Normally, I like to have this exercise done in groups of four, but in the spirit of the beautiful grace and splendor that Mr. Long has brought into the room today, let's go ahead and switch things up by pairing off. And I'll ask of you, Zach, to please choose someone other than Mr. Komsa to pair with, as it seems you two are already acquainted."

"I'll pair with him," came a soft enunciation from the opposite side of the circle. This was the voice of the actress Angela Lui. Her hand waved in the air.

Toast of the town only three years prior, with starring roles in most every teen rom-com released in the second half of the '90s, it became almost impossible to escape her wide smile plastered on buses, magazines, and subway platforms whenever a movie of hers was in the theaters or for rent on DVD. And to the casual observer picking up a copy of whatever rag had her face on it in the checkout lane, Angela appeared to be the epitome of a Hollywood success. What daughters aspired to. But like the Catholic Church and Jeffrey Epstein, the youngish actress possessed secrets so dark the writers of her scripts wouldn't have even bothered. It wouldn't have been believable.

And then she disappeared from the limelight with no explanation or crumbs to follow, a crime scene absent a crime. She was simply forgotten about—the public's attention span unable to withstand her absence for longer than a year—and, by the looks of it, had forgotten about herself too.

Zach had seen healthier-looking cancer patients.

The two grabbed chairs and placed them in the farthest corner of the room, and the actress wasted no time with introductions.

"Cocaine?" she asked as if popping Tylenol were no different. "That's it? Shit, man . . . I was blasting close to an eight ball before I left the house in the morning. Washed it down with half a handle of Beefeater. You ever shot up black tar heroin before? Fuck out of here with your gram-a-day habit."

Squeezing her right eye shut like a pirate, she frightened Zach more with each new syllable and he could hardly contain the shock.

"My manager forced me into some rehab up in Sonoma County, but it ended up being easier to score drugs in there than on the street. I OD'd my fourth night and had to be resuscitated by one of the nurses. Was in a coma for three weeks. When I came to, I was informed the state had taken my son away and that my husband was filing for divorce less than a year after we got married. My second divorce in three years. Thank the Lord my last movie did well. Only way I could afford this fucking place."

"Wow, Angela," Zach said, desperate for Bud's attention, looking to ask if he could switch partners if it wasn't too late. "That's messed up. I'm really sorry to hear that."

"Yeah, it is." Her right eye was tighter than a NASA O-ring. "Sooooo what? You finally got a little bit of fame and couldn't handle it? Or is it just the clichéd drug addict musician thing you were trying to go after?" She put her hand on his upper thigh. "I must admit, it does look good on you."

"Nah," he said, and peered down at the track marks that constellated Angela's right arm. "None of that. If anything, it made me a worse musician, not a better one."

"Funny, isn't it?" Angela mused. "Here we are. These 'celebrities.' But it's really all a bunch of bullshit. I mean, I can remember being a little girl and staring at my posters of Janet Jackson and Molly Ringwald and dreaming about leaving that trailer home in West Virginia and becoming them. Living their life. A fairy tale. And then I did. And then I saw how fucked up those fairies were." She scratched at a scab on her elbow. It fell off. "I used to have friends—now I don't. The people I knew grew up, started families, and created meaningful relationships. I moved to Hollywood and blew any producer willing to give me a role."

"How's everything going here?" Bud asked, standing behind Angela and placing his hairy hands onto her defenseless shoulder blades. "Seems like you two are diving into some great stuff."

"We are, thanks," Zach answered, hopeful Angela knew Muay Thai.

"Great to hear! If there is anything I can help with or guide you through on this practice of immaterial learning, please let me know. And remember, Zach—we're all friends here."

"I think we're good," he answered back. "Thanks."

"Sure," Bud said, "onward then," and kept his hands on Angela's shoulders for three more uncooperative seconds before trotting away like a horse who won fourth place at Yonkers Raceway.

She wiped his dirt off her shoulders like Jay-Z.

"That guy is such a creep."

Zach agreed. "What were we talking about?"

"How fucked up I am. But let's talk about you, the *rock star*. Why is it your pathetic ass ended up here?"

"Well, I have no wife, no kids, and just OD'd in Hawaii off some shit a dude at a brothel gave me."

Angela ignored his life's torment and downed the last of her coffee in one swallow. "I need a refill. Want one?"

"I'm all set."

"All right, everybody!" Bud yelled from the front of the room, center stage. "Let's quiet the voices please and get back into our circle to discuss the 'walls' we were able to break down."

An appreciated pause in the action, sufficient time was allowed for everyone to grab more organic fair-trade artisanal coffee, bagels with lox, and fruit smoothies before seating themselves down for another ring around the rosy of drug-dependent egomaniacs balanced on a tightrope with oiled shoes during a windy day.

"Angela, it looked like you and Zach were digging deep for a bit there. If you wouldn't mind starting us off?"

Still standing by the table full of luxurious delicacies, Angela asked, "Uh, are you sure?" between watchful sips of a light-roasted espresso.

"Yes, I'm *sure*. Please"—he extended his hand out to offer her the floor—"and without being too specific, but making sure to include plenty of detail, go ahead and explain the 'walls' you were able to break down in your 'dialogue' with Zach."

Angela took a hearty bite of her everything bagel with lox, and with a mouthful of brined salmon and poppy-seeded carbs, she answered the question to the best of her ability. "We talked about how fucked it is to have everything you always dreamed of yet still want to destroy yourself in the hopes that said destruction leads to some other kind of screwed-up happiness. Or acceptance. Or something like that." She took another bite, smaller in size but louder in sound. "This lox is fantastic, by the way."

Each of his fingertips touched softly together in front of his barrel chest, the digits forming a small sphere of influence before him, and he spoke like the god he believed himself to be. "Yes, that's good," Bud said. "I see where you're coming f—"

"Like, I had everything. And now I have nothing. My career is, how would you say it . . . hors de combat? I mean, this is exactly when I should be doing drugs, right?"

Angela's joke landed and gathered a good response from the audience.

"Very funny. Thank you for sharing. And, Zach, what 'walls' were you able to break down in your 'dialogue'? Were Angela's expressions of her own dejection and fear ringing true within your soul?"

The kind of gas that forces air through your cheeks like a muted trumpet passed across his digestive tract, stopping for no one. "Yeah, I think so . . ." Zach said, more confused than confident. "I don't know. This is really intense, to be honest." His heart thumped harder. "I think I need a little more time . . . I actually feel light-headed."

Breathing in a creepy old-man yogi manner—the kind who wears ankle bracelets and toe rings—Bud said, "Zach—is it all right if I call you Zach?"

"You already have been."

"Zach, when a soul is new to this world, a sober world, one must let go of past flows and enter a new flow. A flow with no dams or hurdles to dissuade you. Please, I ask you to close your eyes . . . In fact"—his attention swayed—"let's have everyone close their eyes . . ."

Zach imagined the Kool-Aid to come any minute now, no doubt.

". . . and imagine that our fears, wishes, hopes, and demons are floating in a crystal-clear pool." Bud waited till every eye in the room was shut before he picked his nose. "Now I'd like for you all to imagine that swimming pool. Maybe one similar to the Beverly Wilshire Hotel's." His hack comic material, stale like doing the same bit in the same city for fifteen years, killed. "Now picture your demons and dark energy embodied in a bowling ball tied tight around your waist, the force so heavy it's pulling you down so that only your mouth remains above the majestic water by barely a whisker."

Florence McCowlan, star of the 1980s syndicated television series *Teething Troubles*, began to sob next to Zach. Her arms and legs were covered with cuts, and she had a noticeable habit of pulling out her own hair. She looked likely to lose her shit at any moment.

"Now imagine that you're suddenly in possession of a sharp knife. Maybe one from the restaurant inside of the Beverly Wilshire Hotel," Bud went on, testing the beat of the room. "Now *cut that rope*! Cut that rope and let go! Let go and spread your arms wide toward the heavens! Spread those wings that will bring you back to the top . . . Breathe . . . Breathe in the air! Breathe in that beautiful air!! Breeeeatttthhhhhee!"

Zach's eyes were open when Bud's body hit the ground.

Two hours later, after the ambulance had carted away his lifeless corpse, Rebecca gathered the witnesses of Bud Spalding's passing back into the same room where he had just died from a massive heart attack for dinner. The dulled shock of fatality was hard to bear, but as bluefin tuna sushi was served, the circle of life felt richly well represented in the wake of its sudden ending.

"Mr. Spalding was a beautiful person and will be deeply missed here at Happy Hills Recovery," Rebecca spoke solemnly. "I'm not sure what else to say . . . We will be offering sessions with some of Los Angeles's most esteemed grief counselors for anyone who feels the need to speak about their feelings after the witnessing of such a horrific event." Choking back tears, she continued: "We will also be holding a candlelight memorial for Mr. Spalding out on the veranda after men's enhancement yoga and ladies' spa rejuvenation treatments. If anyone would like to speak a few words, by all means pl—"

"*Motherfucking shit cunt fucking fuck!!*" Florence McCowlan stood up and, with a giant clump of her own hair squeezed in her gripped fist, screamed even louder. "Life is *fucked*! Ha-ha-ha-ha! We're all gonna *die*! Don't you fucking *see*, you blind pigs! You all *follow* this *system*! Your *fear*! It's not blind to everyone!"

"Ms. McCowlan," Rebecca said tenderly, lifting her eyebrow to one of the security personnel, "if you'd please relax, this is a very sensitive time for everyone."

"Fuck you, *bitch*!" Florence yelled, pointing her index finger like a wand of reckoning, its knuckle bent in maniacal fashion. "They used to worship me. All of them!" She proceeded to pull out more of her hair. "But not Mr. Big Shot. No, no, no . . . he wasn't impressed. Told me I wouldn't get the part if I wasn't his *plaything*."

Rebecca remained calm. "Ms. McCowlan, if you could please refrain from bringing up such dark memories. You should be concentrating on your path forward no matter the situation at hand."

A security guard snuck up behind Florence and shoved a small needle into the side of her neck.

"*Ahhh! Get off me!*" she screamed, and fought for three more seconds before succumbing to the powerful tranquilizer.

Her limp body dragged away from the room to the joy of everyone there, the rest of the meal went by as Zach imagined it would have even if Bud Spalding hadn't dropped dead and Florence wasn't 5150'ed. Then, like the last day of school before summer break, with the agenda Rebecca had planned out the window, the group dispersed, and Zach peeled away with ease, looking forward to his king-sized bed and detoxification process alone in a dark, moist, silent room.

Safe from sound and tucked in tight, he skimmed through the pages of Stephen King's *On Writing* by only the light of the moon. His eyes fluttered in the soft illumination, ready for a journey through dreams and new schemes. The warmth of heavy slumber was moments from overtaking him and the flashes of past days were before him, when there was a knock on his door.

"Open up!"

Zach dreamed harder.

The knocks became louder.

"Open up!!" The voice was growly.

"Char, I'm sleeping. Go away."

"It's not Char, you idiot. It's Angela."

"Huh? Angela?"

The heavy down comforter suffocated his limbs, but surprised at his surprise guest, Zach sludged his torso up like a man emerging from quicksand and searched for the lamp's light switch. "What's up? I'm sleeping."

"No, you're not. You're talking to me right now. Let me in."

"Can this wait till tomorrow?"

"Open this door, or I'm going to kick it down."

Zach got up, put on a microfiber bathrobe with plush lining to cover his fever-ridden skin, and opened the door enough to see Angela's still-tense right eye.

"Is everything all right?" he asked, caring as little as he would for a dead fly. "I really don't feel well and very much need to sleep."

"Can I just come in and talk for a bit?" she asked genuinely. "I'm still pretty spooked about what happened earlier."

He cursed under his breath but groaned out loud. "Uuugggh, all right . . . but not for long. I really need to go to sleep."

She let herself in, and Zach sat himself down at the end of his bed and lit a smoke. Angela sat across from him on an Eames lounge chair and asked him for a light. "That was some fucked-up shit earlier," she said. "I keep trying to get the image of Bud's body out of my head, but I can't."

"Yeah," Zach said, cracking his back to the left. "I thought he was joking at first"—a fresh crack the other way—"definitely not."

With perfect little feet, Angela kicked the Eames ottoman out of the way and spread her legs out wide in front of her. Her loose dress flowed with inducement. "Wanna take some acid?"

"*What?*" Zach checked that he'd heard right, cleaning out his ear. "Do I wanna what?"

"You heard me. I have two hits. This place gets so boring."

"You want to trip on acid in a drug rehab facility?"

"Yeah. You got a problem with that?"

"I mean, no. Just seems counterproductive, is all."

He turned on the TV for no reason, yet for every reason, and Martha Stewart's face popped up on the screen, a fresh tray of brownies on the table below her, a prison sentence ahead of her.

"But wouldn't you rather do that in the woods or something? Aren't you also getting clean? This *is* rehab." His voice was higher-pitched than before.

"What is this," Angela mocked, "Haight-Ashbury? I'm looking to go *deep*, man"—she tapped her temple—"and unlock the real shit inside this sleepy house."

"I'm going to take a hard pass on all of that."

"Pussy."

"What?"

"You heard me."

"I won't even dignify that with an answer."

"Come on . . . It will be fun!"

Fun wasn't anything Zach was in the mood for. *Fun* was the polar opposite of going to sleep. A heavy, deep sleep void of any pleasure or amusement.

Pulling a pack of gum from her purse, Angela revealed two small pieces of blotter paper stashed inside. "Open your mouth," she said.

"Angela, Bud died, like, three hours ago."

"Oh, come on! I'm gonna take mine right now, see?" She placed a tab with the Cookie Monster from *Sesame Street* onto her tongue.

"How strong is it?" he asked, and then asked himself, *Seriously?*

"How am I supposed to know? One of the security guards gave it to me." She handed him the pack of gum. And then she spread her legs a little more. "I was serious about what I said before."

Zach took hold of the pack, opened it, and then became distracted by Angela's red-painted toenails. His penis took over shortly thereafter.

"It can't be that strong, right?" he asked undecidedly, the power of his cock pulling him much further than our Milky Way galaxy held capable. "Maybe I'll just take a quarter of it. Might help me sleep too."

"Whatever."

After unsuccessfully trying to cut the tab with his long, dirty fingernails, Zach began to search around for a pair of scissors or a knife, then quickly recognized that such instruments weren't likely to be floating around a building of recovering suicidal drug addicts. Hallucinogens were easier to find apparently. As he bit into one of the tab's corners with an accurate lateral incisor, ready for a fast tear in half, Angela screamed,

"Mouse!" and Zach's mouth swallowed reactively as he jerked his head back.

"What! Where?"

"I'm sorry!" she squealed, hopping on one foot. "I thought I saw a mouse! Maybe I didn't—I don't know . . ."

"Fuck! I just swallowed that entire hit!" Big Bird's profile dissolving into his bloodstream, the anxiousness of a very bad decision quickly gripped his chest with well-represented fear.

"This should be fun."

With the TV on mute and the hallways of Happy Hills Recovery silent, the down-and-out actress would go on to talk Zach's ear off for over thirty minutes about her failed attempts at career revitalization, the branded water bottle/lifestyle products she sold, and her Beanie Babies collection. Despite slight obstructions in his senses of touch and sight, he felt a category of good, almost dizzy, listening to her babble on and on about nonsense and figured he had a handle on the present condition.

Not that strong probably.

Moving their way to the balcony for a smoke, the change of scenery felt hospitable to both, and Zach noticed a change in Angela as she lit his lighter; its flame brightened up her unmade face in a made-up way. "I still can't believe I married that asshole," she said through her first drag, the smoke curling around her tongue.

"Married who?"

"Very funny. You know who I'm talking about."

"I have no idea who you're talking about."

"Jim Weeney? That little-dicked actor in all those Snapple commercials? Doesn't matter." She lit the lighter again. And then she snuffed it out. And then she lit it again. "After I got pregnant, we had to get married. Hollywood doesn't like single mothers."

Nothing about this conversation made Zach feel particularly spiritual or free from negative thought, and then he was hit with a brief reminder that the sole reason he was even talking to Angela Lui at all about her B-list ex-husband, on acid, immediately following a stranger's death, at a rehab facility in Malibu, was because he'd come within moments of dying himself. This abrupt awareness caught him in a panic.

And then the drug took over.

That recognizable feeling right before all goes to shit tickled his newfound worries, and Zach excused himself, went back inside and to the bathroom, splashing some cold water on his face to stifle the oncoming terror buoyant in his throat. The faucet turned all the way cold, he generated a pond inside his cupped hands and threw more water onto his skin, assuring himself, briefly, that this would be the cure for any of Angela's bad vibes or, worse, his own imminent ones. The few drops that remained on his face somehow felt challenging to pat dry with one of the six monogrammed towels available at his disposal. It also became a challenge to breathe. He looked at himself in the mirror—his first mistake—blinked hard, and then saw Bud Spalding standing firmly behind him.

What the fuck?!

He spun around to see nothing but the shower curtain, its pattern of seahorses stupefying. A thin shaft of moonlight shone through the skylight and immersed the drapery with a turquoise glow.

Angela heard his commotion from outside and was drawn to it like a moth. "Everything all right in there?" she asked.

His heart exploded with alarm. His breath became labored. "Yeah. Yeah—everything is all right. I just . . . I thought I saw something, is all."

"Was it the mouse?!"

His heartbeat was visible through his shirt and ready to burst into spades. Zach did what little he could to grab hold of himself, contemplating whether a shower would be too startling a task or that much-needed centering of his concentration. Left with little other alternative for immediate inner peace, he rotated the shower's spigot far enough to the left to burn the hair off a cat and allowed a steam to gather in the room. Condensation thick, oxygen thin, and a brain sautéing like onions without oil, he wandered back into the bedroom for another Camel Light.

Angela sat on the bed smoking his last one. "Why are you taking a shower?"

He stepped out to meet her, pins and needles running through both arms and legs, and the clock liquefied into the orange wall behind her as he slipped on its numbers. "I'm not . . . I don't know . . . This feels weird . . . Is that clock melting?"

"Zach, chill out. You took a huge hit of acid . . ."

The mattress began to waver and come alive underneath her. Its movements were slight but plenty enough to question the laws of physics—that cushioned objects won't move unless being exerted on by an outside force. Angela sat motionless on top of it like an oil painting.

"Actually," he said, "I am going to take that shower. You can hang here, or . . ." He watched a small herd of seahorses swim around the bedsheets beneath her and almost lost it. "I don't know. You can do whatever you want. I really need to shower."

"You're a fucking weirdo." The seahorses dispersed as she stood up and gathered her belongings in a hurry. "It's always the musicians too. Why can't any of you just be normal for once?" Her white Airwalk sneakers, untied and loose around her delicate ankles, made leaving difficult, and as she struggled with her exit, she screamed, "Screw you and your micro-penis!" before a stomp of both feet on the carpet and a slam of the door shut behind her, its hinges scared of her possible return, the doorknob injured.

His head transfixed with a cavernous worry, Zach returned to the sauna his bathroom had become and stripped off all his clothing how a snake sheds skin. He wiped away the moisture on the mirror with his forearm and snuck another glimpse of his reflection long enough to lock eyes with it.

The worst of ideas.

In the hollows of Zach's reason, scents and muffled sounds of Bud Spalding came back once again, boring a wide hole deep into his already guilty conscience. Appearing in the mirror of his mind as the drill instructor from *Full Metal Jacket*, Bud soon began screaming at him as if he were one of his soldiers, his voice stern and mortal.

"YOU TOOK DRUGS IN A DRUG REHAB FACILITY, ZACH LONG?!"

"Yes, sir! I'm sorry, sir!" Zach shouted.

"I CAN'T HEAR YOU!"

"Yes, Mr. Spalding, *sir!*"

"AND WHAT THE HELL MADE YOU THINK YOU COULD DO THAT?!"

"I don't know, sir! It was peer pressure, sir!"

"PEER PRESSURE?! WHAT IS THIS, MIDDLE SCHOOL?!"

"Sir! I swear, I'll never do it again, sir! I swear I will never touch another drug for as long as I live, sir!"

The shower still running, his deliriums running faster, Zach stared down at his hand, which looked to have seven fingers, and the conversation lost place in his skull.

"What in God's name is going on here?" A new voice—human and softer in its howl—entered the fray.

His depth perception marginally off-kilter, Zach rotated to face the shower curtain he was positive had spoken and, in the process, lost his balance, slipping off the edge of existence and tumbling into the drape, the material coming down into the bathtub with him and cloaking his naked body, protecting his skin from the life-threatening hot water that blasted above. He heard a woman's voice ask, "Mr. Long, who are you screaming at?" before extracting himself from the tub upended, ass-naked, and with a new welt on his head.

Rebecca's being took shape in the entry of the bathroom. He was positive her hair was on fire, the dyed-red flames of her mane ashing into its natural gray, a kaleidoscope of autumn season no pumpkin spice latte could ever make you feel. Exposed, he admitted his wrongdoings as a sinner in a confessional might. "I took acid and I'm having a bad trip and—oh my god is your hair on fire? And when did I grow a seventh finger?"

"I'm sorry . . ." Rebecca stalled. "Did you just say you took LSD in a drug rehab facility?"

"I did but it's all right because I told Bud I would never do drugs again for as long as I live. I'm going to take another shower and everything will be fine."

A true professional, Rebecca said, "Let's have you relax," her voice soothing in a maternal way as she handed Zach his discarded clothes. "Cover up and follow me, please. I'd like to get you into a cozier environment and apply some apple fig compresses."

She led Zach down the only hallway he had seen in this entire place, the back of her head a painter's palette of oranges and yellows, red and purples, luminosities and hums.

"You're not angry at me, right?" he asked. "I told Bud I would never do drugs again—this is so beautiful, I can feel the walls breathing."

"We don't believe in *anger* here at Happy Hills Recovery," Rebecca responded. "We believe in *restoration* and *revival*."

A door opened.

A small room appeared.

"Please, sit down."

Four Eames lounge chairs, unanchored and delightful, sat

in the small space, bare of almost all else. He sat down on the farthest one as she lit a Sparkling Cinnamon Yankee Candle, dimmed the lights, and pressed play on the room's entertainment system. The soundwaves of traditional Chinese music muted his mind.

In a voice appropriate to the situation, Rebecca said, "We have procedures for these kinds of things."

"Do people take acid here often? I still can't believe I did it—I'm so sorry—but your hair—I can't believe how red it is."

"I appreciate the compliment, Mr. Long, but let's please focus on you. Make yourself comfortable. This will all be over soon enough."

Flipping open a little white box placed at waist-height, she punched in a code, and a projector screen descended from the ceiling, the soundtrack of flutes and bells transmuting into the theme song of the television show *Friends*. She lowered the lights to that level right before total blackness.

"One of the cast members spent some time here fighting his demons with us," Rebecca said. "And as a thank-you gift, he had Warner Bros. send over copies of his fun little show *Friends*."

His seventh finger turned into the claw of a chicken. "Oh cool, yeah, this is a good show, my ex-girlfriend watched it all the time."

"Ha-ha . . . I know when I'm feeling scared and confused, a couple episodes of *Friends* always help to make me feel grounded. Let me leave you be, and I'll be back after episode nine of season three to check in on you. You'll be amazed how quickly time flies when this show is on!"

The Eames chair Zach sat in started to levitate off the ground. "Do you want to watch some episodes of *Friends* with me? I think it would be nice."

Rebecca blushed, almost embarrassed, and smiled politely.

"Mr. Long, thank you. In fact, there's nothing in this world I'd love to do more than watch *Friends* with you."

But before he could register his own smile, his joyfulness dissipated when she *also* said, "Let me go knock on Angela's door and see if she'd like to join us. I think she was in a couple of episodes!"

7

Second National Bank Amphitheatre at the Fulton Distillery Gardens presented by Ohio Mobile Energy Partners & Associates LLC
Cincinnati, OH
8/31/2005

Capacity: 10,500
Tickets Sold: 5,477

"Ye believe these twats? I mean, they smashing cunts, but my lord, they didn't even read the fookin' sign. It says only *artists* past this point! Where these broads even come from anyways? Sken fancy they been eating cheese and pancakes their whole lives . . . And what the feck's with ye Yankee cunts? All ye eat is cheese and pancakes. Maybe that's why everyone here is the size of a whale. What state r we even in? Alfie, where r we again? Ahhhh, yes . . . Ohio, where 'with God, all things are possible.' Well, God certainly made it possible for all these bloody Yanks to eat an enormous amount of shite. Why can't everyone just drink Guinness and smoke fags? It's been a blessing for us folks in the UK, let me tell ye now. None of this processed gobshite goes into our bodies. Alcohol and some fried fish 'n' crisps, ya know? But hell, a little fish 'n' crisps ain't never killed no one. Nope. Not a soul. But Twinkies? Laddie, I bet those kill thousands of bloater fucks a year. What the feck is a Twinkie anyways? And why r they serving us this cack backstage? I mean, how can ye eat this stuff and think you're going to live a long and plenteous life? Fags and alcohol, my mate. It's what keeps ya young. Keeps the pipes flowing and yer trouser snake working. Hell, I'm fifty-six and can keep an erection for three minutes straight *without* a break. Tell me what other fifty-six-year-ol' can dae that, eh? I bet ye can't keep yer willy up for that long. And fookin' hell, these broads ye got out here. Seriously, fancy they were born straight from the twat of a cow. A bloater cow. Butters cow at that, ya know? Anyways. I'm just 'bout out of ale. Can I get ya one? Oh, yeh. Couldn't handle the stuff, could ya? Yeh alreet, noting wrong with that I suppose. Not meant for everyone if ya can't gripe it. Well, I'll catch ya another time, yeh? Time for our set. Be smashing, lad . . . Always a pleasure."

Black leather pants stuck to the sofa like a waffle to an ungreased pan, the man pried his old, fat, wrinkly body off Texas Flip's tour bus couch, yawned sideways, farted length-wise, and took a final sip from the last orange juice container left in their fridge. White boots embellished with actual spurs, blue denim jacket, and blond hair balding only on the crown of his head in a skullet, this chap presented himself more like a dead-tired cowboy rather than the has-been rock star he actu-ally was, fastened to the dark memories that kept him up most nights, burping up citric acid and repentance. He stretched himself forward a mere two inches and, with no more thought on the subject, continued out of their bus and onward to his own bus parked fifty feet away, crop-dusting his evening's chicken cordon bleu upon departure.

His name was Oscar Thomson, and he was the lead singer of the band Dusters Blunt.

An incarnated legend of the road surviving off a string of hits from the mid-'90s—that moment in time when the world championed loud guitars and Europeans with poor dental hygiene—Dusters Blunt was one of eight bands that, packaged together with Texas Flip and other forgotten bits of meat, filled out the lineup of this traveling circus they were all on called the Rock of Cages tour, presented by the country's third-largest professional wrestling organization, World Professional Wrestling (WPW), a multinational corporation based out of Hartford, Connecticut. WPW's earlier success with a similarly themed music festival in Buckeye Lake, Ohio, had become a deadly weapon in the hands of greedy players, who decided to further extend their reach into the music production world with a concept never properly placed into action before.

Heavier heads in corner offices concluding, *Why not?* after chilled seafood towers on early afternoons, the WPW brass thought it best to combine the two greatest things in the world —live music and professional wrestling—into one transportable package the middle of the country would eat up like a buy-one-get-one corn dog special. Cage wrestlers performed simultaneously in amphitheater parking lots while bands that people used to like played on stages bigger than their current popularities warranted. Each avenue of entertainment a profit monster in its own right, the idea was that the two together were more than guaranteed to rake in piles of cash on merchandise alone, not to mention sales of Michelob Ultra and overpriced bottled water.

What WPW thought would be a river of treasure pouring into an ocean of gold.

What WPW got was a stream of liabilities and budget deficits.

Day after day, rain or shine, these WPW wrestlers were expected to bang their bodies into oblivion for the gap-toothed, pink-haired, disability-receiving public who were mostly in attendance to shove funnel cake down their diabetic gullets and ignore their parental responsibilities for yet another day. The cities changing but the damage done not, these wrestlers played out the same rehearsed acts as the musicians up on the stage did, injecting steroids and swallowing Percocets at rest stops in Missouri, Iowa, you name it, far enough away from the banal guitar riffs and salty, middle-aged women flashing their saggy, sunburned tits for no one.

Oscar and Zach had made acquaintances after the latter provided the former with an urgently needed cigarette at a most opportune moment. Zach happened to be standing offstage, smoking and watching Dusters Blunt's set, right as Oscar walked off, the final notes of their biggest song, "It Never Fucking Ends," fading out in the fumigation of his eggplant Parmesan lunch. The man had marched up to him, unsure if the younger gentleman was a performer or someone's brother, and there was a beating fear in Oscar's eyes when he asked, with a voice within four more screams of being completely ruined, "You got a fag, you fag?" and then took the lit cigarette from his new friend's mouth, smoking its remains in five drags and flicking the butt back onto the stage.

These two musicians, in a bond of unity stronger than that with their own respective bandmates, would soon become inseparable: hanging out on the bus after gigs, shooting the shit and talking shit about jack shit. Oscar Thomson was an unaltered glimpse into a world of regret and bad judgment the likes of which Zach couldn't get enough of. Happy Hills Recovery paled in comparison.

But as joyous as he was to be back on the road himself, all the other players involved—from the bands down to the wrestlers, production workers, bus drivers, and caterers—were over the Rock of Cages tour before that first week had even finished. A laundry list of complaints and no soap to cleanse them away, with a noisome tinge of *please let this be over*, could be smelled not just in the wrestling cages and porta-johns but also from the stage. But not expressly thrilled to go back to an empty apartment and guaranteed boredom, Zach counted on touring as the one thing to keep him busy.

Because keeping busy was his new drug.

Immediately following his releasee from rehab, Texas Flip had gone right back into the studio to pump out a joke of a record, *A Farewell to Farms*, that would barely crack the Top 200.

And then Bart died.

Drunk on his motorcycle during a vacation in South Carolina, cruising 80 mph in a school zone on a weekday morning, he unsuccessfully evaded the oncoming train that took his life.

Spin magazine wrote a small obituary.

There was no funeral.

By a long shot their most musically talented member, the band went on an immediate hiatus after his passing. That was until they were reminded that they were still under contract and needed to get back in the studio and on the road if they wanted to keep their jobs. They soon released the rushed and even more disappointing *Sharing in the Groove*.

And then Harry quit the band after an epiphany (and messy divorce), deciding that he wanted to go to med school at the age of thirty-two.

No one said this game was fair. And Robin Williams

already warned us about golf. But this helps to explain how a band that actually "makes it" can very quickly wind up in a traveling carnival, produced by a professional wrestling company, in Ohio, sunburned and sad.

And as with most everything that involves money, opportunity, and musicians, it had all started on a wrong note months previous.

"Listen, guys, I'm gonna be frank here. You haven't had a song the radio gave a shit about since the Bush tax cuts. Your last record sold . . . Shit, I just had the . . . okay, yeah . . . here they are—sorry . . . 36,144 copies. And you not only lost money on that album's recording but on both of its tours. I'm honestly amazed Mountain View hasn't dropped you from their roster yet. Thankfully they haven't. Means I can still book you some decent-paying gigs."

Silence filled the world. Filled the solar system. Filled hell.

With a voice sweeter than Honey Nut Cheerios and coated with sugar, Felicia, in the nicest of ways possible, was only doing her job: reporting to the band that they were, quite simply, fucked.

"I know this is not what you want to hear, but this is the best I could get you guys right now. Truth is, this is the best tour I'm going to be able to get you until the band has anything that even comes *close* to another hit."

No news here, as Texas Flip had been fucked many times throughout their career, either by their record label, a venue, or sometimes both simultaneously. Felicia informing them they were fucked once again wasn't a shock to anyone.

"The pay is decent, though. It's a forty-three-date, fifty-day North American tour with eight bands from your era."

"Era"—a sticky note that held pertinence only to the people who were there.

"The lineup will change every city," she continued. "The promoters are doing this to ensure that no one specific band is favored, although WPW is relying heavily on Dusters Blunt to do the big lifting when it comes to ticket sales. I'm guessing their wrestlers aren't strong enough."

No one laughed.

The band sat in a warehouse in the Ozone Park section of Queens. Luke rented an apartment nearby and had made friends with a local wise guy who helped keep an eye on the block where he lived and helped him purchase things not available at your corner bodega. The warehouse's ground level used to store freight, appliances, and what looked like stolen cars, Todd was appreciative of the price of rent for the second floor, and so the band signed a three-year lease to take over the offices and an isolated storage closet they converted into a rehearsal room. There were two windows that had bullet holes through them and a boarded-up window that had had a body thrown through it.

If they could have picked a more appropriate place to die inside, they would have been dead already.

"Who's Dusters Blunt?" Luke asked.

"You know who they are," Felicia said, her voice crackling more than the phone's connection. "They're that band that had that song . . . Damn, now I can't remember the name of it. It had the video of the talking guitar and the talking fish in some dude's bedroom, and they would talk to each other all day while the dude was at work."

"Oh yeah!" Luke yelped. "I remember that video! And the guitar and fish would sing the chorus, right?"

"Yeah, that one. Anyways—those guys. I can send over the rest of the information once I get a confirmation from you."

"We'll do it," Todd answered.

"Hi, Todd," Felicia said, the sweetness of her voice turning to vinegar. "How about you give them a second to think about it before we commit? It is a gig, but it's also a very long stretch of time. I don't want you all disintegrating out there."

"We're doing it. Send over everything we need, and we'll discuss it all next week. Thanks. Bye."

"Bu—"

Todd hung up the speakerphone, sunk in his chair, and, with arms wide open, whistled loud enough to fill the spaces between the murkily lit room and the bookies downstairs. "Finally, some good news! Jesus goddamn Christ, did we need it too."

With obvious apprehension, as if he had bitten into under-cooked chicken, Luke asked, "Are we sure we can do this? We haven't been on the road for that long in a while."

Both were right. And that was a problem.

"We all appreciate your concern in the matter," Todd said. "But it doesn't make much of a difference when this boils down to basic economics."

And again, he was right.

They'll teach you calculus, chemistry, and cooking in school. They'll teach you how to play dodgeball and ways to dissect a frog. They'll even teach you languages that people no longer speak. But what the public school system fails to teach each passing generation, at a time when their brains are sponges for such instruction, is how the most critical possession in this world operates.

Money.

Cold hard cash.

And provided with the same elementary teachings in regard to the operations and pitfalls of those little pieces of powerful green paper—that is to say zero—Zach and Luke were both of an equal insolvency.

Texas Flip's lead singer, in nearsighted fashion, had made

an investment known the world over as the worst you could possibly make and opened an ambitious multilevel New American restaurant with some childhood friends in Edgewater, New Jersey. A money-losing failure before doors even opened, the business would bleed him dry of the little fortune he had amassed doing something completely different—playing bass guitar and singing in a band. Knowing nothing about the restaurant business, and even less about starting one, he would be forced to sell off his stake at a major loss and go into even more debt with a loan shark in order to pay off the rest.

Maintaining the financial well-being of a ditch digger with a bum shoulder, you'd think Luke would have been the last person interrogating Texas Flip's ability to suffer further. Todd —with a wife, three kids, two dogs, and a house in Westchester County—was dually fucked, because no matter how much money he made off of them, it wasn't ever going to be enough to afford the solid level of comfort that he and his stay-at-home wife had acclimated themselves to with no regard for the future of a business centered on entertainment value and not skill.

At least not without "another hit" as Felicia so bluntly pointed out.

Zach? Well, he'd sadly spent all his earnings on substances, then Happy Hills Recovery, the only thing more expensive than drugs being the money paid to get off them. His body aloof on the sofa, he scrutinized the ceiling like a stoned teen. "How do *you* feel about all of this?" he asked, peering over at Luke, the only other person whose opinion actually mattered. "Can your voice handle that many shows?"

"Bro," Luke said, too lazy to move his eyes from the ceiling. "I was thinking. And I think I got this."

Todd rolled his eyes. "Great to hear. I'm assuming everybody else feels the same?"

The "everybody else" that Todd was speaking of were Texas Flip's freshest hired guns, Rurik and Matthew.

Rurik joined the band exactly a month after Bart died, and if he needed to be described, he'd be called a man who "wasn't for every woman but was all the man for some." Dirty white sneakers, tight black jeans, and a black Metallica T-shirt covered his body, and his hair was parted down the middle in a way that made it uncomfortable to look at. His playing ability was of less importance than his genealogical connection; he was the long-lost nephew to some music mogul the history books described as "chewed up and bankrupted." Rurik was a keyboard player who had fumbled around the scene long enough to land the kind of gigs that mattered. Or rather, that paid. Joining Texas Flip as a momentary stop between something that paid less and something better, he kept his plan of an early departure a secret, playing the same game his employers had been playing for decades.

Matthew joined the day after Harry had quit.

His Jamaican-Iranian blood mixed with a buzzed head bleached blond and a lankier build than Gumby. His drumming skills on par with that of an eighth-grade enthusiast, he was hired mostly because he was pleasant to look at onstage shirtless and even more pleasant to photographers, and he made the band look a lot cooler and thus made people think they were better than they actually were. Like an attractive woman with the personality of an oat bran muffin, Matthew added a touch of spice to a beverage diluted by melted ice and served with a squashy paper straw. The dude even played open-handed. Lefty.

And so, through a series of unfortunate occurrences, bad calls, awful decisions, and legitimate losses of life, these soggy grinds now sat around a circular table made of plastic, deciding whether they were desperate enough to go on a tour of has-beens and hardly weres, or prideful enough to say fuck it and continue on their path of lamentable career suicide.

Zach—single, no kids, and holding stock of nothing but

free time—deposited a vote of "yes" speedily into the ballot box.

Matthew and Rurik, in it for only money and not a platform to spread their enlightened opinions, smiled and spoke nothing.

Todd smirked at this whiff of assent.

"This is going to be big for us," he said. "I got a good feeling about it."

Three months later, before another run-of-the-mill show in another second-rate city, Zach was in a strange mood, having trouble finding something to light his cigarette with. The Reds played the Dodgers on TV while the sound of grown men in purple spandex wrestling outside drowned it out. The Rock of Cages tour was only six shows deep when grave news trickled down to all those concerned. A smallpox outbreak would have been more welcomed.

Due to the popularity the tour was seeing in cities you'd never want to perform in, let alone live in, additional dates were added in Des Moines, Tulsa, Fort Worth, Corpus Christi, Cheyenne, and Fresno, and all without informing any of the bands until that particular morning. Notes slid under the doors of buses with "Attention Artists!" written in lime-green Sharpie alone served as notice to the musicians, many of whom, hungover from the night before, believed it to be a prank. Reading *Stoner*, by John Williams, with a freshly lit cigarette and a cold cup of tea when the dispatch was slipped through, Zach would be the one to report these new developments to Todd, clad in Simpsons pajama bottoms and Nike flip-flops and holding a stuffed sea otter, having freshly rolled out of his bunk already on the wrong side.

His features were more offensive than his Garth Brooks T-shirt.

"What's up? Something wrong?"

"You're not gonna like this."

"What?" he asked, and lit a smoke. He took three drags in quick succession and ashed into a used red Solo cup, its contents of warm Diet Coke and chewing gum snuffing out the hot ambers—much like how this news would be snuffing out six more days of his life.

"WPW added more dates."

"No, they didn't."

Rubbing his eyes raw as Marges and Homers took a steady plunge toward his ankles, Todd pulled up his pants, tied them tighter than they needed to be, and then took a sip from the Solo cup that he had just ashed into. "You're messing with me."

"No, I'm not."

There was no sun outside, and if there had been, it'd be hesitant to say hello just then.

"It's no sweat off my back," Zach said, and handed Todd the notice. "But I'm kind of worried about Luke."

Reading with a soured expression, Todd asked, "Why?"

Unsure if their singer was on the bus, and unsure if what he was about to say was even accurate or true, Zach went down to a whisper. Critical creature speaking speculation. "I think he's doing more than just banging that chick . . . I think he's been popping pills again."

Todd grabbed an egg from the bus's mini-fridge, cracked it open, and poured its yolk into a fresh Solo cup. A dab of hot sauce, some black pepper and salt, and he lifted the hillbilly demitasse and swallowed the creation in one gulp.

"Dude!" Zach said, appalled. "What the hell was that?"

"What? You've never heard of a prairie oyster before? This hangover is killing me. And I only had two glasses of zinfandel last night!" Shook from this new dawn forced upon him, Todd's attention narrowed, anger subsided, and the faith in a brighter side to the morning prevailed. And then he remembered they were in Cincinnati. "I'm worried about Luke too," he admitted. "I swear, sometimes I think he's actually mentally challenged."

"Does he seem whacked out to you?"

"Always. But in what way do you mean?"

"I don't know. Something's off with him. Especially this past week. Dude looks high whenever I'm around him. And his voice sounds like shit too. He also had that pill thing a while back."

After getting clean, Zach had grown a new sense. A sober sense.

When you're sober, you're not fucked up.

And when you're not fucked up, you can see how other people act when they're fucked up.

They act fucked up.

Todd grunted in agreement with this rundown. "Should we ask him what's up? Like an intervention? Worked for you."

"I OD'd at a whorehouse. You guys didn't intervene in shit. Let me go talk to him, see what's good. The way this is going, I'm not sure he's even gonna make it another six shows. I think he legit fell asleep during our set yesterday."

"He did," Todd said, stubbing out his cigarette on the bus's gray carpet. "I saw it. But yeah—you should definitely be the one to talk to him. The guy hates whenever I say anything touchy."

Out of all the road warriors Zach had known through the years, Luke Strange—his best friend, his brother—was without question one of the toughest and most dependable you could find.

He was also one of the dumbest.

Like any improper lothario, Luke, on the tour's second stop

in Myrtle Beach, had struck up a sexual relationship with a female backup singer from another band on the tour, Louie Spritzer and the White-Hot Griddle Biscuits.

A swing revival act still riding high on their one and only hit from a decade prior, "Rise Rag An' Howl," the band continued to effortlessly surf that long, steady wave they had caught for themselves over a decade of touring nothing but states that ended in a vowel.

Heavy footsteps marching up their bus's stairs stifled any further findings.

Sounds of boots carrying the weight of the world would be Oscar, not Luke, and Oscar would indeed stroll down the front lounge of their tour bus, hair matted with sweat, and sit down on the couch next to Zach like a salamander on vacation. He smelled like compost and looked worse.

"Ahh, sken at these cunts! Still waiting around here, ain't ya? How goes it, Zak? And you?" He pointed at Todd. "What's yer name again?"

"Todd."

"Ah yes—smashing boobarse, ye are. Well, gents, another night, right? Bloody hell, my hip has been killing me too. Ain't fancy the ol' days, that's for sure." Detecting a tension from both Todd and Zach, he continued with an air of incertitude: "Now what r ye cunts moping about? Looks fancy the ol' lady just left ya for the dog walker!"

"We were talking about Luke," Zach said.

"Who's Luke?"

"Luke is the singer of our band. We think he might be getting high again."

"On what? Ahh, come on now, gentlemen, a little Colombian fire does smashing for the soul!"

Zach shook his head in annoyance. "Pills. He had a habit a couple years ago but kicked it. Could be the chick he's hanging with. One of the backup singers in Louie Spritzer and the White-Hot Griddle Biscuits."

"Louie's what?" Oscar asked, confused. "Dey serve cheeseburgers onstage? The bonk thinks up these shitty names?" He coughed up blood and spat onto the floor of their bus. "Is Duke fookin' up the shows?"

"It's *Luke*," Todd said. "And yes, he is. Haven't you heard him? Guy sounds like shit."

Oscar looked offended. And for good reason.

"Nah, blud, I haven't heard a second of yer set. Or any other band's set, come to that . . . I've heard it all, man. I'm done hearing." His response all too familiar, there was a clarity and character in his voice he'd never displayed before. "This is just a payday and a chance to get away from the missus."

"Gotcha," Zach said. "Well, yeah . . . He's been singing like ass and can barely last our whole set. It's been going on since the tour started. Dude almost passed out while he was singing last night."

Oscar scratched his chin and looked like he needed to fart. And then he did. "Drugs and women—always been my mole grip too. But hell, ain't that why we all started doing this anyways? Let me tell ye, laddie . . ." Archaic memories marched past his eyes, frosty but visible. "The broads I used to pull back in our day? Sweet bless . . . Now the only thing I pull is me back and me own trouser snake. But after a whilst that shizz gets old, ya know? Starts eating away at yer soul. Got to thinking about settling down. Found myself a noice quine who gave me my first poppet. Year later, I find out the bitch copped the porter of our building whilst I'm out playing some corporate gig to fashion execs in East London. I almost kicked her arse straight through the door of our flat! Haven't spoken to that wench in a year. She's been holding custody of me little laddie too. Wouldn't let me see him on his second birthday. But that's the life we chose, am I right? I started dating her sister instead."

Painful how right he was.

Before Oscar could go on further about his wife's adulterous tactics and his lack of parental duties, the attention of all was grabbed by the crunching of gravel and Luke's hurried footfalls outside the bus. Joining their sphere of terrific losses, he sauntered past Oscar as if he were a wax statue on loan and over to the mini-fridge, his NOFX T-shirt fresher than his face. "What's up, fuckers? Where's the OJ?" The fridge empty besides energy drinks and coffee creamer, Luke dug around for a couple seconds more until he realized that there was no orange juice and that the dude standing beside him wasn't made of wax. And wasn't in their band. "Oh shit, Oscar Thomson!"

"How dae yeh dae?"

"Dude," Luke spoke nervously, "I love Dusters Blunt! Been watching you guys play every night. My name is Luke." He extended his arm out for a handshake.

Oscar reciprocated the gesture with a braceleted wrist and four Navajo ringed fingers. "Noice to meet ya, chap. But from the sounds of it, seems fancy you been catching less sets than I 'ave . . . Hope you aren't catching anything else, brub."

Luke chuckled uneasily and gave Zach and Todd a cautious look, the dark bags under his eyes that of a cadaver. "Ha-ha. Guess I've been a little preoccupied recently."

"Is that what you ring up swallowing a bunch of pills and shoving yer willy in some lassie every night?"

Luke looked at Zach in shock. Zach looked at the floor. "Excuse me? I literally just met you. All I wanted was some orange juice."

A boozy reassurance flowed through Oscar's veins, and he pointed at Zach. "You might want to talk to yer laddie then. I wouldn't shoot the messenger."

Not sure whether to look at Oscar or Zach, Luke turned to Todd. "What's going on here?"

The cat was out of the bag.

"Dude," Todd began, "what the hell is going on with *you* man? You've been singing like shit every night, you always look like you just woke up from a three-hour nap, and you've been hanging with that chick from Louie's band nonstop. You legit fell asleep onstage last night."

The lid of Luke's left eye began to shut. An eyelash's length away from closing fully, he snapped to and drank a little coffee creamer. "You saw that?" he asked, ashamed but not surprised.

"Did I see it? Of course I saw it! I also heard it, seeing as your forehead hit the microphone."

"I remember pissing myself one time at a show in Hamburg," Oscar reminisced. "First couple of rows saw, but no one in the back could tell. Hell, just kept on playing!"

"Cool story."

"Oi now! Don't get smart with me, you little twat. I just met ya, too. Hold yer titties."

A skip in the soundtrack, Luke took this rift in emotions to sit down on the couch and procure the last cigarette from Zach's floating pack, lighting, lounging, and crossing his legs. "I'm just tired guys," he said truthfully, and the smoke only added authenticity to his claim. "Getting older too. This dude knows." He waved his cigarette toward Oscar. "And what are you going on about Rita for? You got that all twisted. She's studying to be a podiatrist. And her father is a pastor or some shit." He searched for a reassuring face and found none. "Fuck . . . you know what the road is like, guys! So yeah, maybe I take a little something from time to time. But come on! No one in this room has any right to judge. And *you* of all people," he said to Oscar, "lecturing me? You're drunk right now!"

"Oi! Listen here, laddie—yeh're the voice of the band. And

without its voice, ain't no one gonna 'ave a job for much longer. It ain't about ye and yer willie getting wet all the time. Get yer cack together, lad! Be a man!"

Zach jumped back into the deep end of this symposium with feet of bricks and a Ziploc bag tied around his head. "Luke, we love you. But whatever you're up to is seriously affecting your performances. And that, in turn, affects all of us."

Luke wiped at a booger with the inside of his T-shirt collar. It remained for all to see. "All right, all right," he said, the snot already crusting. "Rita is leaving the tour in three days to go back to Rutgers. Or Princeton. I forget . . . One of those Ivy League schools."

"I don't think Rutgers is an Iv—"

"So once Rita leaves, you're telling us you'll get your shit together?" Zach asked, blowing off Todd with a shotgun blast of termination. He needed Luke to confirm. "Is that what you're saying?"

"A hundred percent. Let me have this one last fling, and when she leaves, I'm back in the game. We're in Chicago tomorrow anyways, yeah? Right down the road. We should go to Pequod's!"

Todd, sick of Luke and ready to go back to sleep, laid down the final words on the matter. "Yeah, Pequod's . . . Listen, you're an adult. I think. But Zach is right—your performance affects everything and everyone. Just please be on the bus tomorrow an hour before our set. For my sanity, if nothing else . . . Please."

With a steadier gaze than earlier, Luke swallowed a stiff taste of affirmation and one last drop of creamer. "You have my word."

8

**TreadBrite Tires Chicago Summer Stage on the Lake
Chicago, IL
9/1/2005**

Capacity: 12,500
Tickets Sold: 7,003

Despite the air conditioner on their bus being broken at 59 degrees, Todd sweated as if he had a fever. He probed tensely the preliminary drawings of an early disaster: "What are the odds he shows up?"

Zach felt the need to deflate what little optimism there might have been left in the band's manager. "I honestly don't know," he said, a kombucha stain on his Neil Young *Rust Never Sleeps* tour T-shirt drawing more of his interest than the loss of all their jobs. He licked his fingers only to smudge the stain even more. "Luke is fucked up. I wouldn't hold anything past him."

On top of the disgusting state of the bus, this tour, and their lives, Zach's source of fire was also missing among the half-drunk water bottles and crusty fast-food wrappers littered about the stiff foundations that they were forced to refer to as "couches." He'd have rubbed two sticks together if necessary to smoke a cigarette, or light the bus on fire. "Who's got my lighter?"

Rusty sat cross-legged, puffing on a newly acquired corncob pipe and unable to sense the unrest all around him, and threw the lighter he stole from Zach back to him. "You know what, guys?" he pondered. "Maybe Luke needs to hit rock bottom . . . Maybe that dumbass needs to realize what he still has going for him." He picked a poppyseed out of his teeth with his tongue. "That chick he's banging is pretty hot, though."

Everyone agreed.

Worrisome sounds were heard as their rather old bus drove over even older potholes in the rear parking lot of the Tread-Brite Tires Chicago Summer Stage on the Lake. It reached its destination next to Dusters Blunt's white Prevost with the drippage of another disappointing morning tumbling from its tailpipe well after the ignition was turned off. His hands flexed and interlocked above his head, Todd creaked his back left and lit an apathetic fart in the reverse direction, a riptide of confluence that pulled the goners into its smelly grip. "Let's get some air in here. It smells like my ass."

Their icebox thus exposed to the elements of seasonal transformation, the blistering hot Chicago morning hit them like a 'roided-up Sosa–hit home run.

The doorway of their bus was blocked by the sudden appearance of a skinny white guy with a bat tattoo that covered most of his throat, a Smashing Pumpkins T-shirt, white Chuck Taylors, and a Chicago Cubs baseball cap. His once brown, now graying, hair trailed down like a succulent into the collar of his record-store-bought T-shirt, and his staggeringly tight skinny jeans scrunched up his nut sack into a yeasty dough folded over a time too many. Along with different-colored eyes, this guy was, by default, *that* dude who needed every living soul in the universe to know that he was *that* dude. He looked annoyed, as if he'd been waiting a long time for the elevator of a four-story building, and did his best to help usher across the heat in the darndest way possible.

"Hey, guys, my name is Charlie." Walking onto Texas Flip's bus without being invited, he asked, "Is there a Todd Shift here?"

Still in the same Simpsons pajama pants from the day prior, the band's manager sipped from a new container of orange juice that, like its predecessors, would never make its way back inside the mini-fridge. "Yeah, that's me. What's up?"

"Hi, Todd. I'm the vice president and cochairman from the midwestern division of promotion and marketing for World Professional Wrestling. Just wanted to introduce myself to y'all and thank you personally for being so communicative with everyone back at HQ during the tour. Enjoying your complimentary bottles of Nestlé water and cherry Laffy Taffy bars?"

Scratching his dick hard enough to scrape it, Todd said, "Yeah, they've been swell. How can I help you?"

"That's great to hear! Our dear friends at Nestlé love providing their products—free of charge—for all our artists, and World Professional Wrestling is very proud to have them as partners on the Rock of Cages tour!"

He resonated like a weatherman from California: speaking in safe, warm manners; informing all that it would be yet another day of partly cloudy sunshine. He felt pointless. His gaze turned anxiously back toward the front of the bus where Zach was standing and then to the back of the bus where

Todd was guarding the entrance to the bunk bed area, still scratching his dick. "I have received word that your singer, Luke Str—"

"What about him?" Todd cut him off.

"We got a call this morning from the manager of Louie Spritzer and the White-Hot Griddle Biscuits informing us that one of their backup singers, Rita Hilaria, was arrested late last night for public intoxication outside of the Art Institute of Chicago. The story I'm getting is that your singer, Luke Strange, whom she was also with, took a swing at one of the arresting officers."

"You're fucking kidding me."

"I'm afraid not. But before you freak out, there is some good news . . . The cop that he tried to punch, believe it or not, is actually a big fan of you guys and let Luke off the hook after he realized who he was. But they booked his girlfriend Rita."

"Wow," Todd said, surprised. "First I'm hearing of this."

"Gotcha. Then it might also be news to you that Mr. Strange then proceeded to trash the presidential suite at the Four Seasons immediately after this incident—a room that he charged to the World Professional Wrestling's house account. He was thrown out of the hotel by security shortly after."

"Stop it . . ."

"He isn't here with y'all now, is he?"

With the hand that had been firmly cupped to his balls now removed from his pajama pants, Todd gave the moist palm a deep whiff, a reflection of sorts, and then wiped away the last evening's fast-food remnants from his chin. The smell of his balls remained. "No, Luke is not currently with us . . . I just told you that this is the first I'm hearing of it. Thanks for informing me, though." He could have strangled a puppy just then. Instead, he strangled himself. "We're all just waking up, so if you wouldn't mind, could you give us a couple of minutes and let me get my head straight? Maybe try and figure out

Luke's whereabouts. In the meantime, you can show Rusty where we load in our gear. Appreciate it, buddy."

In the forty-three seconds that Zach had come to know Charlie, he had penned a chronicle that was no doubt closer to accurate than not: some dude who once played in a moderately successful local band—probably called A Last Beating Heartbeat, My Love—that had hopped in the van for a couple of tours through Nebraska, Montana, and South Dakota before breaking up after their drummer knocked up his girlfriend. Charlie had regrettably tasted what the life of being a touring musician was kind of like—this sample of ruin, however small, going on to make the next fifteen years of his existence longer than death.

Turning his hobby into his passion (always a mistake), these years of *that should have been me* envy would not surprisingly grind him down to powdered clay, and he would eventually ease off the dream and at long last "sell out" to the "man" by applying for a newly created position at a professional wrestling organization through backwater connections, becoming one of the few lucky dudes who could actually play the part of vice president and cochairman from the midwestern division of promotion and marketing on the Rock of Cages tour. A guy stuck in a character he had created for himself a decade prior, his unsureness in himself and his job title affected his ability to be comfortable around the talent. His whole identity had been built around a once imperishable love for music. Someone else's music.

And then he grew up.

Consequential life decisions fleshed out by the way lyrics in a song had once made him feel, Charlie was yet another victim of this falsified art form. Every breath he took reeked of diffidence. He was the opposite of a Police song.

"Can do," he said, "although we will need to discuss the Four Seasons hotel bill at some point. But we can talk about that stuff after your performance this afternoon. These kinds of things happen all the time! Rock and roll, am I right?"

"This *afternoon*?" Todd asked. "What are you talking about? My itinerary says six forty-five P.M."

Charlie's face contorted with discomfort, like he'd swallowed a bone from a fish. "Gotcha . . . There was a slight change in the day's schedule. No one told you?"

Todd placed his hand back inside his pajama pants and gave his nuts a good wiggle: a signal that no one had told him shit about anything.

"M'kay, I'll take that as a no. Sorry to be the bearer of bad news once again, but y'all are on at three twenty."

Retracting his hand from its warm safe space, Todd held a clammy middle finger and thumb to his temples and pointed with his other hand to the bus door with disgust. "Please leave."

Rusty gave Charlie a harsh slap on the shoulder. "How about you show me where the gear goes?" he suggested, and escorted him off the bus before this hole could be dug further.

The door still wide open, Todd shouted loud enough for all of Illinois to hear: "I can't believe this goddamn shit! Total amateurs on this tour! Everyone. Fucking morons!" Pacing the bus's lounge like a rodent trapped in a maze, his catwalk spoiled by Burger King bags and a scattered deck of Uno cards, the man was close to a stroke, or worse, more debt. "If Luke doesn't show up, we can't play. And if we can't play—"

"We don't get paid," Zach finished. "Yeah, we know how it goes. So how about rather than complain about it, we all instead try to figure out a solution?"

A Whopper wrapper stuck to his foot and clung to his toes for dear life. "You're right," Todd said, then speaking as if it were his idea all along, "We should start with the hotel, give them a call and see what happened. They might know where Luke went off to."

Outside the window of their bus stood Charlie, doing nothing to help Rusty with any of the gear. The air was humid, and the rush of work was replaced with the passiveness of acceptance. Zach opened the window and yelled over the sound of stagehands bolting and screwing together the wrestling ring, cage, and stage off in the background. "Yo! Any chance you have a number for the Four Seasons?"

"Actually," Charlie said, adjusting his hand to block the sun his hat failed to, "I do! It's on their invoice. Here you go." He produced the document from his front pocket.

Standing up to reach out the window, Zach stepped on a packet of honey mustard by accident; the gooey substance fired out like a Bliss–Leavitt Mark 8 torpedo and hit the bottom of Todd's pajama pants in defiant devastation. "Thanks," he said once the invoice was in hand, and kicked the packet away.

Todd dialed the number on his Motorola Razr.

After six minutes of trying to get through to a human, a pubescent-sounding kid broke the soft jazz on-hold music that played over the speakerphone in a monotone jelly. His voice sounded like warm bread.

"Hello, this is Jesse and thank you for calling the Four Seasons Hotel Chicago. How might I be of assistance?"

"Hey? Hello?"

"I can hear you. How might I be of assistance?"

"Oh, sorry, took me a while to get through to someone. Wanted to make sure I hadn't lost the connection."

"Is there something I can help you with?"

"Yes, there is. I'm calling to get in touch with a friend of mine who I believe is—err, was a guest in your hotel last night."

"*Was* a guest?"

"Well, yeah. He might have left recently."

"Name please."

"Mine or my friend's?"

"Your friend's. Why would I need your name?"

"Mike Rotch."

"Excuse me?"

"His name is Mike Rotch."

"My crotch?"

"No. Two names. Mike. Rotch."

"That's from *The Simpsons*. Is this a prank call? Listen, sir, I have a lobby filled with guests waiting to check in and half the Minnesota Twins tearing up the hotel bar with prostitutes. I don't have time for this."

"I'm sorry. His name is Luke Strange, but he usually checks in under the name Mike Rotch. He's a musician. Kinda famous."

"Never heard of him. And why didn't you say that in the beginning? Could have saved us both a lot of time."

"It's only been twenty seconds."

"Sir, please."

"He sings in the band Texas Flip. I am their manager, Todd Sh—"

"Never heard of them. Let me place you on a brief hold. Thanks."

Click.

In the "entertainment business"—a term people tend to forget is two words, not one—an artist must always remember that when the forces that be, those all-mighty individuals who decide it's time for you and your band to no longer matter and that your "art" is of no more value to their pocketbooks— when they finally determine that it is game over, then that's it. No questions asked. The stock of your importance sold like long positions during a margin call. Your clout purloined out from under you quicker than Aladdin's rug. You wake up one day conscious that this daydream you've been living, this fantasy, is now just a footnote to a story you weren't quite done reading. And now you've lost your place, the bookmark having fallen behind the bed, the first edition too precious to earmark —a hardcover for a paperback legend.

"Hello, sir, and thank you for holding. I have been informed that security escorted Mr. Strange out of the hotel a couple of hours ago. It's noted that he caused substantial damage to our presidential suite, and then when asked to leave, he refused and was subsequently dragged out of the hotel."

"Are you shitting me?"

"I'm afraid not, sir. I wasn't here when this all happened, but my coworkers tell me he was wearing nothing but a Phish T-shirt and a Four Seasons embroidered hand towel wrapped around his genitalia."

"Motherfucker . . ."

"Excuse me?"

"Sorry. Nothing. You're saying that was a couple of hours ago, yeah?"

"That's what I'm saying, sir, yes."

"Any idea where he might have gone? Did he say anything to anyone? Maybe the security guards on the way out?"

"Not that I'm aware of, sir. It sounds like he was pretty intoxicated, possibly upset about a woman. Happens all the time here. Might explain the hand towel thing. Not the Phish shirt."

"Appreciate the help." Flipping the phone closed hard enough to break its hinges, he shoved his palms into his eyes, breathed in through his nose, and cursed out his mouth. "The fuck we gonna do now? Luke doesn't have a cell phone and was last reported to be roaming the Magnificent Mile with a towel on his cock."

Keen to not let any more of this hot mess ruin an otherwise pleasant midwestern morning, Zach stood back up, peeked out the window, and lied. "I'm gonna go outside and help Rusty with some of the gear."

Rusty and Charlie hadn't left to load in any of the gear and stood in the parking lot side by side in that way strangers forced to converse at cocktail parties do. The looks on their face held the emotion of drywall, their tones cautious.

"Isn't Chicago beautiful in the summer?" Charlie commented. "I've been living here for the last six months and am such a fan of this time of year. The best."

Rusty spat on the ground and packed tobacco into his pipe. "If you've only been living here six months, then isn't this your first summer here?"

"Well, yeah . . . But it feels like I've lived here my entire life for some reason."

A nod to Zach as he parked himself next to the duo, pleased with some fresh blood, Rusty persevered out of pure boredom. "Where are you from originally?"

"A little town in Texas called Levelland."

"Know it well." Rusty spat again, closer to Charlie's foot than he would have probably preferred. "Zach, ain't that where they had the burger place you got sick from? Fuckin' guy was curled up, puking in a Costco bag of tortilla chips in the back of the van all night."

"Nah"—Zach's stomach gurgled—"that was Lubbock."

Three grown men standing around a parking lot in a circle jerk of poor choices, all could sense the impatience in the air how a dog senses where to shit.

"But yeah," Charlie said, "you guys can bring all your gear through this way. And," he asked with an awkward dip of his shoulder, "it's Crusty, right?"

"Just show me where to put the damn gear," Rusty said before ashing the hot coals from his pipe into his palm. "Let me know if you guys hear from Luke. I'll start setting up in the meantime."

The unease was too much to address and the sun's cancerous rays too much this early in the day, so Zach became eager once again for the bus's air-conditioning and Todd's irrational distrust of everyone around him. Back inside, Matthew and Rurik played each other in a game of Uno on the small front lounge table, the cards dirty from the bottoms of all their sneakers. A reverse Uno card was being played. The game's rules were lost on everyone.

Their manager, still in the same spot he had been when Zach left him, stood and watched CNN, contemplating all options and breathing heavily. He glanced at the watch he was now considering pawning on the South Side.

"Our set is in a couple of hours, and this band's lead singer was just dragged out of the Four Seasons with a dish rag on his cock, and I'm almost out of weed. Tell me how any of this ends well."

"A hand towel," Zach corrected. "Embroidered."

"Whatever it was, his dick is about to fuck our paychecks straight in the ass. What do we do if he doesn't show up?"

"He'll be here," Zach assured. "He'll be here."

Playing chess by himself later that afternoon, Zach was closest to the door when Charlie knocked and then entered once again without invitation. "Hey, guys!" He scanned the ceiling and floorboards as if Luke were there to be found. "Any word from the man in question?"

At the end of his rope, Todd did what he did better than everyone else in the band: lied. "He'll be here soon. I talked to him less than an hour ago. We're all good. Thanks."

Not entirely satiated with the plate of fabrication he was just served, Charlie burped up another question. "Great! So, he'll be here any minute then, right?"

"That's what I just said," Todd fibbed further. "Now if you'd excuse us, the band has some other matters that we need to discuss. In private."

"Sure thing. Then I'll leave you all to it. Excited to see Texas Flip rock Chicago today! Going to be a beautiful afternoon."

Rusty opened the bus door—"We can't wait either"—and motioned in a curt manner for Charlie to get off their bus. Todd held off till the coast was clear. "Soooooo, obviously that was a lie. But goddamn, what wouldn't I say to get that twat out of here?" Dropping to a murmur in case Charlie was snooping outside the window, he said, "I'm also going on the assumption that Luke isn't showing up. And if that's the case, then we need to prepare ourselves for the consequences."

"Couldn't we just play without him?" Matthew asked.

"Well," Todd said, "since he's the singer of the band, and nobody else here can sing worth shit, it probably wouldn't behoove us to do that. Oasis might have pulled it off, but you guys ain't Oasis. And Luke also happens to play b—"

"I can play his bass lines with my left hand," Rurik chimed in. "They're not that hard."

The opinions of hired hands like dogs that annoyingly pull too much, Todd capitulated like a bad owner, the real victims being everyone else. "Okay . . . But that still doesn't answer the question of who is going to sing. Luke might be an unreliable moron, but he knows how to sing somewhat on key."

Zoned out from yet another conversation about something beyond his control, the tap on the window behind Zach's head startled him. "Cunt!" Oscar yelled in an accent strong enough to cut an overcooked beef Wellington, his fist-sized bald spot soaking up as much vitamin D that it could. "Let me in!"

"Could you open the door?" Zach asked Rusty.

Like a sodden piece of chicken fried steak, Oscar stood motionless outside their doorway in a gravy of sweat, absorbing the inevitable four-step journey ahead of him with a meager reluctance. Grabbing a hold of the handrail Zach didn't even know was there, he placed his right foot onto the bus's first step like a newly wakened coma patient. A clear distrust in his efforts, he proceeded with this basic demonstration of flair to the best of his ability, grunting harder with each movement upward, his hips cracking to the rhythm of his heart, and if he had perished right there, no one would have blinked. "Why the fak . . . they make these . . . goddamn stairs . . . so *blooming* steep for? Cack's killing my hip!"

The top of this mountain summited, the man regained his serenity and, with the hesitance of someone already dead, hobbled his sack of bones into the bus's lounge. Plopping down onto the couch next to Zach, he crossed his right leg over his left and placed his left arm behind his buddy's neck, tugging his ear and blowing air into the other for the pure annoyance of life. Costumed in a black leather jacket, black leather pants, black leather vest, and a white button-down shirt opened halfway down his chest, he looked and smelled like a spoiled eggplant.

"Dickey bird on the street is yer laddie hasn't showed up yet. What ye bonks going to dae?"

"We actually haven't gotten that far yet," Todd replied. "Maybe you have some suggestions we haven't thought of?"

"I can sing for ye chaps," he suggested back, smacking his lips like a grandfather chewing an old piece of gum.

Zach, momentarily distracted by the singular hair that stuck out from Oscar's right nostril like a black candlewick, asked, "Do you know any of our songs?" unsure if he himself even knew all the words to their songs.

"No. But how hard can they be if your moron singer does?"

Hit with a wave of interest and a second wave of desperation, Todd said, "Hold that thought," and jolted off the bus, returning before Oscar could finish bumming a cigarette from Zach. In his hand was a copy of Texas Flip's *Greatest Hits*. He pushed the CD into Oscar's face.

"Here."

Oscar's knuckles crunched loudly as he took the plastic CD case, flipping it over and around. "You hae a greatest hits record? I honestly never even heard of you chaps till we started this tour."

The band, having had only two of what could be considered "hits," should never have been scheduled for a career milestone such as a greatest hits record, but working the loophole that had been so widely exposed to them, they had shut their mouths and went along with the game plan anyways.

Another dupe of commerce for the labels, a greatest hits album used to be an assured way to wring out yet more money from a record-buying public. Released in conjunction with the holidays or the celebration of a band's finality, a greatest hits CD was akin to receiving a Rolex after twenty years on the force or a Grammy nomination. An honor for those who deserved it. Not Texas Flip.

Yet since both of their "hits" were from two different records and since they'd released multiple albums after said successes, Mountain View Records felt gracious enough to throw the band a bone and release a *Greatest Hits* anyways, as it would cost no money and only generate more income. The record had also been optioned in their original contract, so in a way, they were kind of owed it.

Other than "Fake News" and "Sight Glass," the rest of the tracks that made up this collection of compost were remixes of the *Mean Smiles* EP, unreleased tunes, and demo versions of most of their Mountain View Records debut, *Friday Night Friends*. Released months prior to the Rock of Cages tour, the album did, however, kill two birds with one stone: it fulfilled the final album of their contract and pushed the group's name forward one last time before it fell off a cliff.

"There's only nine tunes on it," Todd told Oscar. "If you

can learn them in the next couple of hours, we might be able to pull this off. All of the lyrics are in the CD booklet."

"*Christ!* My eyes are shite! How dae ye expect me to be able to read those tottie arse words?" the craggy singer pleaded, squinting at the size 5 font with pupils dilated the size of nickels. "Aye . . . alreet"—he gave Zach a noogie—"let me give her a spin and see what I can fancy up. Gonna be fun flexing the olde pipes, tussling around with some of ye youngins! I'll see ya cunts in a tad, aye." He handed Todd a red Solo cup filled with Canadian Club, Diet Coke, and visible saliva and, stretching out his mangled lower back, walked off with a nod of his head.

"Is that dude *always* drunk?" Todd questioned. "Doesn't matter. Do you think he can actually do this?"

"I mean, the dude is a singer," Zach said. "But I've watched him screw up the lyrics for the same song at least five times on this tour already, so who knows . . ."

"Well, if Luke doesn't show, we literally have no other alternative."

Extending a branch of optimism covered in thorns and lubricated with castor oil, Zach said, "This will work out, guys. We'll be fine."

~

One hour later, and no Luke.

Or Oscar.

Interrupting their game of *NHL 2004* on Xbox, an anxious Charlie, now sporting a Chicago Blackhawks hat and a Wilco T-shirt, once again made his presence known like a bunion on the first day of vacation. "Hey, guys. Where's Luke?"

Todd, the first to react, sat up straight as a board, dropping his controller and Jaromír Jágr's breakaway. "Oh, you didn't see him? Yeah, he was just here . . . I think he went to take a jog or something," he lied, tossing the verbal grenade sans its pin. "Isn't that right, Zach?

"Uhhhh, yeah," their guitarist also lied, the puck gliding into Martin Brodeur's control, the red of his team's jerseys the color of his face. "Something about going for a run over by Millennium Park, I think."

"Millennium Park?!" Charlie yelled. "You go on in an hour, and your lead singer is taking a jog around Chicago? Are you joking? This is a joke, right?"

"It's all good," Todd assured. "He's probably on his way back right now. But if you wouldn't mind, it's time for our preshow band prayer. Sorry, but no outsiders allowed."

"Your *what*? Listen, guys, I need to know what the *fuck* is going on here, right now. Is Luke a no-show?" The anger rising in his voice akin to water beginning to boil, Charlie's manner shifted as soon as business was discussed: "You do know the stipulations of your contract if you miss a performance, right? You are *also* aware that your management begged us to include you on this tour, right?"

"Charlie!" Oscar's voice squeaked through the bus cabin. "My smashing flop! Please, all is well."

Turning in the direction of this newest accent, Charlie widened his eyes in surprise. "Oscar? What are you doing here? You're supposed to be at the radio tent doing press right now."

"Oh, bang! That's today, isn't it? Shite, my bad, mucca. Hard to keep track of everything, ya know?"

Charlie's head turned around like an owl's. "Am I missing something here?"

"What? These buggers didn't tell you? I'm singing for them 'cause their singer can't keep his cock out of some floozy." He threw a friendly elbow into Charlie's rib cage. "He been riding the rails, if ye know what I mean."

"What?!" Charlie yelled. "You're saying Luke isn't showing up?"

Opening one of the many boxes of day-old chicken nuggets and eating its sole remnant with crusty ketchup, Todd spoke through mangled poultry and sugary sauce. "Yeah, see, the thing is—"

"What's the big deal, gents?" Oscar burped into the side of Charlie's face. "I can sing better than that momo anyways. Nothing to worry about, chap."

"Oscar can't sing for you!" Charlie's tantrum escalated. "He's not in your band! The contract you signed states that Texas Flip is to perform, not Texas Flip and Friends. This isn't some hippie jam-band circuit!"

"Ay! Chill the fook out, mate. Who got yer panties all bunched up, eh? None of those idiots out there will even suss I'm not the singer of the band. Lighten up."

"We really have no other choice," Todd added, "because my watch says we have to be on that stage soon. I gave Oscar a CD of songs with all the lyrics, and he's been practicing them for the last hour"—Todd glanced at Oscar with a hopeful look in his eyes—"haven't you?"

Another burp and pat of the belly. "Yep. Sure have." Oscar lied better than Todd and Zach ever could. He slapped Charlie on the back loud enough to know it would bruise. "Let's get this show on the road, shall we, gents?"

"I don't know about this," Charlie said. "I need to run it past the higher-ups. I don't think they're gonna let it fly."

"You go and dae that, and we'll get ourselves a-going to put on a stonking show. Carry on now, buddy. Orff you go."

"Shit, guys," Charlie whined from outside the bus like a kid picked last for dodgeball. "Why are you doing this to me?"

Oscar slammed the door in his face and locked it. "My god, what a blooming twat he is, 'm I right?"

"How are you feeling about the tunes?" Zach asked their newest lead singer, the strap of his cherry-red Les Paul Standard hanging heavy on his shoulder blade. The hunk of wood was the root cause of a decade-long chronic nerve pain that ran down his left shoulder and into his pinkie; the discomfort was at least familiar and predictable, unlike their yet-to-be-performed set.

"Eh, pretty good, mate." Oscar laughed, cementing in everyone's head that he had given each tune at most one spin. If they were lucky, he might have even read the lyric sheet. "How much time we got?"

"Not long," Rusty said.

"Righty-oh. Well, let's hae a drink then, shan't we?" He raised a fresh red Solo cup. "To Luke and to Charlie and to every blinking boink who thought they couldn't get things done, because that's what matters most. Doing the things that need to be said and saying the things that need to be done. But first most and so on, let it be whispered lastly that all things come, and bad things stay for mint. So, to that, and to Cincinnati!"

"We're in Chicago," Todd corrected. "We were in Cincinnati yesterday. How fucked up are you?"

"That's . . . why, yes, Rodd . . . Don't mind that. Let's just, alreet, let's dae this . . . Mitts in!"

Stuck in that weird interval between morning and evening and grasping for any crumb of reason to schlep their asses up onstage to survive uncertainty in front of a ravaged pack of hammered hyenas for the next fifty minutes, all hands in was the only option if they wanted any chance of getting paid. Together like an unprepared army walking into a battle of vague outcome—Napoléon at Waterloo, Hitler on the Eastern Front—this formation of Texas Flip marched off the bus, traipsed through a field of cables, staff, and directionless musicians looking for the free beer tent, and arrived at the bottom of stage right with little time to spare. They could hear the hum on the other side of the fence that protected the backstage area from a sea of drunk rednecks.

Oscar tripped up the stairs.

"Let's dae this, ye cunts!"

Before Zach knew it, they were plugged in and standing in front of four thousand sunburned examples of all the reasons to hate America.

"Are you ready to rock, Cincinnati?!" Oscar screamed into the microphone.

The next fifty minutes proceeded to be the longest fifty minutes, in the worst of ways, of Zach's entire existence.

Holding up the CD lyric booklet in front of his face their entire set, Oscar stuttered confusedly through every song and scratched his ass no less than thirty-one times, his anus begging for forgiveness the way the crowd begged for it to end. His back turned to the audience for most of their performance, shielding him from the sunlit visual of disappointment and perplexity in the crowd, Zach mostly fiddled with the knobs and buttons on his Marshall JCM2000 DSL100 amp until he ran out of combinations to keep pretending and then intentionally popped his low E-string with his pick, trying his hardest to give off the impression that this whole charade was nothing but one big technical difficulty, or, at worst, the end of their career. While wrapping up this shitshow, the crowd dissipated in a steady flow between each tune, and Zach's shame in his incinerated soul nearly caused him to put down his guitar and leave for the bathrooms with them.

And then he looked to the side of the stage.

And then he saw Luke.

Arms folded across his torso, the singer stared the guitarist down with the look of Lucifer woken up early on a Sunday. The booing twenty feet away was an ideal soundtrack for the look of disbelief in his eyes, and from fear more than anything else, Zach mechanically shot his gaze back at the heckling spectators, praying Biggie was right and that this *was* all a dream.

It wasn't.

And by the time they finished that last song, half the audience had left.

As had Luke.

"I think that went alreet, aye?" Oscar addressed the band at the bottom of the stairs behind the stage.

"Oscar, you started singing they lyrics to 'Billie Jean' during the first song," Matthew said angrily.

"Hold it now there, sonny lad! Where'd you even come from?"

"I'm the fucking drummer!"

"Listen, I did ye chaps an effing favor. Don't get all pissy because it wasn't my most stellar performance!"

"Did anyone else see Luke?" Zach came running up to the group frantically. "He was standing on the side of the stage but bounced."

Todd was nowhere in sight.

Over Oscar's shoulder, he could measure Charlie fifteen yards away, approaching them with the caution of a BASE jumper without his wingsuit. Stepping in between himself and Matthew, Charlie's eyes spindled an emotion his words were incapable of. The weighty look of dissatisfaction he wore said more than what he was about to.

"I gotta be honest, guys . . . I really don't even know what to say right now. I mean, I want to be angry. But, like, truthfully?"

"Fuck off, Charlie."

Biting his lip to keep from spilling out laughter, he said, "I'm sorry, I am. But that was *truly* one of the worst things I've ever seen in my life. It was so bad, it's hard for me to even be upset with you guys. I mean . . . y'all managed to get two-thousand-plus people to stand up out of their seats and walk away . . . They were sitting. In seats. Do you know how comfortable it is to be seated at a concert?"

Zach held his hand up to Charlie's face to stop. He should have slapped him. "Charlie, please. Not now with any of this shit."

"Yeah. Yeah, okay. I get it." He continued the conversation with himself as he walked away from them and back to the production trailer: "Take all the time you guys need."

It was then that Todd arrived.

"Did you see Luke?" Zach asked him.

"I did."

"Great. Where is he now?"

"Heading to Minneapolis."

"What?"

"He's heading to Minneapolis," Todd said again. "I'm assuming by airplane."

"What are you talking about?"

"Well, Luke got here in time for the set. You guys went onstage seven minutes early, is all. My watch was wrong."

"Fuck . . ."

"*Fuck* is right. Luke flipped his shit when he saw Oscar up there. I had to hold him back from running out and choking him to death with the mic cable."

"Puhhhh—I'd fancy to see that slimy floop sucker try!"

"Why is he going to Minneapolis?"

"Because he's a Prince fan? Hell I know. Why would anyone go to Minneapolis? Doesn't his mom live there?"

"She does."

Silence.

"Shit . . ."

"*Shit* is right."

"So, what do we do?"

"I don't know."

"I know what you guys can do," Charlie said, back again

and standing too close. "You can pack your bags and head home, because you've been kicked off the tour."

"Excuse me?" Todd asked.

"Eileen from artist relations—she was going to let this whole farce slide. That was until your actual singer stormed into the production trailer and threatened her because he thought she was part of some grand plot to screw him over and have him replaced by Oscar. You guys know you went on seven minutes early, right?"

"Oi! That lad must be on some damn smashing shizz!"

"So, I'm here to tell you, ahead of Eileen telling you, that this stunt was indubitably in breach of your contract, and since that's the case, WPW must unfortunately expel Texas Flip from the Rock of Cages tour."

Todd's jaw nearly hit the floor. It didn't because his shoes were in the way. "You're shitting me."

"I can assure you the only *shit* involved is the one I will be taking in the bathroom once this conversation is finished. Any other questions can be directed to HQ. Sorry it had to end this way, guys." He looked back toward his work pod. "And if you can also offload any unused Nestlé products from your bus and bring them over to that production trailer, right over there, that would be great. Safe travels home!" he yelled as he climbed into a golf cart parked ten feet away and slammed his foot on the accelerator, spraying up grass and mud in a vegetative discharge.

Looking on in disbelief at ending on the same flat note they had started this all off with, Zach was sad, confused, and, primarily, hungry. So, with little hope for the future and no submitting to the past, he set his sights on the only comfort the Rock of Cages tour had provided all along: leftover Burger King on their bus.

The honey mustard on Todd's pajama pants would have to suffice.

9

Japan ROCKS! Festival
Hokuto, Yamanashi Prefecture, Japan
8/13/2008

Capacity: 40,000
Tickets Sold: 28,469

rritated from a summer of Asian rock festivals with no weed to smoke and a hemorrhoid more persistent than a bedbug outbreak, Todd, like usual, was in a bad mood.

"Where is my Pellegrino? Did you see where it went? It was here a minute ago. Why is it my crap and no one else's that always goes missing? I turn around for one second, and poof, something else is gone. Every time! Do I need to just never take my eyes off anything? Ever? Seriously . . . What the fuck?"

Mount Fuji flaunted its grandeur off in the distance, but

the beauty of the world did little to settle Todd's temper back-stage at the Japan ROCKS! Festival, and Zach's arsehole was red like the Japanese flag.

"Can you shut your damn mouth for the love of my sanity already? This place is filled with free water bottles, and you're losing it over a warm Pellegrino you lost?"

The two were supposed to be taking a break from the Asian-Pacific heat and the rest of the band, but that plan had failed. The sun's warmth had turned the Poland Spring Artist Village tent into a noxious goop, pounds of water weight lost in sweat and anxiety constituting the majority of Zach's Genesis T-shirt, and Todd's complaints were out of touch and imbalanced, tickling the wrong funny bone and wrong hemorrhoid. "How do you know *I* lost it?" he asked. "How do you know someone working here didn't throw it out? Maybe someone working here threw it out because it *wasn't* a Poland Spring water bottle. Ever think about that, Columbo?"

Perspiration dripped from his forehead and from his armpits onto the weathered copy of *Sabbath's Theater* in his hands, and the war of botheration raging inside Zach's flesh all morning would require a third change of scenery if he were to survive the rest of this day, let alone the rest of this tour. "I'm going outside."

A lingering ACL pain doing its utmost to remind him that age forty was right around the corner, he stood himself up from the wooden lounge chair filled with cheap one-inch padding he had hoped would be his home for the expectable future and snagged a bottle of Poland Spring from a mini-fridge that sat atop a large table covered in a promotional banner, before endeavoring out into the humidity for another smoke and better look at what everyone who worked here kept referring to as Fuji-san.

Only in Japan for six hours, he already wanted to leave.

His beefy tits and perpetually sweaty ass crack enjoying

most of his insecurities, Zach pulled out his second-to-last cigarette and turned around to face the American-sponsored/Japanese-run monstrosity that blocked the only view of the one positive feature this seventeen-hour stop on their tour had to offer: a private observation of Japan's highest volcano. The 12,389-foot peak was hidden behind a tent the size of a Home Depot; it was this trade-off of aesthetic for luxury one tolerated when most in need or when least deserved. These tents, or what promoters might label as a "village," were numerous in their appearance backstage at most any major music festival with a ticket price over sixty-five dollars and nine different headliners. Enough metal framing to house half of Florida's homeless population—they were an essential measure to a constant demand: privacy for the talent.

These tents were also where bands who didn't help to sell any tickets spent all their time before their set. And, in most cases, after their set too. A haven for smaller acts on their way up to hang and shoot the shit with other established, midsized groups on the bill; many multiple hours of life would be allocated to doing absolutely nothing inside these communal grounds other than getting drunk, getting high, and maybe getting laid on another band's bus. And that's because those fans in the field who paid good money for tickets weren't here for them.

Unless you were one of the festival's bigger names, from the moment your band arrived till the moment you left, your day consisted wholly of subpar catering, conversations with people you didn't know (and wouldn't meet again), and more than enough time to read that book you started at the beginning of the tour but were only twenty-three pages through a month later. The morning's coffee still coating your throat, you'd hit on some girl who "fucked Tommy Lee once" but had never heard of your band, and then you played your set—a set that was never longer than forty minutes and almost always the same—to an under-enthused crowd, drunk at 11:00 A.M., sitting on lawn chairs, blankets, or each other; a crowd who promised themselves they remembered your band, even grabbed a free sticker, but would forget you the moment the next one took the stage. Hanging around behind the gates and mucking it up with the rest of the untalented yet "semifamous" morons who had also managed to land a record deal and a 2:30 P.M. slot—everyone getting wasted off double IPAs from the tap well after the final aftershocks of the night have rung out—your band becomes the thirteenth floor of a building: there but not there. The normality of an anomaly. How it's supposed to be.

But what happens when against every right move and false trail, your band becomes one of those acts at the festival that people "used to come see"? That band people feel fine telling their buddies they saw even if it was from the comforts of a picnic table half a mile away from the stage? A nitty-gritty example of what the business was really about: this display of significance, a totem pole indicating a band's rank crucial in keeping the grades correct. Crucial because where a band landed on the day's schedule flagrantly showcased their ability to sell tickets. And a band's ability to sell tickets is the only thing that will ever matter.

Never forget that.

The music business is the money business. One dirty hand washing the other. And as it's always more fun to start at the bottom where the dust settles and the shit rolls down to, let us go ahead and introduce the lower class of this pecking order first: a space where up-and-coming bands reign supreme in a land most people know not a damn thing about, playing when doors have just opened and participants are still cultivating their pre-afternoon buzz.

These bands roam the festival grounds freely after sets with laminated all-access passes hanging by lanyards around their necks, starry-eyed at all their little group from Bakersfield has accomplished. Of these bands, 96 percent are living in a twilight zone of insignificance and will never be heard from again. The ones who remain after this necessary purge (out of a need for progress of the art form) might sneak through the veil in mediocre ways, maybe scoring a minor hit or a song placement in a video game, pursuing the dream long enough that people eventually give them a chance at making a living. A minuscule carrot on the end of an invisible stick keeps them going as the rest of the heap naturally break up, acquire jobs at Trader Joe's, and reminisce with coworkers about that time their band played the side stage on the Vans Warped Tour for five dates. The view from the bottom might look sad from a long way off. But if one can stand the wait, the boredom, and the guaranteed failures in a life of playing live music for a living, then maybe the view from the top might be worth it.

To some.

Boring like a dude who still wears his college sweatshirt seventeen years after graduation, the real meat of any festival bill beyond these low-level entertainers and rookie all-stars is a doggie bag full of bands that have either seated themselves in the public consciousness during recent times or acts past their sell-by date, skiing down an avalanche of forgetfulness, unable to stop the backward momentum of their once-lauded repute. A way to fill up space and justify the steep ticket price, these bodies and songs satisfy the vacuum of attention in between pizza and red wine drunk in plastic cups, fulfilling a purpose how duct tape fixes a leak. The sounds emanating from the stage on an early Saturday afternoon, weaving in and out of coherence, are all just background accompaniment to patrons walking from entrance gates to friend groups they won't find for another hour. Never a point of focus, but never not needed. Who else would concertgoers have to make fun of until their favorite band came on at 7:45 P.M.?

For the briefest of moments, Texas Flip had once balanced atop this totem pole. But be that as it may, gravity, like death and taxes, was a surefire bet, dragging down their name (and skin) line by line on the festival poster until even Zach had trouble reading it from a few feet away. The "cookie-crumbling" flavor an acquired taste for people with no taste, the rosiness of survival smelled foul and, as usual, had been served to them in a double dose. Wasn't it a pity? Their set time for the second day of the three-day Japan ROCKS! Festival was at 2:45 P.M., and that meant they had to arrive at the festival around 10:00 A.M. to load in their gear, set it up (with no sound check), and then hang around backstage doing nothing till their allotted performance time. No shock there.

Sad thing was, if this had been seven years earlier, the band could have been caught lounging around at their hotel, sipping beers and watching PGA golf highlights at the bar till they had to load into a passenger van, their equipment having been set up hours earlier, and be driven to the festival grounds by some nameless runner who only took the job for a free backstage pass and maybe a chance to pass his demo off to Thom Yorke.

Shame the future hadn't bothered to wait up for them.

"Dude, I can't believe Cat vs. Duck is headlining tonight! And we get to see them! Did you see their new video? It's so sick."

Blaine Robat was the group's third pianist and annoyed everyone he met the way sand gets into everything. He'd joined immediately after Rurik quit the band following the Rock of Cages tour and had been a member of Texas Flip for five touring cycles by the time they had reached the shores of Japan. Blaine had been introduced to them through some mutual friends during an open audition they held at their rehearsal studio in Ozone Park. One of three serious contestants who had tried out, and in a crunch to have literally anyone fill the spot, Blaine played their songs well enough and didn't irritate Zach and Luke initially—all that was needed to win him the gig.

Fools once again.

"No," Zach said, stubbing his cigarette out in a dry patch of grass. "I haven't seen their video. I don't own a TV."

"Yeah, man, it's something else! Think we'll make a video like that soon?" Observing the pack outlined in Zach's front pocket, he couldn't bother waiting for a response. "Mind if I bum one? I only have two left."

The pack of smokes moister than his chafed inner thighs, Zach took stock of his last heater after giving one to his bandmate and tried to remember why he had picked up the habit again after a year off. Then he looked at Blaine.

They took in life together through carcinogenic inhales, and the kid, despite all warnings to the contrary, kept at it. "This is crazy. I can't believe we're in Japan! I never thought this band was that popular." O-rings of smoke propelled from his pierced lips—black hoops that rested in both corners of his mouth begging to be caught on a shirtsleeve or pillowcase. The long blond hair resting on his bony shoulders was unbothered by the wavering wind. His smoke held more movement. "You can see Mount Everest right behind the tent too!" He outlined its peak with his cigarette.

Wishing he were in Hiroshima at the end of the war, Zach corrected him. "That's Mount Fuji."

"Mount Fuji? Nah, bro, I'm pretty sure it's Mount Everest. Mount Fuji is in Cambodia or some shit."

"You couldn't be more wrong. That's Mount Fuji. Mount Everest is on the border of China and Nepal."

"Nepal? That's a country? Whoa . . . Anyways, I think you're still wrong."

Blaine's mannerisms attached themselves to the headache

Zach had been rocking since they landed at Haneda Airport only hours before. Life felt painful. Being alive seemed wrong. "I'm right. You're wrong. Please stop talking."

"Wrong?" Blaine asked, and sucked harder on his free cigarette. "What makes you so sure, Christopher Columbus? How do you know I didn't major in geography at college?"

Wanting nothing more than to rip both lip rings from out of his face and force him to swallow the repulsive metallic loops, Zach took control of his emotions before responding. He thanked Happy Hills Recovery. "Because I know you are wrong. If you had majored in geography, you'd know that you were wrong too. And you wouldn't be in this band. Why are we still talking about this?" An exit from this conversation was needed. Turning hard on his verbal steering wheel, he took the next off-ramp. "I gotta start warming up."

A Gibson Les Paul Special Tribute P-90 served as his main ax for this current tour across the world. Intimate in his hands, the strings were dull and unworkable, and Zach relocated himself into a corner of Texas Flip's trailer and began to stretch out the cramped, pre-rheumatic fingers that he would be paying the toll for soon enough. The knuckles of each index creaking and cracking in ways that concerned him more than amused, he swallowed the fact that more amicable days were behind him than would be in front. Strategy his strength, what it came down to was this: if one were talking years and ages prior, Zach would have been well into his fourth hour of practice for the day. Charts and scales, verses and outros, closed voicings and inversions—a sandbox filled with guitars, beer, joints, and precious time—treasured moments he had fallen out of love with long ago. The short warm-ups of his days now were noodling Mike Bloomfield and Jeff Beck riffs fifteen minutes before they got onstage and hoping he had wiped his ass well enough. Gone were the weeks and months lost to better understanding an instrument, an art form. The lessons of financial ruin and conclusions drawn about the back nine of life were more up front and forward, and his putter was broken.

The previous day they had been in Kuala Lumpur—a set played to 2,300 sober Muslims at 1:30 in the afternoon. Then a fifteen-hour journey complete with an eight-hour layover in Hong Kong: a blur of airline pretzels, cocktail napkins, and stingy servings of soda on melting ice. Rumors heard earlier in the day about possible thunderstorms seemed an accurate forecast as thick dark clouds covered their arrival in the Land of the Rising Sun. Landing through deep mists and low mountain ranges, Texas Flip's touchdown was greeted as warmly as a Hot Pocket bitten too early. The ten pounds of sweat Zach had lost in the last week had begun to affect his ability to give a shit about anything or anyone. A shuttle from the airport to a field hours west of Tokyo provided him his best block of sleep in weeks. Then the band settled into common surroundings backstage, he into another couch. The morning turned into that sticky pocket of time right before noon, and it was only luck that they had arrived early enough for the food being served: breakfast burritos. The assemblage of workers behind the scenes came to life as those who were paid to be concerned became increasingly worried about the impending doom seen in the sky, checking the AccuWeather reports on their computers every four minutes. The bottom-barrel apple juice provided in catering held a sour a taste. Like rotten sauerkraut. Like flat lime seltzer. Quenching as sodium.

Mustiness and ass sweat the flavor of the day, the appearance of a very short Japanese woman in their trailer, without any knock or forewarning, was worrying to those with a propensity to concern. Mainly Todd. Therefore, she marched up to Luke to avoid any politeness.

"You guys are Texas Flip, right?"

Thinking on his feet for once, Luke replied, "That is what the sign on the door you just blasted open says, right?"

"My name is Misato, and I'm the talent manager for the Japan ROCKS! Festival. We're getting word that the forecast is calling for heavy wind and possible thunderstorms, and by the looks of the sky, that seems like a pretty safe assessment."

Out the trailer window, Zach could see branches breaking off trees, whipping through the air like lost scenes from *The Wizard of Oz*. Perhaps worried the band might freak out over her meteorological report, or that maybe they were out of Poland Spring water bottles, her tone mellowed. "You guys should be all right, though, so long as the stage and your equipment don't get wet."

"You're telling us there is going to be high winds, heavy rain, and possible lightning, but we'll be all right so long as the stage and our equipment avoid getting soaked by an oncoming monsoon?" Todd asked.

"Are you their manager?"

"What the hell does that matter?"

"Yes. That's what I'm saying." She grabbed a bottle of Poland Spring from their mini-fridge, cracked open the plastic top with difficulty, and dribbled a little on her chin with an ill-aimed sip. "I'll be back if any major developments happen. If not, then it will be business as usual, and your set will be at its original scheduled time. Thanks for your patience and coop-eration."

The wind's force on the other side of the door keeping it shut, Misato had trouble upon her exit, which troubled Todd even more. He opened the door for her, peering his head up and shaking it. "Yep, looks fucked . . . Thanks, Misato."

"Is it that bad?" Zach asked, unplugging his guitar and laying it upright with the neck rested between the edge of a chair and the edge of a table.

Like a high school soccer coach on the last day of a losing

season, Todd did his best to pull it back together for one more go at it. "Yes. But listen, we're on in thirty minutes and only need to play for thirty-five minutes. There's no way it can get that bad by then." Cracking his neck to show he was serious and not because he needed to crack his neck, he added, "It should also go without saying that we need this paycheck . . . The show tonight is not even close to being sold out."

To make the most of a two-month-long expedition through the majority of Asia, Felicia had booked the band various club dates in between festival dates, sometimes on the same night. As Texas Flip almost always played before 3:00 P.M., this was a generally easy task to pull off, and tonight they were booked for a show in Tokyo at Club Quattro, a 350-capacity room in the Yakuza-run Kabukichō district.

"I don't care if it starts hailing bullets," Todd spoke through gritted dental work. "You guys stay on that stage. If we cut the set short by even a minute, they'll negate our guarantee."

"For fuck's sake," Zach said. "We get it."

Written out on three separate pieces of paper towel, a set list Zach had drafted minutes prior was handed out, and as usual, Luke didn't like the opening song.

"You sure we should open with 'Chocolate Toothpaste'? I think it's too slow for an opener. Might put people to sleep."

"'Put people to sleep'? They opened the gates an hour ago. And we've started with that tune before anyways. It always got a good response."

Licking his thumb to smudge some dirt from his Dr. Martens—the boots already a dark brown, the grime only improving the ugly things—Blaine asked, "'Chocolate Tooth-paste' is in B flat major, right?"

Todd stopped this foolishness with little care. "No time to argue, guys. And, Luke, please make sure you remember to thank Red Dragon Entertainment when you're up there."

"Who?"

"Seriously?"

Silence.

"Red Dragon Entertainment are the ones putting on this festival."

Luke nodded his head in agreement. "Right on, right on."

Red Dragon Entertainment was the promotional vehicle behind the Japan ROCKS! Festival and the Asian partner of Texas Flip's booking agency, Beaten Path Touring.

Seven years previous, Red Dragon Entertainment was working with the mildly popular Japanese heavy metal band Death by Sushi around the same time Texas Flip was hitting their own peak in popularity and could still provide a positive impact on spillover audiences around the country. After scoring a surprise crossover hit with their song "猫と一緒につかむ," or "Neko to issho ni tsukamu" (more commonly translated to "Grab Them with a Cat"), Death by Sushi were set to start a nationwide tour in the States—the band's first time overseas and first time playing to people who didn't speak their native language. Luck on their side, this same song would also be included in the soundtrack for the American-made movie *Deep in the Grass*, which would make its premiere during the band's run. A bomb in the box office, and total piece of crap overall, the film became immortalized when, by more dumb luck, it was parodied by a Japanese pornography company in its motion picture お尻の奥深く, or *O shiri no okufukaku* (more commonly translated to "Deep in the Ass"), a movie that would also feature a Death by Sushi song in the soundtrack.

Slipshod amateurish work on their end, or perhaps destiny, Death by Sushi's management was unable to secure the proper American work visas for the band in time and was forced to cancel their entire tour just days before the first date. Red Dragon Entertainment—terrified at the prospect of losing all that easy money and leaving a bitter taste in the mouths of numerous concert halls around the country—reached out to Felicia, who in turn reached out to Texas Flip and asked if they could help Red Dragon Entertainment with a couple of East Coast dates that were gaining interest on its books. The timing for the band none more perfect, as they were in between a record cycle, they took this chance to wipe the dust off some of the old tunes (and some old times) and announced the shows via their mailing list. The gigs a total surprise to their fans, they sold out within days of being put on sale and saved Red Dragon Entertainment a huge embarrassment.

Now, they had pulled that timeworn favor from out their pocket seven years later like a $500 casino chip found after doing laundry. This also helped to explain how a once popular band ended up in a foreign country, playing to a one-third capacity audience on the main stage in the afternoon, with only breakfast burritos in their stomachs.

Their trailer thirty feet from the stage right entrance—a dicey trek through jungles of thick audio cables and battery-powered golf carts and almost no speakers of the English language—there was no way they could back out now unless lightning was gracious enough to strike them before they reached the rear stairs. Flighty thoughts lost in tenebrous clouds, the band climbed the rickety stepladder to the stage and waited behind the floor-level speakers for the festival's MC to finish screaming in Japanese what unmistakably was a promo for Poland Spring before announcing *"Texas Flip!"* to the less-than-half-filled audience.

Few applauded as they walked on.

The weather having turned from bad to worse in the time it took the band to travel from the trailer to the stage, growing stronger and more savage by the second, it seemed as if the crowd's thoughts were more focused on an overall safety protocol than an overall good time. Rain hitting Zach's shoes in an off-beat repetition as he clicked through a couple of his foot pedals with caution—all too aware of the forcible electric current running through his amp, through his guitar, and perhaps then through his body—the high probability of losing his life on this stage entered his thoughts—not because he wished it, but because it was close to a guarantee. Most of the audience scattered about the large, swampy terrain, using this performance for the purchase of concessions and alcohol. Zach's own dissolution felt welcoming.

Mental stopwatch started, the band blasted through an unsatisfying set of easy cuts with no major hiccups other than a couple of missed cues by Blaine and a thick burp into the microphone by Luke, and they found that the time moved quicker because of it. Because of the numbness. Another unremarkable thirty-five minutes of work finished, the rain dropping in ways that signaled worse things to come, back to their trailer they went, where inside, sitting on a stool and fuming with restlessness, they also found Todd. He was dry as a bone. "Great set, guys."

"Did you even watch it?" Luke asked, and opened a bottle of Poland Spring, pouring its liquid out onto the floor for no reason.

"I didn't. Weather is awful." Luke's river of carelessness trickling toward him, Todd stood up and did a tight jumping jack. "Rusty is going to start breaking all the gear down. I'll have the van come around and scoop us once he's finished. It shouldn't take more than two hours to get to Tokyo if we leave right now."

The plan had been to be loaded up and on their way to that night's gig as soon as their set was finished. But plans are just an idea of what you believe the future will hold, not what will most likely happen.

"Remember, there's no opening band tonight and the club won't let us play two sets for some reason. So that means you're going to have to play one two-hour set, like the old days."

Toeing the water and unsure himself why he had poured the bottle out, Luke looked sad. "Two hours? Seriously? We just played for half an hour."

Before Todd could respond, a roaring sound of thunder shook the trailer; the blast producing ripples in the puddle on the floor and wrinkles across his face. "You gotta be kidding me," he said, and walked over to the window, peeking one eye through the shades and then the other.

BOOM!

The trailer illuminated and the power went out briefly.

"Holy shit! You guys see that? Lightning just struck outside our door! Like, right there!"

And then, as if the gods themselves broke their seal on a lifetime's worth of beers drunk, a rain started to pour harder and faster than the earth could absorb. The water in the sky pelting the roof of their trailer in drops the size of golf balls, it started to come down so heavy that the previous view of their thirty-foot hike to the stage was no longer. Todd took action fast. The water was faster.

"Okay, okay. No big deal," he mumbled, trying his best to reassure himself that although there was no way they were going to get out of there on schedule, they would still make it to the club on time. "Rusty should be done with the gear any minute. Everyone, grab your shit and get ready. We can beat this storm if we leave immediately."

The logistical location for the festival about as unfavorable as possible—an empty plot of land in the sticks—this locality also happened to be placed in an elevated highland that was heavily forested and had only one road in and out. Why this site was chosen for a festival was anybody's guess, but this unforeseen rain was going to make it near impossible to get out in time for their sound check at Club Quattro, let alone load-in, let alone a mudslide. Safe to assume that a fair number of patrons in attendance at the festival would also be heading to drier pastures—be it there on the festival grounds or back in the comfort of their own homes—the backup in foot and car traffic was certain to be a nightmare in any case.

Before Luke could say they were screwed, Rusty erupted into the trailer, drenched from head to toe but with a lit cigarette in his mouth somehow. And then *he* let them know they were screwed. "I just got soaked out there! Weather is god-awful. No way we can drive in that." He sat atop Zach's Fender practice amp, shaking himself dry, his mouth chimney puffing away.

Todd walked over to Rusty. "You're lying."

"I'd be amazed if that van is going to get us down this mountain and through that mud. Look at my boots. I was sinking ankle-deep in that shit!"

The rain crashed harder with each passing second, and they all mutely hoped, waiting for someone to say anything positive. After what felt like a decade, one of the Red Dragon Entertainment big shots—an older, heavyset, bald Japanese man named Frank—made his way to their trailer, popping his head through the door but leaving the rest of his body outside. Looking down at the stagnant puddle of Poland Spring water in the middle of the floor, he said, "Shit . . . has it already started leaking water in here? Let's hope not, because it is *not* looking good out there. We've had to cancel the next two acts due to lightning strikes."

"Do you want to come inside?" Luke asked.

"No thanks," Frank said. "Just here to tell you that the entire audience has been forced to take cover in the emergency tents we have spread out around the festival grounds and that the road leading out has become completely flooded as well. We're currently waiting for emergency support from the local police and fire department to help clear it. I'm making the rounds and letting all the bands know to sit tight, because we might be hanging inside for a while." An indecipherable crackle of English or Japanese came from his walkie-talkie, a bit about "refusing to go on" and "they also demand their guarantee," before he turned the dial to silent. "Total shit-fest out there. I'll be back in a bit, gang. Hang tight."

Another door closed on them; Frank's departure left room for their previous silence to return with a vengeance.

Todd picked up a chair and heaved it clear across the trailer, crashing into a mirror and missing Blaine's head by an inch.

"*Fucking motherfucking fuck!!*" The chair (and his self-image) taking more damage than the spiderwebbed glass, he screamed the dangerous truth: "Club Quattro is going to be up my ass farther than a prostate exam if we don't make it to this gig tonight!"

Getting struck by lightning a preferred alternative to sticking around a bunch of momos yelling about a matter clean out of their control, Zach had his jacket already in hand before he headed to the exit. "I'll be back."

"It's raining, bro!" Luke yelled at him.

"Thanks for the weather update."

His breath deep upon departure, he threw on his denim sheath and walked outside with no desire for an umbrella or shelter from this storm. The rain would only help wash off the disappointment the rest of this night was sure to present them. He went to the concessions tent and ate a sashimi meal among thousands and wasn't recognized by a single person as a member of a band that had performed for them not even an hour ago. He smoked three cigarettes, drank two Coca-Colas, and walked slowly in the fast-pouring rain back to his trailer because that was all there was for him to do. If he caught a cold, so be it. He was already dead inside. Twenty-four minutes had passed.

Blockaded by a collection of officials covered with more umbrellas than there were people, Frank, Misato, six firefighters, and three police officers all stood in a circle in front of Texas Flip's trailer entrance, their demeanors the least bit reassuring. A blank space where his mind should have been, Zach walked closer to get a better take on the situation, already soaked with regret before he could take a bath in it. The nearer he inched, the sooner it became clear that Frank—both hands waving wildly about—was looking for something to be done, pronto. And the more that Frank looked like he was asking for something to be done, the less likely the firefighters and police officers looked to be doing it. Zach was uncertain of what the significance of this convergence of views would have on the rest of the nights moves.

"They have to be able to play tonight! Look"—Frank pointed up toward the tremendous speakers towering above the stage, the pair swaying back and forth in a pendulum of death, one gust away from falling from the rafters and smashing through the stage—"it's not even that windy anymore!"

Everybody spoke in English for some reason, and one of the firefighters put her arm around Frank's shoulders, stating sweetly, "We understand your financial concerns, but it's obviously not safe for the performers, the stagehands, or anyone in attendance to be near such a safety hazard. The lightning may have subsided for now, but these winds are too unpredictable."

"Fuck their safety!" Frank screamed. "Do you have any idea how much money I'll be losing if they don't get on that stage? I'm already screwed because of that goddamn Pocky promo!"

The Pocky promo . . .

For this momentous musical occasion, the Japanese snack food brand loved by millions around the world had teamed up with Red Dragon Entertainment for a promotional giveaway as part of the Japan ROCKS! Festival's advertisement scheme. Simple really, it went something like this: with every three-day

VIP ticket bought, the ticket holder would receive a free box of Pocky upon entry. That's it.

Why would I drop a couple of yard sticks for a free snack? Sounds like a bum deal, would be logical reasoning.

Unless there's a catch . . .

To keep it interesting, one out of every hundred of these randomly dispersed Pocky boxes would contain a pink piece of paper inside that would act as a coupon for one free beer and 30 percent off any item of food, as well as an entire year's worth of Pocky. Pretty bad promotional technique when you considered that a one-day ticket cost $100, but Pocky had helped foot some of the expenses that goes along with putting on such a large event, its gaudy advertisements everywhere the eye could see, so this little giveaway was the least of anybody's concerns.

Unfortunate for Frank, someone at the processing factory fucked up their only job, and instead of putting one pink piece of paper inside every hundredth box, they put one pink piece of paper inside *every* single box. This, in turn, created a fever pitch at the concession stands; none of the workers had even been told about the promotional giveaway to begin with, and soon they were inundated by the thousands of people descending upon them with coupons for free beer and discounted food. The crowd engulfing and overpowering the employees with a tsunamic wave of openhanded interest, the workers had no time to ask their managers if what they were doing was even correct. Word eventually got to Frank—the damage already done—and an announcement was made over the PA system broadcasting: *"Any pink Pocky coupons yet to be used will no longer be accepted."*

Tens of thousands of dollars in food and beverages lost before the first band had even hit the stage, the Pocky promo was not something Frank needed to rehash.

"Sorry to hear about your monetary difficulties, but we're

not letting any artists up on that stage with the wind and rain like this." The firefighter radioed to someone and then refocused her attention back to the group. "Listen, we'll wait another half hour. If this storm can calm itself down, and I feel comfortable enough, then we can proceed with the show. If not, then I ask that either yourself or Misato write a statement that can be conveyed over the sound system to the audience."

Frank, livid, yelled, "Write a statement? What is this, the Jewel Voice Broadcast?"

Misato, in an effort to save Frank from his second heart attack, grabbed his forearm to calm him down. "We completely understand, Ms. . . . I'm sorry, what is your name?"

Thrown off by the sudden kind gesture, the firefighter blushed. "My name is Katarina."

"Katarina. That's beautiful," Misato said. "That's my mother's name. Katarina, if it's all right with you, I'd like to speak for Frank and say that we would be happy to have that statement ready for you in the next thirty minutes. In the meantime, let's have everyone take a quick break, and then we can reconvene with a better strategy to best deal with this situation."

All in agreement with Katarina's new game plan, both parties dispersed, going their separate ways and dragging bits of Frank's soggy annoyance along with them. Discovering himself with a bellyful of scrumptious gossip and a big ladle with which to dispense it, Zach sprinted back to his trailer. What he entered was a caravan of disorderly musicians. His pack of smokes was missing, equal to cookies without their fortune.

"Nah, dude. It's a G maj there instead of that C sharp minor . . . Yeah, that's it. And strum it more like a reggae tune. Upstrokes, baby! Just like stroking your dick."

In the depths of the trailer, on the other side of a smoke

cloud too thick for a machete, sat Todd, stoned silly on the couch. Luke was to his left, taut and wiry. Next to them sat Phil Leigh, the guitar player from that night's headlining band, Posole, seated on the fold-out chair that Todd had thrown across the room earlier, Zach's Les Paul strapped around his shoulder. Also sharing this small space inside the stuffy trailer imbued with cannabis exhaust were the three female backup singers from the band Sleigh Doll (one of the acts to have their set canceled because of the inclement weather).

Blaine stood beside them.

Luke's face was close in Phil's grill. "Yeah, dude! Get that Joe Strummer feel on it!" he directed eagerly.

Fingers pressed hard against the fretboard, eyes closed tight, Phil began singing the words to Texas Flip's song "I'm Trying to Do My Best," playing rhythm guitar better than Zach ever had. The chord progression written on a paper towel in front of him in chicken scratch harder to read than smudged hieroglyphic—Luke's handwriting assuredly—it felt wrong to intrude and spoil the mood of such a natural jam session. So, Luke did instead.

"Zach, perfect timing! Show my man Phil here how you play the pre-chorus."

Todd puffed a joint that held more hash than flower. "The girls had ganja too!"

The gossip mill turning in his pocket, Zach grabbed his guitar and an Adamas two-millimeter graphite pick from Phil, the plectrum's twin feathers posted on either side of his thumb the most agreeable part of his day, and began to strum the end of the song's second verse. Phil, picking the cadence right up, started in on the chorus lyrics:

> *And I'm trying to do my best baby,*
> *just one more time.*
> *If I give up now,*

this old ghost is gonna get up,
and march on back down the line . . .

Without batting an eye, all three girls from Sleigh Doll started to sing the chorus harmonies with an emotion Zach never knew could exist in this song. Their angelic voices suffusing the little oxygen available to them, the moment so good his face hurt from smiling that hard, Zach forgot why he had even returned in the first place, brought back to a time when the music made him feel alive, before the contracts and thrown chairs. No audience. No microphones. No outside forces to taint the purity of the instant. Musicians in a rain-soaked trailer, taking refuge from the spoils of a war their own music had brought them. Happiness.

"Do you repeat the chorus here, or do you go to the bridge?" Phil asked.

Before Zach could answer, there was a thick knock on the door. Thicker than mercury. He had yet to move from the entrance because of the lack of room, but he opened it wide enough for Frank's bald head to peek through like an ice cube in a bottle. "Sorry to interrupt, everyone, but I have some news. The fire department, along with the police department and every other fucking department on this island, have made the decision that Posole and all the other bands' sets will be delayed. They claim it's 'too unsafe for bands to be on the stage,' whatever that means."

Phil sucked hard on the soggy joint and exhaled slow. "It's all good, man," he said. "We're putting on the show of the century anyways."

Frank, choosing to ignore the illegal drugs being smoked, couldn't help but smile. "I can see that. Anyways, Red Dragon is going to set up some temporary lodgings with beds, a masseuse, and a private bartender over in the Poland Spring tent for you and the rest of the band."

"What about the these dudes?" Phil coughed up admirably.

Frank glared at Luke like one would at a dog that shits on the rug. "This is just for Posole and your crew. But I can give the girls a lift over to their trailer as well. This trailer will be sufficient for Texas Flip and a couple of stagehands I need to put in here. If you'd like, I can take you all over there in a golf cart now."

Phil leaped at the compromise—"Sounds good!"—and gave consideration to Luke and Zach, joint still in his mouth. "Take care, dudes!" he said, walking out with the three backup singers and all their umbrellas. Frank patted him on the back. They took the weed with them.

Blaine, witness to everything and not one to let things slide, pulled Zach aside and whispered in his ear.

"Phil thought it was Mount Everest too."

10

Greens Ballroom
Hoboken, New Jersey
2/27/10

Capacity: 500
Tickets Sold: 221

They used to have fresh strawberries in their dressing room every night. Todd always made sure of it, although nobody in the band had eaten one in at least eight years.

A footnote buried deep in a tour rider of needlessness length, like Van Halen and their M&M'S, this small request was included only to make sure the venues did their jobs for once and not just supply the band with sorely needed vitamin C.

They also needed a reason to keep paying Todd.

The dressing room of the Greens Ballroom was a cramped, untidy kitchen besieged with stuff no one ever uses: a blender, stevia packets, a twelve-pack of Dasani water, and a plastic tray of a dozen stale cupcakes (one mysteriously absent). The sole couch was even missing a cushion. These needless items sat on a wooden picnic table that clogged up the flow of banquet trade, the setup more in the vein of a military mess hall than a place for performers to unwind. Zach, Luke, Cameron (their fourth pianist), and Noah (their third drummer) ate a flavorless band discounted dinner in silence. Flyers displayed were for shows from five weeks ago, and a garbage can full of bloody tissues, broken strings, and exhausted dreams showcased the venue's lack of professionalism; it hurt to expect so little and to be given so much less. A sugar-free dessert after a vegan meal. Decaf espresso.

The night may have been young, but most of them weren't.

Occupied with cold penne alla vodka and emptied checking accounts, it was no coincidence they ignored their manager walking in and out of the room three times in under thirty seconds. An easy guy to miss if you weren't looking for him, Todd was impossible to ignore when he was looking for you. A hole in the shoulder of his Rush *Moving Pictures* tour T-shirt revealed the edges of a regrettable barbed-wire tattoo. It wasn't till he screamed, "Are you kidding me?" that anyone in the band bothered to raise an eye from their paper plates. "Who didn't read the contract? Our rider *specifically* says that we have strawberries back here. Not whatever the fuck these are."

The beat of "Crosseyed and Painless" on the house PA egged him on further, and he was soon singing out of rhythm with David Byrne. The fruit snafu consumed most of his thoughts, and absent a person within earshot who gave a shit to respond, the words from Todd's mouth stuck to the small room's concrete walls like poorly tossed darts of syllables. The verbs and nouns widely missing the faded pictures of Bon Jovi, Whitney Houston, Frank Sinatra, and the Boss that covered every square inch of the place. One couldn't forget they were in New Jersey no matter how hard they tried.

And they were all trying their hardest.

Collapsed with the only other failures who could suffer defeat like he could, it eased Zach's state of mind knowing he was at least, for the meantime, in similar company. Same cut of loser but with a different seasoning. It also helped that no one else in his band seemed to be in a foul mood other than Todd, which was fine since that was technically still his job. A job the man had done very well for very long.

Zach felt a swishing of his entrails in the backstage area of the Greens Ballroom thirteen years after they had first head-lined it and instinctively knew he would have to go to the bath-room shortly. A sudden chill ran through his legs, up his shoulders, and down his arms—a premonition of things to come—and he brushed off the feeling of naïveté and played the fool, keen for a break in the dressing room's monotony and the mildness of another gig on another tour. Ready for an emptying of his intestines, he stood up, but the floor caught to the soles of his shoes as he walked over to the open doorway where Todd was posted, and he wondered why the floor was so sticky. He didn't bother to think if maybe the floor was stuck to him.

Todd stood like a building waiting for demolition, blasting off emails from his cell phone and ignoring texts from his wife. Producing a pink Bic lighter and joint from his jeans, their manager toasted the spliff he had rolled minutes before and gave a shifty look at the bowl of berries soon to go to waste. The rest of the band lost in the distractions of their modern world, Todd's mind lost in the cloud, it was also no surprise that not one of them noticed the stage manager *also* standing inside the room.

A ghost of Christmas past and there to bring only the greatest of great news surely, the young-looking boy/man (hard to tell since his facial hair looked like he had shaved his pubes and glued them back onto his face in the dark) implanted himself into the center of their smoldered hell, stuttering with an *it's my second week here* tenor. He approached Todd with the caution of one coming upon a bushmaster in the rain forest. His words stammered out before his panic could: "Y-yo . . . You guys go on twenty minutes after they're done."

Right leg bouncing as if waiting for an STD test he knew would produce positive results, Todd pointed at the bowl of fruit and began his prosecution with a frightful tone. "What is this?" he barked. "Our contract states that we have strawberries. Not raspberries, or whatever crap is in that bowl."

"Um . . ." The stage manager hesitated. "I think they're blackberries."

"Blackberries?" Todd asked, his voice at a loss for silence. "Good to know . . . Now listen to me and listen well. Either you, or someone else who works here, is going to go down to Whole Foods, and they are going to bring us back *S-T-R-A-W-B-E-R-R-I-E-S*. Otherwise"—his arm pointed in the opposite direction of the stage—"my guys don't go up there."

Confused at Todd's hostility over healthy sugars, the stage manager took a large step back for such a small length of stride. He was pale and thin, a red STAFF jacket engulfing his tiny frame, and had small teeth. His mustache was blonder than his hair, and his eyes held less health than Rusty's liver. He was a scary person to look at but not be scared of. He was a perfect employee. "Sorry, man," he said, "but I don't know if there's a Whole Foods in Hoboken yet."

In a display of bafflement, Todd turned to Zach, the blood vessels in his eyes pulsing with exhaustion and alarm, and at his limit, he snapped. "You believe this guy?!" he asked with a sideways thumb of sass. "Not only does he screw up our rider. He then tells me he can't fix it!"

"Dude," the stage manager said, "I'm standing right in front of you." He breathed in deep through his mouth, exhaling long from his nose. "I don't know what to tell you guys, but y'all are on soon. The strawberries ain't happening. Sorry." Unfazed, the venue employee posted his hands inside the pockets of his jacket to free himself from any possible microaggressive gestures. "And make sure you settle up with me after your set."

The hardest part of his job done, he spun around as if on ice skates and walked away from another band whom he couldn't care less about. Another one of the thousands of dumb mucks he'd be dealing with for the rest of his career in midlevel live entertainment, nothing to look forward to but two stiff after-work drinks and a *West Wing* binge with his cat and pet lizard. Texas Flip would be an annotation in his life diary by the next night, and they still would have no strawberries.

Fuck 'em.

The sound of a lethargic crowd bubbling over with doubt came from the next room over. They were anticipating a performance they hoped might transport them back to a time when the biggest anxiety in their lives wasn't babysitters and 401(k) valuations. These tunes were a transistor to an older way of life, melodies and notes that harkened back to summers between semesters and bad decisions in seedy bars—a youthful respite when the circus came to town once a year. This was the function the band served.

The wall clock clicked to 9:08 P.M.

They were scheduled to start at 9:15 p.m.

An opening band the club booked called The New York Dimes, an all-female Strokes rip-off from Williamsburg, had started their set on time. But after eating up the first fourteen minutes of it tuning their instruments, adjusting drums, moving monitor wedges, and doing anything other than play their music, they in turn pushed back the rest of the show, which then pushed back Texas Flip's load-out time, and further pushed back the time that they could arrive back at the Sunny Days Hotel. Bored with nothing to do but hang out and wait for their turn to phone it in, Zach craved a drink, a rip, anything that would fuck him up and fuck up years of sober living, and hopefully just kill him already. Then he remembered something that he had learned in rehab: *Drugs like boredom. People don't.*

Then he remembered he was in New Jersey.

Well before the temper tantrums over fruit, there were preshow shots of Jägermeister and bumps of varying powders. But following the revolving door of band members, rehab stints, deaths, and a general understanding that drugs consumed on an idiotically stupid level over decades will destroy everything in your life, Texas Flip's preshow ritual these days consisted of room temperature bottles of water and avoiding eye contact with one another for as long as possible. Looking at his guitar, but empty of any desire to pick it up until he absolutely had to, Zach turned his attention back to Luke and Todd instead, the pair both standing in the doorway.

The singer picked his nose absentmindedly.

The manager frowned deeply.

Before the guitarist could emphasize the dietary fiber content of blackberries, the Talking Heads came back on the PA, and The New York Dimes walked offstage arm in arm, shuffling through their dressing room without a care in the world and out to the rear parking lot of the club, where they continued the party accordingly by chugging cans of Pabst Blue Ribbon and smoking weed out of an apple pipe. Trying to put himself in their shoes, to be twenty-four again and have no obligations, to truly not give a shit—to love life and music just the same—Zach, with little effort, failed. His feet too bloated to fit into such old kicks at this age, he was astonished to think that was himself at one point. He shrugged it off, lit another cigarette, and rejoined his troupe among the fold-out chairs and packets of sweetener in the dressing room meant for them and not the opening band. Picking a strand of someone else's hair from his pants, he did his best to elude the passionate stare coming from Tony Bennett's snapshot on the wall and began to feel like a stranger lost in some long, silky, crazy night. He felt as if he were stumbling blind around the grooves of a Charles Mingus vinyl.

Todd was still muffed from his earlier dealings with the stage manager, arms crossed tighter than an anaconda on a wild pig. Ready to sing a million verses in ragtime to whoever would listen, he said, "I can't believe that guy . . . You hear how he talked to me?" His speech came off guttural and was listened to by nobody. He wasn't sure he heard the words himself.

"Yeah, man," Luke answered, his eyes glued to his phone. "Not cool."

Todd bent his head to catch a glimpse of The New York Dimes throwing a football outside. "I wonder if those chicks have any more weed." Beside himself with annoyance, he instead grabbed a half-drunk bottle of Captain Morgan left over from the previous night's band, put the flagon to his lips, and, arching the back of his head to the top of his back, tilted the sugary foulness down his throat. A giant swig and wipe of the mouth later, he grinned and was caught by surprise as the candied liquor traveled through his esophagus and cooked a thin crust on his thick kidneys; vomit burped up but was forced back down.

Four minutes left till their start time, the band walked out of the dressing room, past the stage manager in his tiny office located directly under the stage (his small workplace decorated with cutouts of Kurt Cobain and the one recognizable guy from Slayer), and up the ten stairs that led directly to stage left. Only a thick black carpet kept them from being seen by the half-filled club.

Cameron, who had been onstage for a couple of minutes already, tinkering with a Nord Stage 2 keyboard he still hadn't figured out how to operate despite being twenty-three shows into the tour, hadn't noticed them slump out there either.

And neither did the audience.

Half of the half-full venue either taking a piss or smoking outside, the band didn't bother to let the Black Keys intro music settle down before they opened their old show with a tune off their new record.

Their first mistake.

Real fans, those people who still buy music, can be welcoming to this change in the game plan. But most fans not. A prompt look of worried curiosity and need for quick reassurance bathing their faces, they were perplexed as a song none of them had ever heard before was played. And this is because fans *don't* come to the show to hear new music. And as much as every band says they don't placate their audiences' wishes for certain songs, they do.

They have to.

A collection of bozos with no other hirable skills, getting these same fans coming back night after night is what their livelihoods depend on. And if that means playing those same drowsy songs every night for the rest of eternity so people will keep buying tickets to the same old song and dance well after the records stop selling but their love for that one album from fourteen years ago hasn't, then it's simply what it is. These tunes, the ones people pay money to hear live and have ingrained in their bone marrow, are the small globules that constitute an ancient band's slowly dying soul, musical notes and cringey choruses eating them away until they simply cease to care anymore, until it doesn't matter, until the caricature becomes reality.

By the time Texas Flip finished their newest unexplored material, thirty or forty more people who had spent their hard-earned cash supporting their last-ditch efforts popped up inside the club and helped fill the void. Sad at the turnout but not surprised, Zach was still in good humor in lieu of being upset over the obvious.

He should have known better.

They would forge ahead and make another fatal choice, kicking off a thrice-rehearsed cover of "Bitch," by the Rolling Stones, rather than playing one of the hundreds of other original songs that were in their catalog.

Their second mistake.

A song that should never be played without a brass section (or without Charlie Watts), they went against better judgment and started the tune anyways, throwing caution to the wind and crapping on the legacy of yet another rock classic. The tasty Keith Richards riff drifting the crowd back into their favor, Cameron did his best to fill in Bobby Keys's saxophone licks on his Nord keyboard as a close-eyed Luke mouthed the words to the tune but could hardly be bothered to sing them, the saliva buildup at the rear of his tongue providing no justice to Mick Jagger's "Pavlov dog" reference. They screwed up the ending, then paused for a tuning break and an opportunity for random people off the street to maybe purchase one of the many tickets available at the box office.

The band wasn't stupid. They knew everyone in that room was only there to hear the four or five songs they understood would be played no matter the show. And Texas Flip had tested their luck by being two songs in and having not yet played one of them. Zach gave Matthew a head nod, his Vater 5A drumsticks hitting the paradiddle intro of their second most successful single, "Fake News," and kicked them off to the races.

Any animosity that might have been held on to from the earlier set list choices was rapidly withdrawn, and the crowd burst forth with animation at the identifiable rhythm, gladly joining in on the stock groove. The room changed in an instant. Zach went about amplifying the thin crowd's energy with a compact head of confusion and allowed himself the pleasure to freely imagine an audience that he used to know. A band, friends, and a life he used to know. To imagine anything that he used to know. Gripping the stage with his sore feet, he tried to remember all these things with every fiber of his being and find belief in their powers. A belief that, with little comparison, was almost as strong as his belief in Luke Strange and their commitment to this life of music they had embarked on together, like brothers, decades prior.

More solid than a dump after a prime rib dinner, Luke, for the twenty-three years they'd known each other, was still Zach's truest friend in the world. They had been through it all. Sausages squeezed through the same broken machine. Front line soldiers on the beaches of Normandy. Or so he thought before Luke said, "Fuck this shit," into his microphone, unplugged his bass, jumped into the audience, and walked straight out the front door of the Greens Ballroom and into another unforgiving night.

Stunned, and with nowhere to go, the rest of the band instinctively stopped playing. Everyone's eyes now targeted the front door, waiting for Luke to walk back through it like this was all a joke.

He didn't.

And it wasn't.

After a tense couple of seconds, the silence in the club became as deafening as it was morbid, and Noah and Cameron—dealing with more than they had signed up for or were being paid for—both tiptoed offstage, leaving Zach, the lone survivor and the only original member of the band, up there. The task of explaining to the audience what was happening would fall solely on his shoulders.

A precarious four-step passage to reach Luke's vacated microphone, the seconds spanned hours as he tramped up to the stinky Shure Beta 58A and cleared his throat directly into it. He held his hand a couple of inches from his eyes, blinded by the hot bright lights positioned ten feet from his face, and squinted, straining to see the barren landscape, his vision a blur of green, red, and yellow circles.

"Hey, everyone. So, um, we're gonna go gather up Luke, and then we're gonna, uhhh . . . continue the show." He gulped hard. "I also want to take this time to say thank you for coming out tonight." Sweat beaded on the back of his neck and dripped farther down his spine with each nervous laugh. "Sorry for the inconvenience—but don't worry, we got plenty more music coming at you in a bit!"

With this abbreviated pile of nothing steamed from his mouth and now puddled on the stage before him, Zach ran, maybe the fastest he'd ever ran in his life, off it.

Unfortunately, he wasn't fast enough for Todd.

Waiting feverishly in the wings, Texas Flip's manager hooked the guitarist by the arm and stopped him from being anywhere but here. His face a lighter shade of already-too-light pale, he screamed, "What the *fuck* just happened?!" at the top of his lungs to the top of the ceiling.

Out of breath from the twenty-foot sprint, Zach struggled to regain his composure. "I have . . . no idea . . . We're playing . . . and next thing I know . . . he's . . . walking out . . . the front door . . ."

"I tried to run after him, guys!" Rusty said, also exasperated. "Dude hopped on a bus and it drove off before I could stop it!"

"He's on a bus?!" Todd screamed.

"Yeah, crazy . . . Dude still had his bass on him too!"

"Fuck me," Todd said, the Captain Morgan bottle gripped tight in his right hand. "This isn't good."

Zach could see the stage manager storming in their direction, a single light illuminating his path—a familiar sight after all these years. Reaching their position feet from the stage exit, and a head bend away from being seen by the angry mob left out on the dance floor, he yelled, "What the hell is happening?!" His facial expression was as severe as his breath. "Why did your lead singer just get on a bus going to Lyndhurst?!"

"Everything is all right!" The nonsense squeezed between Todd's teeth like warm toothpaste. "There is nothing to worry about."

"*Everything is all right?!* Your singer just walked out of the club in the middle of your third song! What do you mean 'everything is all right'?" Static crackled from the radio set hung an inch below his right ear. Something about a guy and his girlfriend fighting in the bathroom. He ignored it. "I have two hundred cold and soon to be very angry people in here who are going to rip this place apart if you guys do not get back on that stage."

"Two hundred?" Todd asked with enthusiasm. "That's great. I thought we only did 163."

Before the stage manager could dig in further, a Corona bottle exploded against the lit-up neon Tecate sign installed above the drum set. "Oh shit!" he screamed, ducking down to waist level and covering his head with his hand. The other checked to make sure his remaining limbs were still attached. "Get on that stage, now!"

A second Corona bottle, faster in its pace, tore a hole through the head of Noah's kick drum, the lime from the cerveza coming to rest in between Todd's Reeboks. "My guys are not getting back up there," their manager said. "No way!"

The audience grew more and more restless the longer this quarrel progressed, the booing beginning to overtake the levels of "Burning Down the House" the FOH engineer had cranked through the PA system, and the only thing louder would have been Motörhead.

"Rusty!" Todd yelled. "Pull the van around. We need to get out of here before there is a riot. These guys will get killed if they go back on that stage!"

"You got it, boss."

The stage manager, who was now standing face-to-face with Todd, came back hard and fast. "You're leaving? You can't leave!"

"Watch us."

"If you leave, I'll make sure of it myself that Texas Flip never plays in the state of New Jersey again!"

Todd took a large stride backward in a sign of slight, his head cocked like a wise guy who'd been disrespected. "Is that your biggest threat?" he asked, peeved. "Is that all you got? Listen, homeboy, I'm sure you love your job, but don't try to play the good cop here and go above your pay grade. This is not the time. I don't know what's going on myself, but what I do know is that I am not sending my guys back out there." Another bottle smashed against a wall behind them. This time a Heineken. "Not a fucking chance."

"You are under contract!"

"I hear you loud and clear. And I hope you hear me when I say you can take your contract and you can shove it up your ass. And while you're at it, shove that bowl of blackberries up there too."

Rusty hotfooted through the emergency exit door looking like he needed to take a shit. "Let's go, guys!" he yelled nervously, before pocketing some fruit, granola bars, Hershey's Kisses, and a bottle of water. "There's already people outside circling the van."

Most of their gear rented (the Gretsch drum kit, Fender Bassman amp, and Nord Stage 2 keyboard), they resolved that it was time to leave it all behind—inevitable, given the circumstances—and get out of dodge before they were put in caskets and sent back home themselves. Everything having gone so bad in such a short period, and nothing they could do to make it cease, the leftovers of the band jumped in their waiting Chevrolet Express 3500 and sped away like it was the last plane out of 'Nam, Todd looking back only to make sure they hadn't run over the opening band. Rusty all but killing three pedestrians as he turned left on Washington Street, he channeled their way onto Route 17N toward Paramus. The collectively high level of adrenaline abated only once they were in the clear and everyone could light up a smoke.

Billows inside the van thicker than its exhaust, the five were mum and all too aware of the financial price they'd be paying for this chain of incidents still unfolding. Not much good could have been said by anyone if he had so chosen.

So, no one said anything.

Except Todd.

Sitting in the front seat, his hair in tatters and skin rum flushed, their manager continued to nip steadily at the backwashed Captain Morgan bottle, most of its contents already inside of his belly, to his heavy satisfaction. He began his line of questioning—"Did Luke say anyytinng to youse guys twoday?"—his speech slurring in that way drunks normally speak when sober. They could comprehend his words, but the slope they slid down was slippery. Adrenaline still boosting the alcohol content of his blood, he sustained his questions like a rookie cop in his first interrogation: "Maybe aahh hiiiint he'd do something thiss dumb? Why was his bass stillll on him?"

"Not a word," Rusty answered for everyone.

A sign for Fort Lee whipped past, and a fart that couldn't decide whether it was coming or going made Zach smile lightheartedly as he watched their driver discharge a snot-torpedo out through the two-inch crack of his window; the windshield of the Toyota Prius driving alongside them assaulted by Rusty's nasal waste.

Rusty coughed up a second observation before coughing up a third lung and a fourth life. "I was with him most of the day, twisting around the piers. Dude was happy as a donkey."

His head pounding and bowels bubbling, Zach lay down on the last bench seat in the van, Cameron's drool-stained pillow his only friend in the world, and dreamed about this night ending. Or their van crashing. Eyes closed for the entirety of this trip back to the Sunny Days Hotel, they startled opened after Rusty lacerated a three-foot scar into the entrance ramp of the parking lot with their van. He was genuinely more stoked the Wendy's next door was still open than he was about masturbating in the shower and going to sleep. The van parked unlawfully in the lot, taking up two spots and blocking half a lane of traffic, Rusty turned off its engine, reclined his chair back, and burped: the smell of sugar and Marlboros pungent. Having the deep need to piss, Todd was out of the van within seconds of the Chevy shifting into P, his fly unzipped and shrunken cock already in hand. The air outside ruthless and with little cover from the Meadowlandic winds, his urination began on the tire of an unlucky Toyota Camry parked next to them, the color of his stream the color of Captain Morgan, and he let out a loud "Hallelujah!" to the gods of bladder relief above.

Too morose to move, and too sober to be awake, Zach breathed a bleary canvas onto the interior of his van window, drawing a large penis with one testicle over Todd's silhouette and tried his best to find an ounce of humor in this lake of fire.

His bladder only half emptied on a night darker than Vantablack, some unseen motorist clicked their unlock button and sent the Camry into self-defense mode against Todd's urine. Amid a free-flowing stream, he reactively swerved, the watercourse's curvature, coming within inches of irrigating the side of the Chevy van, and body fluids sprayed onto the ground outside the front passenger door like a hose to a blaze. Force-finishing his reprieve, with dribbles down both legs, he zipped up his dick safely and wiped his mouth with the same hand. The clouds had thickened in the meantime and so had the alcohol in his veins, and with the added confidence of an inebriated sailor covered in his own piss, he blustered up to the front entrance of the hotel, humming the lyrics to "The Rain (Supa Dupa Fly)," by Missy Elliott, because it was the last song to be played in the van.

Zach peeled himself from the bed of his own making and followed Todd like a fearful deer through the parking lot, the wind blowing sharp fumes of parched piss his way. He navigated the cheap lawn job and even cheaper lobby furniture with little difficulty, affixing himself as the lone hanger-on to another conversation between dullards, the lobby empty of anybody else, and was in awe at the combined stupidity that lay before him.

"Whettt's de whinefi passwerrd?" Todd slurred.

"The Wi-Fi password, sir?" the taller and more attractive of the two female concierges asked.

They were both brunette and both dumb as rocks.

"Fuggin' whinefi!" Todd persisted. "What esss it?"

"The password is 'password,' sir," the second concierge responded. She was much shorter and had a much uglier face. Everything below her chin a solid eight, what existed above fast fell off the that ten-digit scale of desirability. "All lowercase."

Closely monitoring the matter and highly aware of the nine different security cameras pointed at them, Zach watched Todd swipe through bookmarks for porn sites and baking recipes on his cell phone before pulling up a stock image of Luke from their *NME* magazine cover shoot in 2001. "Hevv you seeeenn diss asshole t'night?" he asked, pointing at his phone's screen.

The girls were both messing with their own cell phones and on a wavelength much different from Todd's. Mobile devices holding much more importance than the dickbag standing across from them, they continued to entertain his line of questioning with a thin line of pleasantry all the while continuing to text boyfriends about brunch plans at the Cheesecake Factory and manicures with girlfriends.

"No such *asshole* has been seen tonight," they said simultaneously.

Todd mumbled under his breath what Zach believed was "buttfucker" but what could have also been "bedwetter."

"It seems like you've had a long night, sir," the hotter girl commented wryly, her Pokémon watch an exposé on the seriousness she had to offer this job. "You should probably go up to your room and chill out."

"Don't tell meee to chilllll . . ." Todd blubbered, and pointed to his left. "I gottsaa pisss enywayy. Iz thattt the—"

"That would be the elevator, sir."

"Yehhh . . . smellevator . . . Smellevator! That'd be a gooood band name!" His interest renewed, he winked at each girl individually, but with equal discomfort.

Zach grabbed him hard by the arm. "And we're off."

Dragging this drunken adult to the waiting elevator, he pressed the button for the hotel's second floor and wished Todd a pleasant sleep and more pleasant hangover, and the creaky pulley system worked overtime to fade Texas Flip's manager from sight and sound. Ready for a double bacon cheeseburger, a Diet Coke, and a deep, dark trip through his spank bank, Zach walked back through the lobby, his gag reflexes activated from the smell. But what he was ready for most of all was another cigarette.

Nothing could have been more appealing.

Rusty, Noah, and Cameron overcrowded the small entrance to the hotel in a triangular formation, three corrupts drinking Red Bull and smoking, and Zach then felt what little light was left inside his body extinguish: a nighttime fantasy of having three minutes alone swept away like trash into the Atlantic Ocean. A crow cawed close by, which was strange since it was past midnight, but not even this bird of death could lift his spirits higher than curb level, and so he lit a smoke, saw through the flame a floating leaf, and tried to gather himself as best he could within his surroundings, taking his spot back within the crew and succumbing to an early submission that this rare chance for withdrawal was no longer available.

On a quest for a nervier night, Cameron interrupted his employer's inner narrative. "Hey, man," he said. "So, since tonight's a bust, Noah and I were thinking about heading over to Satin Dolls. There's a couple of girls over there that he knows, and, well, yeah . . ."

Eyes on the prize of the Wendy's sign behind Matthew, Zach said, "Go for it." His stomach rumbled with foresight and pleasure. "I'm gonna hang out here."

"Wanna come see some tits with us?" Cameron asked Rusty.

His eyes observant but moody, their roadie pointed them at Zach's nipples and lifted his brows to his chin. "Not my thing, guys. Thanks, though. Zach, care to join me at the bar?"

Left to choose either saturated fats and a quick beat sesh in the shower or a no-tequila sunrise with his roadie in an empty bar, Zach, through much debate, decided on the least soul-sucking option. "Sounds good."

The Sunny Days Steakhouse, a restaurant/bar/Albanian money front attached to their shit-box hotel, was a batty phantasm of what life fancied when you finally gave up. The staff (and clientele) playing their respective parts in the miserabilist of ways, no one in there wanted to be there from the owner down to the plants. Ponying up to the vacant bar right as the local news started, Zach lit a cigarette and then extinguished it in his cup of water, remembering it wasn't 2006 anymore.

"What are you thinking?" he asked Rusty, his interest in the question equal to his disinterest.

"I'm gonna have a Tanqueray and tonic. Probably a double."

"I meant about the band."

"Oh yeah. My bad. Luke really screwed us tonight, didn't he?"

Zach combed his uneasy hands through his hair. "He jumped off the goddamn stage, Rusty! You must be thinking what I'm thinking at this point."

"What?"

"Is this it?"

"Is what it?"

"Is this the end?"

"*Beautiful friend . . .*"

"Please don't."

"*The end . . .*"

The bartender, with her breasts pushed up to her tonsils and an attitude just as busty, asked for their order.

"He'll have a double Tanqueray and tonic. And I'll have a no-tequila sunrise."

"A 'no-tequila sunrise'? Does that mean there's no tequila in it? Or is that some hip drink kids order today?"

She was younger than him.

"It means there's no tequila."

"That'll be thirty-three."

"Thirty-three dollars? We ordered one drink and an orange juice!"

"I don't make the prices, honey . . . Thirty-three."

The last fifty-dollar bill he'd likely see for a while leaving his wallet, she scoffed at his two-dollar tip.

Pain from the undiagnosed piriformis syndrome in Zach's left leg—the cause of many sleepless nights—activated. Nothing and everything felt right at the same time. *My Aim Is True*, by Elvis Costello, played on the jukebox in shuffle mode. A man, alone in a booth, choked on a tough piece of sirloin. The bartender turned the TV on mute.

"If he quits the band, I don't know what I'm gonna do. I'm forty years old and I don't have a single employable skill other than playing guitar. And the place I work at is, like, a week from going out of business."

"He ain't gonna *quit*, dude," Rusty said. "And plus, you ain't broke. You made plenty of money. Should be fine to skirt by on."

A new pain joined the numbness in Zach's leg. And that was because Rusty had pressed on more than his sciatic nerve.

With a savings account drier than a sleeve of saltine crackers with no water, this tour was supposed to float him for the next couple of months until he found steady employment —most likely at an ex-girlfriend's real estate office or, worse, as a sober bartender. The neuralgia increased with his concern. "But seriously, I don't know if he's coming back. He got on a bus for Chrissake."

"He'll be fine by tomorrow. Don't worry, dude."

"But what if he isn't? What am I gonna do? What are *you* gonna do?"

"We're hiring," spoke the bartender.

"Not now, miss."

The female news anchor on the TV explored her camera's lens with a poker face, perforating the last edges of their humanity like a bull on parade.

Zach swallowed more of the bar nuts he was eating like candy and wiped his salty hands on his pants leg.

Rusty drank.

Life moved on.

At that moment, a burly redheaded gentleman stepped up to the bar and leaned his left elbow on its edge, posting up to the right of them. "Excuse me," he said with a bass voice. "Sorry to be a bother, but are you gentlemen with the band Texas Flip?"

Rusty held out his arm. "No autographs now."

"I don't want your fucking autograph," the man said. Zach then noticed his jacket was embroidered with the word MANAGER. "I want the drunk idiot who's with your party to stop pissing in our bushes."

Sooner than Zach could laugh at the easily believable thought of Todd urinating in a bush, the man himself appeared at the bar wearing nothing but boxer shorts and a Replacements T-shirt. He threw his arm around Zach's shoulders, Captain Morgan and vomit odorous on his tongue. Closing his eyes, his face looked pure. He licked his lips and inhaled long. *My Aim Is True*'s first track came on, and Elvis laid down the law. Todd started to sing along to the words he heard coming from the speakers. Nothing had changed, yet everything would be forever different.

"*Now that your . . .*"

Words to a song once cherished sung in his ear with the musicality of a prune and now ruined for all of eternity, Zach felt the need to make a stand, for Todd could not go on.

This night could no longer go on.

This life, this act, none of it could keep going on.

The end of the road.

"Please don't," he begged.

"*And you can . . .*"

"Stop . . ."

"*All you gotta . . .*"

Before the meter ended and the band came in and the rush

of doing something with so much love, so much passion, so much confidence in the future could still spin his world around with joy, Zach downed his thirteen-dollar glass of sugar in one sip, stood up, compartmentalized his existence, and faced his coworker with empty eyes. Finishing the lyrics for him, and for himself, was the least he could do.

"Welcome to the working week."